THE CIRCLE OF
MYNNIA

ALSO BY L. L. BLACKMUR:

Love Lies Slain

THE CIRCLE OF
MYNNIA

By L. L. Blackmur

St. Martin's Press ● New York

THE CIRCLE OF MYNNIA. Copyright © 1991 by L. L. Blackmur. All rights reserved. Printed in the United States of America. No part of this book may be used or reproduced in any manner whatsoever without written permission except in the case of brief quotations embodied in critical articles or reviews. For information, address St. Martin's Press, 175 Fifth Avenue, New York, N.Y. 10010.

Library of Congress Cataloging-in-Publication Data

Blackmur, L. L.
    The circle of Mynnia / L.L. Blackmur.
        p.   cm.
    ISBN 0-312-06420-9
    I. Title
    PS3552.L3426C57 1991
    813'.54—dc20
                                                                91-20479
                                                                CIP

First Edition: September 1991

10 9 8 7 6 5 4 3 2 1

To George

─PART ONE─────

1

She couldn't have been wetter had she been swimming in it. It was hard not to be. A few feet from where she stood a million and a half gallons of water a second were roaring over a cliff a mile wide and four hundred feet high. Standing on the same spot almost a century and a half before, David Livingstone had named the falls Victoria, for his queen. The African name made more sense: *Mosi-oa-tunya*, or smoke that thunders. Thunders, and rains constantly for a hundred yards in all directions, which is how the cooling waters of the Zambezi River, otherwise bound for the Indian Ocean nine hundred miles away, had come to drench Joan Cook to the skin.

Another local name for the falls was *Chongwe*, or place of the rainbow. This one was fitting as well, as vapors swirled out of the great chasm a thousand feet into the air and refracted the morning sun into half a dozen disappearing washes of color. Joan mouthed the syllables as she turned away. Chongwe, she whispered. Chongwe. Chongwe. *Damn*.

It was a haunting, magical African word, but there was no way around the annoying realization that she hadn't learned it here. That, by some irksome coincidence, the first time she saw it she'd been sipping a beer on the man's miserable flagstone terrace almost eight thousand miles away.

Joan was trying to ignore the irony of this as she made her way soggily along the cliff-side path, which bore like a tunnel through a dripping chaos of fig trees, acacias and wild date palms tangled with liana vines. She found some distraction in the white-bearded face of a vervet monkey, whose worried red eyes were peering at her from the stump of an ebony tree. Stepping over the PLEASE DON'T FEED THE ANIMALS sign, she fished through her pockets. The monkey came closer. She dropped to one knee and extended an arm, but, startled by the sudden appearance of another human on the path—this one sensible enough to have brought an umbrella—the animal darted back. Joan glanced around and started to rise. She got as far as a low stoop. Changing branches overhead a violet-crested turaco gave an excited *kurru kurru kurru.* Frozen like a garden statue amid the orchids and ferns, Joan gave a muffled squeak. She blinked, but the dreaded picture did not change. Barely ten yards away and closing fast, Philip Dumas was striding directly toward her.

2

Uncle Eldon may have had many talents, but sailing, while his greatest love, was never one of them. The single most significant flaw in his aptitude for the sport was probably as much a function of personality as misapprehension: It was his pride, and his vanity, that he never motored into any harbor, no matter how small or congested, if there was a breath of air on which to sail. He never even turned on the engine as a precautionary measure, which was particularly dangerous if there was considerably more than a breath of air, as there was that day. He hadn't yet damaged his boat, nor any member of his crew, but it was tacitly agreed among them it was only a matter of time. The boat in question, a forty-foot ketch, named *Priscilla* for his late wife, had been a consolation present to himself upon her death twelve years before. It was the only remaining passion in his life and at its helm was the only place he was ever truly happy.

This, at any rate, is how overnight cruises had come to be the weekend fare while the Cooks were on Martha's Vineyard, which they had been in one form or another ever since Joan could remember. Once a mid-size family, they'd dwindled now to three: Frances Cook Hicks—known once again as Fanny Cook—a semiretired social columnist for a suburban Boston newspaper; her brother Eldon, a fully retired mid-level New York banker; and her daughter Joan, an illustrator who after a ten-year absence from the island had recently quit her job in the city and agreed to come up for the summer. She'd arrived just in time for this, their first cruise of the season.

It had started on a peaceful enough note. The wind on which they left Edgartown Harbor that sultry June morning was lazy and out of the west. With the exception of a faint marbling of high clouds, the weather remained fair as they ran north along the eastern shore of the island, past Oak Bluffs, Vineyard Haven and West Chop. Fanny buzzed about the boat wiping things with a sponge while Joan painted watercolor horizons on the foredeck. No one would ever have taken them for mother and daughter. Although not so bad looking in her youth, Fanny at fifty-five had grayed and grown broad in the beam. Her boxy red face was hung with jowls and a fatty nose, and her eyes, once winsomely dark, had faded to a marshy hazel and were shrunken by a puffiness that made her perpetually appear to have just finished crying. Joan, on the other hand, may have inherited the eyes of Fanny's youth, but the narrow nose, demure mouth and olive complexion had come from her father, Arnie Hicks, who had been good-looking in a delicate smooth-skinned sort of way. Joan's hair, however, was entirely original, worn long and convincingly bleached, including her eyebrows, the color of butter. The roundness of her face was a stubborn but not unattractive remnant of an overweight adolescence that, even in her late twenties, Joan had yet to completely shed. (To her frustration it lingered as well in full hips and thighs.) But the soft lines of her face may also have been a throwback to Fanny and Eldon's sister Katharine, who was cursorily described as "cheruby." "Be glad, dearest, those kind of looks *age* so well," Fanny liked to say, though whether they ever did in Kate's case, she didn't really know, nor much care.

It was at about two o'clock, off Tashmoo Bight, that the wind changed. Fanny had just emerged from the galley with a tray of sandwiches. "I've been *dying* to get into that thing and see what they've done to it," she was saying with a nod toward a sprawling, newly shingled house that had just come into view on the island's northwest shore. "She's spent a fortune and I hear it's a wreck. Of course, *he* can afford it—he's in the Fortune 500, you know."

"I think you mean the Forbes 400, dear."

"Whatever, it's all family money anyway. *Old* Long Island money. His father was president of the New York Stock Exchange. *She* on the other hand comes from the other side of the tracks—practically the other side of the planet. Her husband met her behind the perfume counter at Filene's—think what that says about *him*—and now of course she carries on as if she were suckled on the tit of the *bel mondo.*"

"I think you mean the *beau monde*, Mum."

"Either way, you could never accuse the woman of good taste. I mean she's got all the money in the *world*, and she looks like she dresses out of a Jake's costume van. I saw her—"

Here Fanny stopped and looked around. The sails had suddenly luffed. Uncle Eldon put down his glass and got to his feet. The boom swung fitfully back and forth for a few minutes, then, seeming to have made up its mind, yanked the traveller hard to one side. The mainsail, which Joan had released, swung wide, filled with cooler air that was all at once coming out of the east, and gave the boat a tug. In another few minutes it was blowing almost ten knots—on its way to twenty.

Uncle Eldon pulled at his navy-blue skipper's cap like a pitcher facing a full count with the bases loaded and no one out. "We won't have to tack once," Joan heard him murmur excitedly to himself. "Not even through Quicks." Quicks Hole was a narrow cut between two of the small islands that separated Vineyard Sound from Buzzards Bay. Fanny told Joan the last time he tried this he ran aground.

Indeed, the wind hurled them on a spinnakered run down the Sound past Naushon and Pasque Islands. On gusts the *Priscilla* pushed ten knots. Between Pasque and Nashawena they raced through the cut on the coming tide and were greeted with the typical big blow and rolling waves of Buzzards Bay, which swept them down the rest of the island chain. At about three, the hazy blue mound that was Cuttyhunk, the last of the main Elizabeth Islands, began to give way to detail, revealing a cluster of buildings clinging to the side of a hill that overlooked a hidden harbor. Climbing halfway out of the cabin, Fanny glanced dubiously around her. "Damnit, we're *not* going into

Cuttyhunk under sail," she said with alarm. "Not on a reach, El! Not in this wind!"

"Joannie, come aft!" was her brother's reply. "Prepare to take down the spinnaker! Someone stow the soda cans and bring me my tide chart!"

On shore, Uncle Eldon liked to affect a curmudgeonly air Joan suspected was modeled on Lionel Barrymore in *It's a Wonderful Life*. At the *Priscilla*'s helm he stole freely from Charles Laughton's Captain Bligh. One look at the man, muttering to himself and running his fingers through an imaginary beard, told both women that effective intervention on either of their parts was out of the question. It also reminded Joan why she'd stayed away from the Vineyard for so long. Carrying the remnants of lunch below, she peered reluctantly through a porthole at the masts just visible over the neck of barrier beach that protected the anchorage. She could tell that the basin was crowded, some already rafting two on a mooring. By the same token, she knew that anyone on any of those decks could see that someone was coming in, down wind, under full sail. The Cooks were assured a rapt audience.

Entrance to Cuttyhunk Pond was through a long narrow channel, which the *Priscilla* tore down as if she were on a bobsled run. On reaching the end, Uncle Eldon let out a jubilant "heave to!" and swung her hard to starboard. He'd meant to say "jibe ho" but the women guessed his meaning and ducked as wind caught the other side of the sail and swung the boom with crushing force from one side of the boat to the other. The *Priscilla* rolled in a terrific heel and was catapulted by its newly filled sail into the congested harbor.

To their surprise they spotted an unoccupied mooring almost immediately but promptly overshot it and were forced to tack back. The *Priscilla* was a big boat and turning it around in such a cramped space was not easy. There was hardly enough room to turn her into the wind so that Joan could snag the buoy with a boathook. Uncle Eldon oversailed the mark a second time, only narrowly missing the stern of a nearby sloop. By the third pass, to shouts from the cockpit ("To port, *port*—that's *left*, Joannie, dear—come back this way—it's right *here*, for Christ's sake!") Joan managed to snare the buoy and with Fanny's help ran the heavy mooring line up through the fairlead.

This, however, meant that no one was taking down the sails. With Uncle Eldon remaining at the helm, fists firm on the wheel, main sheet firmly gripped in the teeth of the chock but the rudder not quite dead on the wind, the *Priscilla* continued to sail. Its momentum yanked the line out of their hands and all but pulled them over the side with it.

It was in the heat of this moment that Uncle Eldon made, for Joan, his fateful mistake. Having headed off to pick up wind and thus more speed for another go at his target, he had a matter of seconds to decide whether to pass up or down wind of the seventy-foot yawl *Finesterre* that was resting sublimely on the next mooring over. His error would be not in his choice, but, in having chosen, to then change his mind.

His initial decision was to pass to her bow. His change of heart came a few seconds later. In fairness to the man, two children in a small sailboat had appeared from behind the big yawl and were themselves crossing her bowline, thus forcing him to veer sharply off in an attempt to clear her stern. Whatever the cause, it was evident almost immediately that at this late date the maneuver would be a close call at the very least. Scrambling aft and leaping into the cockpit, Joan grabbed a rubber docking fender and threw it over at midship where contact between the two boats was most likely to take place. Her mother braced for the hit; her uncle, fast at the helm, slowly winced.

In the chaos of the next few seconds Joan was only vaguely aware of what went on in the other boat. She heard various exclamations and had a sense of people darting about, but the only face she actually saw was the one that for an instant seemed close enough to kiss, or at any rate to slap. At the same spot Joan was throwing the fender over the side, a man with short dark hair and alarmed blue eyes was reaching for one of the *Priscilla*'s stanchions in an effort to ward her off. She heard him grunt and in an impressionistic flash saw the muscles in his neck and arms strain, pushing up thick veins under sun-reddened skin. He yelled something as well but it was drowned out by the agonized groan of the fender, which was all but torn apart by the rub. This, however, was by some miracle the only point at which the two boats ever touched.

The same, unfortunately, could not be said for the *Priscilla* and the yawl's ribbed wooden dinghy, a nautical antique its owner had not only kept afloat for fifty years but had maintained in pristine condition. The drift of the bigger boat had left it in the path of the Cooks, who with a *crack* now hit it dead on. Looking reluctantly back over their stern as they sailed away Joan could see it already shipping water as it got ready to sink.

3

"Of all the boats in the *harbor*, Eldon," Fanny moaned. "The Du-mases'. *Jesus.*"

The Cooks were below decks, having finally fetched their mooring and at long last pulled down their sails. The only sounds now were a wind-worried halyard clinking against the aluminum mast and the muffled clap of light harbor waves breaking against the hull. Through the cabin door pink clouds slid gradually back and forth across a pale blue sky as the *Priscilla* swung easily on her mooring line. Joan was digging out the sail covers. Uncle Eldon was combing his hair. Fanny was pouring herself a drink.

"I've *written* about these people," she went on. "They probably *know* me! I can't believe this. Do you have any *idea* who they are?"

"Well, I'm about to find out. Who's coming? Joannie?"

"I think I'll skip it, thanks."

"Fan?" He looked around. "Fanny, *don't* do that!"

"My dear, what do you think these things are for?" his sister answered from behind the binoculars she had aimed through a port-hole at the cockpit of the *Finisterre*. "Besides, they of all people should be used to this. Oh, look, look, there he is! Joannie, honey, come here!"

If Joan did not particularly admire the scavenging of personal information about what Fanny liked to call the *bel mondo*, she did not begrudge her mother her profession. Fanny had fun at it, and as much as Eldon liked to make a show of taking the high road in matters of other people's privacy, Joan herself couldn't claim to be so pure. At least, she was not above accepting the binoculars and bracing them against the little circular pane.

"That's Charles Dumas," Fanny murmured in her ear, "better known as Chick, though it sure doesn't fit him. Man, has *he* gone to seed!"

She'd directed Joan's gaze to a hulking man in his late sixties or early seventies in baggy khaki shorts and powder blue V-neck T-shirt. His thin white hair was pulled tightly back into a strained-looking stub of a ponytail, which made his head appear too small for his body. Then, given the thickness of his neck, which dropped like a curtain from his chin to his collar, and the spreading girth below that, the proportions would have appeared wrong no matter how he wore his hair. He bore a passing resemblance to a bullfrog as he sat, chin pensively raised, staring out to sea. He was probably thinking about his dinghy.

"He's the archeologist," Fanny said.

"You're kidding!" Joan would have guessed him to be almost anything—a crane operator, a pastry chef—before an archeologist.

"Sure, you remember. *National Geographic* did a cover piece on him a dozen or so years ago? There was that dig in Turkey? Some big search for—Oh! Now *that's* Charlotte Jessup. His *wife*, if you can believe it . . ."

A slender woman—wispy by comparison—had climbed out of the cabin, dressed almost identically to her husband. She had perfect posture, a square face with a wide, curling mouth and shiny, umber-colored hair cut bluntly, Cleopatra-style. She might have been forty-five. She handed her husband a glass, smiled at whatever it was he said, then swung back to the cabin as if someone below had called to her.

"May-December," Joan murmured.

"At least."

"I take it he's rich."

"Archeologists always are."

"Are they?"

"Well, *that* woman's sitting on a fortune. All she has to do is wait for the old boy's heart to give out, which it almost did last winter. . . . That is, of course, if her stepdaughter doesn't beat her out of it. That's her there now in the hat."

"The hat" was a white straw affair that looked like a fireman's helmet but which Hayden Dumas Channing wore backwards. Tall and buxom, she looked to Joan to be about the same age as her father's wife. She had come out of the cabin, drink in hand, to drop into a deck chair in the abruptly fatigued manner of an overfed cat. She had a long straight nose, thick black eyebrows and a clearly defined jaw to which the slightly backward tilt of her head lent an overtly arrogant air. In another context she might be sniffing the breeze.

"Sort of like a cross between Joan Crawford and Bette Davis," Joan said.

"Not close up."

"She does look familiar."

"You've been reading the tabloids."

"I don't read the tabloids."

"Excuse me, then it must be your fantastic memory recalling a Dialing for Dollars movie you saw when you were ten. She was a B actress before she *wisely* got into producing. The only attributes she ever brought to the silver screen were those Brunhildic breasts."

Joan watched as the woman tossed her head back in laughter and then turned suddenly to look right at her. Involuntarily Joan ducked.

"What are you *doing?*" her mother said. "You ninny, *they* can't see *us! Give* me those. . . . Oh, dear," she said, pointing the glasses back out the porthole, "poor El."

Joan glanced around Fanny to see that her uncle had reached the *Finisterre.* He had rowed over to assess the damage he had done to Charles Dumas's little boat. One hand on the ladder Charlotte had lowered over the side, he was now standing in his pram dressed in his madras Bermudas, daisy-yellow knee socks, crested flag-red blazer and inevitable skipper's cap. With a reluctant pang of tenderness, Joan could just hear him "Requesting permission to come aboard, *Sir!*"

She also saw that two other men had appeared in the cockpit. One was a reddish-blond in loose white pants and top; Fanny said his name was Walter Hudson ("as in *Sonoma Valley* Hudson. He and Hayden have something going on but I think he also used to work for Chick. Anyway his winery is about to declare Chapter Eleven. . . .") The other was a tall thin darker-haired man. He could have been the one she'd seen at the *Finisterre*'s side when the hulls brushed. Philip Dumas, according to her mother, the "blue-eyed boy" of the antiquities department at the Met. . . .

Joan watched him reach down and take Eldon's outstretched hand to help him aboard.

"Of all the boats in the harbor, Eldon," Fanny muttered to herself. "Christ."

4

When Joan met Philip Dumas in person two weeks later, it was not, from her point of view, under greatly improved circumstances. She had taken the painting class she was teaching for the summer out to Wasque, the southeastern tip of Chappaquiddick where winter storms dug into the island and created clay cliffs that left the cover of pitch pine, scrub oak and bayberry brambles suspended over its long surf-smoothed beach. The vistas that resulted were spectacular. So much so that they completely overwhelmed her students and after a dismal showing she decided to abandon the spot—it also looked like it might rain—and start next time at a more manageable venue.

She arrived back on the other side of the island just as the *On Time*, the two-car ferry that was Chappaquiddick's primary access to the main island, was pulling out on its return run to Edgartown Village. With a several-minutes wait before it completed the trip, she left her bicycle against a piling and, pad and pencil in hand, climbed down the landing's bank. The narrows were picturesquely crowded with sail-boats returning from afternoon races, but what had caught her eye was a family of swans gliding with the current toward her. Hoping to intercept them as they traced the curve of the beach, Joan kicked off her sneakers and waded into the water. As they came abreast aways off shore, she swung her arm in a halfhearted attempt to appear to be throwing crumbs into the water. To her surprise the birds turned abruptly and began to chug toward her.

They came to a stop barely half a dozen yards away. Joan had never noticed the variation in the color of their feathers before, how the blue-white of their breasts and wings took on a green tint along their serpentine necks. Swinging her arm again, she inched her way deeper, her pencil hissing against the pad. Their downy heads were like heavy blossoms on soft stems, she mused. They were almost too beautiful, the curves almost too sublime. She swung her hand and took another step. *This* was Nature at her most serene . . . the epitome of dignity . . . the picture of peace. . . .

She might have stretched the description even further, had at this point the adult male not attacked. A gosling had drifted too close? She'd waded too near? Joan had no idea. All she knew was that there was a bowels-of-the-earth hiss, a lightning crack as the massive wings snapped open, and all at once the thing seemed to be running on top of the water, straight for her. With a cry, she whirled and splashed desperately back toward shore, not stopping until she was three-quarters of the way up the bank.

From a four-point crouch she turned back to see the birds cruising calmly away, not a ripple on the water, not a feather out of place, her sketch pad floating on the surface behind. She smiled, picked up a rock and threw it at them. She didn't miss by much, but to her annoyance her effort drew no notice. Not at any rate from the swans. From the opposite direction someone started to laugh.

"You have quite a way with animals," she heard as she swung around to find a man grinning at her from the driver's seat of a green Jeep. She had no idea who he was. At least not at first. It gradually dawned on her, however, that she had seen him somewhere before. Only after she'd fished her things out of the water and was halfway up the bank did she realize where.

The revelation was as welcome as the cold drop of rain that just now splashed on the back of her neck. If perversely funny in retrospect, the Cooks' performance in Cuttyhunk Pond two weeks earlier was something she'd just as soon forget. Killing time with Philip Dumas—she saw in a glance that the ferry had only just left the opposite shore—could hardly fail to dredge it up.

"Yes," she said cautiously as she approached the car, which he had parked directly beside her bike. "It's always been one of my strengths."

"I'm impressed. Frankly, they terrify me. Can I give you a lift?"

"Thanks"—she reached out and gave the handlebars a quick shake—"but I have this."

"But it's raining. You'll be soaked."

"I am already." Glancing down, she noticed that she was also covered with sand and short black strips of dried eel grass that clung to her skin like painted lines.

"Don't be silly," he persisted, nodding toward the channel. "It's really about to come down."

Joan looked reluctantly around only to see that he was right. Already pocked by the now heavy drops, the surface of the sea was blackening as the deluge swept inevitably toward them. As she was taking in the hopelessness of the scene, however, she suddenly realized something else: that she may have recognized Philip Dumas on sight, but unless the Dumases were as shameless with their binoculars as were the Cooks, he had no way of knowing who she was.

Joan turned back with a smile and accepted his offer. He lifted her bicycle into the back and slid in beside her just in time for a sheet of water to envelop them.

"You're an artist," Philip said nodding to the pad lying limply on Joan's lap. A hasty and now faded pencil study of birds covered the exposed page, which she began mechanically to dab with a corner of her T-shirt. "Do you show?"

"Oh, well, in books."

"An illustrator? Locally?"

"No, New York."

"Who do you work for?"

"Various publishers. I freelance."

"Really. We're always looking for illustrators."

"We?" As if she didn't know.

"The Met . . . ropolitan Museum of Art."

There was something disarming, as well as rather charming, about his quick, self-conscious smile. Approaching him as he leaned out of the Jeep's window, she'd recognized, of all things, his neck, which was strong-looking and sunburned. The rest, from the speeding deck of the *Priscilla*, she'd never gotten much of a look at. What she saw now as he navigated the ferry's gangplank was a long thin face shadowed with a day-old beard; a large, slightly crooked nose that looked as if it might have once been broken, and sharply defined sun-reddened lips. If the mouth added a little delicacy to the picture, direct, pale blue eyes lent it the appearance of intelligence. It was at any rate an interesting, if not conspicuously handsome, face. The rain pinged pleasantly on the roof.

"What do you do for them?" Joan asked although she knew the answer to this, too.

As Philip shut off the engine and turned in his seat to look at her, Joan realized inconsequentially that she had seen him once already that afternoon. He had been almost a quarter mile away, but the figure on the open slope of Wasque Point had been wearing a blue shirt like his and she thought she remembered now seeing a Jeep parked along one of the driveways off Pocha Road.

"Nothing at the moment," he was saying. "But until recently I was with the antiquities department."

"Really. I was just reading about your infamous East Greek Treasure. Has the suit been resolved or do you still have it?"

If the subject of the Met's latest legal war with the Turkish government was a sensitive one, he didn't seem to mind. If anything, he seemed pleased. "As a matter of fact we do."

"And you're going to keep it."

"Not personally, but yes. It belongs at the Met."

"Possession being nine-tenths . . . ?"

"Well, there's a little more to it than that."

"There must be, but I find it hard to imagine what an American museum's case could be for keeping another country's national treasure in its vaults."

"Aside from the question of *how* it was acquired, the pieces we have are all duplicated by those currently in the Turkish museum. Also the Met's better equipped to restore the artifacts than the Turks, not to mention properly house them."

"Ditto the Elgin Marbles, I suppose."

He grinned. "You sound passionate about this."

"Not especially. It just sounds like another example of the weak being bullied by the strong, or," she concluded, smiling back at him, "the poor being taken advantage of by the rich."

"Yes, it is, but this time it was a case of the rich *buying* from the poor. From the Turkish dealers themselves. Which way?"

Joan looked around. She was surprised to see they had arrived on the opposite shore and that the ferryman was already hauling back the chain. "Left," she said, thinking suddenly how strange it was that neither of them had yet offered his name. Not that it mattered terribly as she was beginning to enjoy herself. "And which, of course, excuses it."

Philip looked over. "You *are* passionate about this."

"I'm not. I just find it a shame that so much art and history has been lost or destroyed in the name of greed. I, for one, would like to have seen it."

"So would I," he said with a slight smile. "Tell me, do you and your parents sail every weekend?"

Joan gazed at him blankly, feeling a blush scorch a broad path across her cheeks.

"You probably don't remember," he went on with perfect tact, "but I met your father in Cuttyhunk a couple of weeks ago."

They looked at each other for a few seconds in silence. Despite every effort to contain it, a confessional smile began to jiggle the corners of her mouth. She'd never been much good at charades.

"My uncle," she said finally.

But if Philip had had any great attachment to his father's dinghy— or to the tenets of safe boating—he went out of his way to minimize Eldon's flamboyant disregard of both. He assured Joan first that no harm had been done ("We needed a new one anyway"—"I don't believe you"—"No, really") and then that he'd actually enjoyed meeting her uncle.

"You exaggerate."

"Not at all."

"In answer to your question," she said as ten minutes later they pulled into the Cooks' driveway, "we've sailed only once since. We ran aground in Robinson's Hole, tore a jib, and dropped a winch over the side."

Philip laughed. "You sound as if you don't really like to sail," he said.

"I hate it."

"Pity."

5

"Is it just the three of you up there?" Philip called above the wind.

He had picked Joan up at the Cooks' dock the following day in an impressive little two-man sailboat that Chick had bought some years back and literally outgrown. Lightweight and streamlined, it was carrying them over the light chop of the harbor like a knife on edge. The spit from the waves that slapped against the hull left a dusting of salt on their bare backs. It was true that boating with Uncle Eldon had taken a toll on Joan's taste for the sport, but this she didn't mind. Besides being easy to talk to and rather nice to look at—his body was unspectacular but attractively fit—Philip was obviously an excellent sailor as well.

She glanced over her shoulder at the Cooks' summer house, which sat back from the bluff at the top of an overgrown field. Its thick shingles had weathered to yellow-streaked brown and the squat pillars on either side of its seaside door needed paint. It looked rambling and rundown from here. Worse close to. It really had become too much for Fanny and Eldon to keep up. The problem was her uncle kept the place going as a sort of shrine—less to his wife than to his youth, Joan suspected—and her mother kept coming back because she couldn't stand the thought of him out here by himself.

"It is now," Joan said. "My uncle's wife died several years ago and shortly after their son joined a Buddhist colony in Nepal." She might have added that her father had started the decline ten years before that by running off to Central America with her mother's sister, neither of whom anyone ever heard from again (which also would've explained how she'd come to use Fanny's maiden name) but decided to leave it at that. She added only, "The problem is everybody seems to feel obliged to take their leave from that kitchen."

Philip cocked an eyebrow. "Your aunt *died* there?"

She'd been thinking about the errant lovers, but in the case of poor Priscilla, the shoe fit closely enough.

"Oh, well, for the most part," she said. "What about you?"

"Gee, we've had deaths here and there, but nothing so dramatic as—"

"No, no, I mean, do you always summer all together up here?"

Philip seemed to find this funny. "Not as a rule," he said with a short laugh. "This year is something of an exception. I have the time because I'm on a writing leave from the Met. And my sister, Hayden—" He stopped and thought for a moment, his smile dimming slightly, "has rediscovered the joys of family life."

"Walter works for your father?"

"Worked. *Ready about*—"

"Your father's retired?"

"For fifteen years. *Hard to lee*—"

Philip thrust the tiller away from him. There was a momentary explosion of chaos and noise but then the wind caught the other side of the sails and they were off on the opposite tack. Joan looked back at him with a cautious smile. "Is it true he found a treasure in Turkey?"

Whether he'd actually been anticipating the question, his smile told her it didn't exactly catch him by surprise.

"He found several," he said, "but not the one you're talking about."

"Oh, really. I thought . . . my mother said that he'd found some long-lost *head*."

"A head?"

"Of a goddess, I thought she said."

Philip looked confused for a moment, then chuckled. "Close—she must have meant the *face*—of Mynnia. Who was not exactly a goddess. More like the kitchen help."

"That's democratic."

"For the times, yes it was."

"What did she do? Shake off her shackles and marry a king?"

"No, but she *saved* a king. You've heard of Croesus?"

"Oh, sure, the J. Paul Getty of Asia Minor."

"Well, one of the reasons he was so rich was because he was perpetually attacking his neighbors—and always won. The reason he always won—or so he saw it—was because he never waged a war without consulting an oracle first. And, of course, he never consulted an oracle without leaving a lavish offering behind. When it finally came time to invade the Persians he prepared his most spectacular offering, a fortune in coins and some statues, all bearing the face or figure of Mynnia, the woman who baked for him."

"She must have been a good cook."

"Possibly, but she was appreciated more for foiling his evil step-mother's plot to poison him. Either way, he left a few statues and bowls at the oracle, got what he thought was a green light to go ahead with the attack, and buried the rest of the treasure outside Sardis, the capital of Lydia, planning to present it at Delphi after the battle. The problem was the kind of advice one tended to get from an oracle was ambiguous at best—which, naturally, accounted for their success at predicting the future. In Croesus's case he interpreted the message to mean victory was assured. Another reading would have warned him that his army would be beaten and his empire overrun. Which it was. The Persians showed up on camels, which were entirely new to the Lydians' horses, and at first sight—or smell—of them, the horses all turned tail and ran."

"Which meant the offering stayed buried?"

"According to the story."

"And this is the treausre your father tried to find."

"He among others."

"Based on this story? It wouldn't seem like a lot to go on."

"Archeologists are funny that way. Watch your head."

They had come to the mouth of Caleb Pond, a shallow inner bay on the western shore of Chappaquiddick. The flow of water between the harbor and bay cut a narrow winding channel through a spit of sand. Philip let the boom swing wide and they glided toward it on the incoming tide. The surface of the channel was perfectly smooth and in the lee of the shore the air was silent. Joan had asked if they could stop here for a swim, but she'd really wanted to see if it was as she had remembered as a child. The scale was all wrong, of course, and the intervening winters had moved things around, but the feel of the place was essentially the same: After the bluster of the open water, it was as if they had passed through an invisible slit in the day.

"I used to come here," she told him as she slid into the warm waist-deep water and began pulling the boat toward a small patch of sand not yet covered by the flowing tide. "But *years* ago. It was different then—a bit deeper and not so wide, and I think this part of the sand bar is new—but it's surprisingly unchanged. . . . I wonder if the sharks are still here."

Philip, who had taken down the sails and was straddling the gunwale, about to join her, stopped and looked up. "Sharks?"

"Oh, there were *loads* of them in here," she said brightly. "My cousin and I used to chase them in our dinghy. It was a very un-Buddhist thing to do, but a lot of fun. Get out and I'll show you."

Philip sat back down in the cockpit. "I don't like sharks very much," he said.

She looked back at him. "You're *not* afraid."

"I'm not? You may not have suffered in the least from early domestic trauma but I'm not above phobias and this is one I'm perfectly proud of. You could take your bathing suit off right now and I wouldn't swim ten feet to you with a shark within ten miles of this boat. As a matter of fact, I wouldn't even wade to you with a shark within ten miles of this boat."

"Philip, there's a shark within ten miles of every boat."

"Which is why I never go in the water."

Joan could not suppress a laugh. The transformation was truly irresistible: Philip Dumas never looked so handsome as he suddenly did now, cowering in his little boat.

"You're really not joking."

He shook his head.

She grinned. "Well then stay where you are and I'll show you from there."

"I'd just as soon you didn't."

"I promise you'll be perfectly safe."

She gave the boat a push into the current and began to lead it by the anchor line, wading into the water as the bar fell away. Leaning unenthusiastically over the edge, Philip watched the bottom drop off until, at eight feet, it leveled out. He could make out the shapes of a flounder, a crab, a large, gray-green eel and several strands of kelp waving like frayed brown flags. Happily, he did not see a shark. Not, at any rate, until he turned back to Joan, who was thigh deep at the edge of the bar trying to lodge the anchor. Not five yards behind her a triangular fin was plying the smooth surface. It was heading directly for her.

"Behind you!" he shouted.

It was a shout Fanny and Eldon should have been able to hear from their front porch. Joan heard it too, but looked instead at him. He shook his head and pointed. She turned finally to watch the fish glide toward her. It had by now cut its distance in half. It came within three feet before turning away and heading across the sand bar in the direction of the boat.

She was smiling broadly when she turned back to Philip. "They're still here!"

"Obviously," Philip said, adding, "What *are* you doing?" as Joan suddenly took several bounds toward it, chasing it to the edge of the bank. He murmured only a weak "Oh, please" as she dove in after it and disappeared from sight.

"Did you see . . . where he went?" she called between breaths after surfacing several yards off the other side of the boat.

"Gee, Joan, I didn't notice," Philip said, adding mildly, "but I'm sure you'll find him," as she filled her lungs and dove again. Peering reluctantly over the side, Philip looked down just in time to make out the blunt-headed outline of the shark, cruising calmly under the boat. In the next moment he saw Joan, swimming toward it. She was of course reaching for its tail. He watched her grab it and for several seconds be towed by the fish, until with a violent shudder it freed itself.

"You know I think maybe you *have* been affected somewhat by domestic trauma," he called to her when in a halo of bubbles she returned to the surface. "In fact, I think somewhere along the line you may have lost your—oh, great—another friend of yours?" Another gray fin was carving a lazy zig-zag toward them across the shallows. "Perhaps you'd like to cut yourself first this time and make it really exciting. I know I have my Swiss Army knife somewhere here."

Pulling the boat with her, Joan was wading clumsily toward the sand bar. Philip watched as with a halfhearted swing of her arm she splashed water at the approaching fish, which veered off in a gradual arc. "God, I hate girls with a death wish," he sighed.

Joan leaned heavily against the gunwale beside him. "They're not . . . dangerous," she said between drags of air. "They're sand sharks. . . . They don't . . . have . . . teeth."

Her eyelashes cradled large shining droplets of water. Her soft round cheeks were flushed, her yellow hair glinted in the sun. She grinned invitingly at him. Philip gazed at her for several moments in silence, then slowly smiled. She braced herself to be kissed.

He handed her a towel. "Just never expect me to come and save you," he said.

Straightening, Joan had to laugh. Mostly at herself. "I'll keep it in mind."

They had just cleared the mouth of the channel when she asked, "Whatever happened to Mynnia?"

Philip headed the little boat off the wind, let out the sails and set them on a broad reach toward the Cooks' dock. "The evil stepmother paid her back for her efforts," he said with a smile.

"How?"

"She had her bodyguard shoot an arrow through her throat."

6

Chick Dumas looked even less like an archeologist in person than he had sitting in the cockpit of his grand boat. Tall and corpulent, he wasn't a bullfrog but a bear of a man with bear-paw hands, appropriately gravelly voice and blunt, slightly upturned nose. Joan could not imagine him tying his own shoes let along crawling around in the dirt dusting things with a powder brush. Then again, she wouldn't have thought him capable of two sets of tennis, either. But not only had he not succumbed to heat prostration—Fanny's comment about his heart had never been far from Joan's mind—he was largely responsible for their 7–5, 6–4 upset over his wife and son.

Invited to join them in a casual game of doubles, Joan had found the Dumas house at the end of a long dirt driveway that wound through pine trees to the edge of a bluff on the northeastern shore of Chappaquiddick. It was a typical old summer estate ringed with overplanted gardens, thick lawn and a wide pillared wooden porch that on the ocean side gave way to an open flagstone terrace. It was here that the group had reassembled after what turned out to be anything but a casual match. Theirs was a victory Chick clearly intended to savor.

"Perhaps you'll grace our courts—on my side, of course—again," he said with a hoarse chuckle as he wiped a dripping brow with one hand and poured Joan a glass of beer with the other. "I'd given up ever beating my son again. And, of course, it's always a pleasure to beat one's wife."

"You've no idea what you've started," Charlotte said to Joan as she patted her flushed face with a towel. She had a slight curl at the corner of her pink lips. "These two have been breast-feeding an ugly little competition for years now. It had, until today, appeared to be dying a natural death."

Charlotte's eyes were the yellow-green of a new leaf and her cheekbones were set high in a face that was otherwise pale and, not coincidentally, wrinkle-free. It was the kind of face whose individual features were forgettable, if not in some cases almost ugly—her chin was tapered severely, her nostrils taut and sharp, her teeth small and a bit turned in—but which put together somehow made for a striking look. It would have been easy to imagine her the centerpiece of Chick's material possessions and, some twenty-five years younger than her husband, emblem and retainer of his lost youth. However, it had been immediately obvious to Joan that Charlotte was no man's conversation piece. Even if the two sets of merciless tennis had not told her as much, the woman's hands did. Large and mannish, with nails unpainted and clipped short, they suggested vigorous use, if nothing else. She was not a woman who gardened or dug through bones, or did anything else for that matter, in gloves. The only thing that didn't fit the picture was her voice, which was as sweetly thin and high-pitched as a child's.

"I warn you, dear," she went on, "you're about to be conscripted into the Edgartown Charity Tournament, which is a misleading title to say the least. Last year's loser was calling for urine samples."

Philip laughed. "Who was that?"

"Your father."

"Well, I very much doubt Ms. Cook could be convinced to come in on our side," Philip said. "It seems she's rather cool on the rape of the Nile."

Chick gave Joan a surprised look.

"What's more," he went on, "she thinks I should repatriate the East Greek Treasure and that you, Dad, should be prosecuted for the desecration of the Ancient World."

"Is that so?" Chick grunted with obvious pleasure.

"It is not," Joan said.

"Yes," his son continued, "she thinks that if you have the Croesian Hoard hidden in a trunk in your attic, you should give it back."

"I never said *that*," Joan said quickly. "Only that it was *unfortunate* that so many countries had lost their *national treasures* due to—"

"Well, you're absolutely right," Chick jumped energetically in. "There's been disastrous loss at the hands of our 'western' antiquarians. That maniac Schliemann, by his own admission, destroyed more of Troy than he unearthed before he realized he was even there. The horse's ass dug right through it. If *it* is what it was."

"And you always have Evans to thank for that lovely job he and his decorator did on Knossos." Everyone looked around. Chick's daughter had drifted out of the house smoking a cigarette and carrying what looked like a souvenir shop ashtray with tourist slogans and a picture of a waterfall painted on the side. Joan had a hard time picturing any of the Dumases carting it back from Niagara Falls. Least of all this woman.

Hayden was even taller and rather more voluptuous than Joan had been able to tell through Fanny's binoculars and the hat she'd been wearing had hidden a head of wavy blue-black hair. Nor did she look anything like Bette Davis or Joan Crawford, though her facial features were pronounced in a stylized, 1940s sort of way. The effect in her case was not unattractive but decidedly and, Joan suspected, deliberately forbidding. Though striking when animated by a smile, which was rarely, the set of her mouth was not exactly friendly. Her eyes, which showed ever so often over her black lenses, were, like Chick's and Philip's, a translucent blue, but in this case blank-wall remote. After one brief assessing glance, during which Joan felt as if she were a cut of beef being examined for fat, they rarely turned Joan's way again.

"My personal favorite was Giovanni Battista Belzoni," she'd gone on in a slightly bored tone that went perfectly with the rest of her presentation. "Before becoming one of the more avid archeologist-slash-collectors of the century, he was, appropriately enough, a circus strongman who went by the name 'The Patagonian Sampson.' " She took a deep drag on her cigarette and blew the smoke out sharply as if suddenly unhappy with the taste. "He used to carry two-dozen people around on his back."

" 'Those were the great days of excavating,' " a voice with an overdone British accent said from the other side of the patio, "as Howard Carter liked to say. 'Anything to which a fancy was taken, from a scarab to an obelisk, was just appropriated and if there was a difference with a brother excavator, one laid for him with a gun'. . . . Or something like that."

"I see you've been flashing the trespassers again, Walter," Chick said putting a meaty hand up to the sun. He'd come from around the corner of the house with a beach towel tied around his waist. Except for a pair of aviator glasses, he appeared to have nothing else on. His dark strawberry-blond hair was slicked back off his large freckled forehead and there were dandelion heads caught between his toes. His smile revealed a set of friendly white teeth. Dropping into a chair beside Joan, he gazed at her for an extra beat and said, "I'm Walter Hudson, who are you?"

"I still say blame for this lies at the door of local governments," Philip went on, "who back then didn't care what was carted away or by whom."

"I've always found it ironic," Chick said, "that in the region where western history *began* there was so little regard for it. We're all so obsessed with the past, while the Turks, and the Egyptians, with all those centuries behind them. . . ."

"It's like having too many pairs of shoes," Walter said, getting up to tint a full glass of vodka with a thin film of cranberry juice.

"Or not enough," Joan said.

"Either way, the worst have always been the nationals themselves," Charlotte said. "Look how much of modern Cairo is built from dismantled temples and pyramids."

Walter leaned over to Joan: "Most mummy cases were broken up and sold for firewood."

"What did they do with the bodies?"

"They were eaten."

"They were not!"

"Well, maybe not the whole thing."

"I don't believe you."

"Oh, yes, dear," Charlotte said in her serene little voice, "mummy had a long and respectable reputation as a medicinal substance from as early as the tenth century. The word is derived from the Persian word *mummia*, a term for pitch or bitumen. Pissasphalt, which was used for any number of ailments, looks a lot like the bituminous materials used by the Ancient Egyptians in the mummification process. When pissasphalt was in short supply, it became common practice to substitute the hardened bituminous materials found in the body cavities for the real thing. From there it was an even shorter step to substitute the dried flesh of the mummy itself. More beer?"

"By the seventeenth century you had a flourishing trade in mummified human flesh," Walter said. "Grave robbers also used to boil the dead bodies—much as you would a sun-dried tomato—until the flesh fell off, then collected the oil that rose to the surface and sold it to the French nobility who were very big on the stuff."

"Is this true?" Joan asked Chick.

"Most of it," he said with an apologetic shrug.

"It's entirely true," Walter said. "The mummy market was insatiable for at least two centuries, and certainly more profitable than agriculture. The market value in Scotland in 1600 was about eight shillings a pound. Of course, today in your average Manhattan drug store"—he glanced at Philip—"it must go for close to what? Eighty dollars an ounce?"

Philip thought a moment. "I wouldn't know."

Walter tilted his head confidentially toward Joan's and, putting up a hand, added in a low voice, "The problem, of course, was always the risk of fraud and the use of fresh corpses when supply was outstripped by demand."

"Thanks a lot, all of you, for that most edifying seminar," Hayden drawled, holding up a long-fingered palm and getting to her feet. "I particularly liked the part about the tomato. I find you all tasteless in the extreme. Joan, it was nice to meet you. Maybe we can do curses next time. There's nothing quite as interesting as an untimely end, don't you find? Now, I'm going for a swim. Walter, darling, you'll come again, won't you?"

He glanced waggishly around the little group, sprang to his feet and trotted after her.

"So this is what your family does for fun," Joan said. "Bring girls home and titilate them with tales of the macabre?"

Philip smiled. "Only the ones we like."

"What a morbid bunch. I was waiting for someone to run inside and bring me out a pouch of powdered flesh."

"We don't like to show off."

They had climbed down the bluff to walk along the shore. The afternoon had quieted into a breathless evening and at the onset of night the still water of the outer harbor reflected the faint pink and orange blush of high clouds as faithfully as a sheet of glass. Even the tide seemed to be standing still: Mooring lines hung slack from the boats that floated listlessly at odd angles to each other. With the gulls huddling silently on the jetty, the only noise on earth seemed to be the distant rumble of Walter Hudson's salacious laugh. Except for that, the scene was glaringly romantic.

"What was that your stepmother was saying about Sir George Rawlins wearing a bag of *mummy* around his neck?" Joan was wading a few yards into the water; Philip was strolling just out.

"She was exaggerating—King Francis I of France was known to do that. Charlotte is not terribly fond of poor Sir George."

"I thought you said he and your father were partners."

"At one time. But their relationship ultimately deteriorated into a rivalry, culminating in a rather nasty squabble over the Croesian Hoard."

"So Sir George was looking for it, too. Tell me, what set them all off, after all these years?"

"Oh, there'd been attempts to find it since the 1800s—certainly documented ones before that. This one was a late spontaneous flow-

ering of a supposedly 'friendly' competition that'd been brewing off
and on in academic circles for decades. Really what it amounted to
was a last stand for a clique of aging archeologists who'd probably
never see the field again whether they found it or not."

"It's almost too bad that they didn't."

"Well, they found something. Or Sir George did, though not until
two years later. My father had quit by then, but Rawlins went back.
He says he had 'a vision'—he can be a little self-important—and
found what he insists was the crypt Croesus was supposed to have
had specially carved for the trove. And probably was."

Joan stopped and looked back at Philip. He added quickly:

"But no gold. It had been looted, most likely thousands of years
ago, within decades of Croesus's death, or even during his lifetime,
with the invasion of the Persians, and the pieces were melted down,
reburied, or simply scattered like dust on the dry Anatolian wind."

"Or never existed?"

"Possibly, though I prefer to think it did. It's more gratifying to
imagine a treasure still hidden somewhere, in one piece."

They looked at each other for a moment in silence. A pleasant
tightness had already crept into Joan's chest. To her annoyance, it was
accompanied by a film of perspiration that began now to creep across
her palms. She stooped to rinse her hands in the water.

"Joan."

"What?"

"You know they shot the opening scene from the movie *Jaws*
practically on this very spot."

"No, they didn't."

"Well, near here."

"On the other side of the island."

"But it *is* true that sharks feed at night."

"Not in twelve inches of water."

"No, but did you know that something like seventy-five percent of
all shark attacks take place in less than three feet of water?"

"I see you've researched this quite thoroughly."

"Yes, so imagine my relief the other day when you dove deeper
down. I'd really have hated to have to watch you ground into shreds."

"Well, I would hope. . . ."

He looked at her a moment in silence. "The whole thing made for a pretty unique come-on."

"Not in your wildest . . ." Joan laughed, but was happy for the twilight as she felt herself blush. It had indeed. There was a pause before she murmured, "Maybe so," and another one before adding, "But it didn't work."

"Actually, it did," said Philip, who began to wade toward her.

Joan chuckled. "I thought you wouldn't wade ten feet if I was stark naked."

"That was a lie. Mmm, clammy hands. Another good sign."

"You mean you don't hate girls with a death wish?"

"Oh, no, that I do," he said as he finally leaned forward to kiss her. "But you said sand sharks don't have teeth."

─ 7 ───────────────

"So, darling, you're obviously sleeping with him," Fanny said looking up. "Are you in love?"

Her daughter only smiled.

Fanny thrust a meaty forearm back into her handbag and continued to rummage. "Let's see, yesterday it was a drive on East Beach, the day before a picnic on Cape Poge. Or was it body-surfing off Wasque? (Honestly, I *have* to get a smaller bag.) And this isn't counting all the romantic walks on Norton Point, sailing in Katama. . . . Really, you two are like a series of Hallmark cards."

Joan chuckled. It was true. "You're keeping a ledger?" They were sitting in a dockside clam bar where for the last thirty minutes Joan, chin in hand, had watched her mother eat raw littlenecks as fast as the man behind the counter could shuck them.

"Well, dearie, he's in my own kitchen half the mornings I come down. *Here* it is! Oh, hell, that's not it. So I have to assume *something's* going on. Oh, at *last!*" Fanny pulled a tube of salmon lipstick out of the bag, screwed it up, shaped an *O* with her lips and in one expert stroke made a perfect application. With that she flicked it back into her bag, glanced up and looked hard at her daughter. "Head over heels, I suppose," she said.

Joan's smile broadened. This was also true. Fanny sighed. "Well, I just can't help wondering—you'll be a mother some day—where it's going. I can't say I'm not relieved to see you happy, after that shit what's-his-name who ran off with the faith healer—"

"Paul 'Don't Tie Me Down' Dorman? She wasn't a faith healer, she was a homeo—"

"But I'd sure hate to see you hurt like that again. Oh, no thanks, Frank, dear, we've had enough, just the bill, please. I mean, what's going to happen at the end of the month when Philip takes this new position at the Louvre? You're *not* thinking of following him to France."

"As a matter of fact," Joan said as gently as she could, "I am."

Fanny stared at her daughter, directed a loud puff of air at the ceiling and threw down her bag. *"Frank!* Another round!"

"I *am* in love," Joan confessed as the first shell clattered onto Fanny's fresh plate. "And I've always wanted to live in Paris."

"Who hasn't?" Fanny said sourly. "What're you gonna do? Knit berets by the *feu?*"

"From what Chick and Philip say the antiquities community is always looking for illustrators, for texts and cataloguing. Without counting the Louvre, it'd take a lifetime to exhaust the Dumas family contacts."

"My, aren't we the opportunistic little thing all of a sudden."

"It's not exactly the reason I'm going. But if it makes you feel any better, I've already lined up some work on my own. My publisher is putting together another travel book on France and they're looking for submissions from Paris."

"It all still sounds like my Joannie hanging ten off another one of her impulses."

"Not this time."

"Well, let's hope it turns out better than the last."

"Paul was a *boy.*"

"And you were a *girl.* From where I sit you're *still* a girl!"

"You were married seven years by the time you were twenty-seven."

"Six. . . . And times have changed. Besides, look at what happened to me."

Joan considered a moment. "You have a point. But believe me, my eyes are wide open."

"Which doesn't mean you have the first idea what you're looking at."

"Which is what?" Joan asked, regretting the question as soon as it was out of her mouth.

"Okay, let's start with Philip," Fanny said, wiping her lips and rounding energetically on her daughter, "who I won't even point out is ten years older than you—"

"Five."

"But I *will* remind you he's had a long reputation as a gay blade and you're crazy if you don't keep *that* in mind. That and the fact that he and his sister run with a fast crowd. His 'Yugoslavian girlfriend,' by the way, was a bonafide princess."

"Yes, he told me."

"Well, then, don't look so impressed—there's nothing trashier than a throneless Balkan royal. Except for maybe Walter Hudson, who besides being an Olympic-class sybarite, has a dubious business reputation, to say the least."

"He puts sulfites in his wine?"

"No, but I've heard things about 'funny' antiquities deals in Guatemala."

"He loots Mayan tombs."

"I don't know the specifics. But one look at the man. . . ."

"I see what you're saying."

"Furthermore, I don't have to tell you what's been said about the old man. . . ."

"No, you don't. And it's old as the hills. Besides, he's retired now, living a harmless life on the West Bank of the Seine, as peaceful and quiet as a monk."

"While the ice maiden and his princess bride duke it out over his fortune like Godzilla and the Monster from the Id."

"That's old too. And anyway, even if there weren't going to be thirty-five hundred miles of deep water between them, it has nothing to do with me." Joan put the last clam on her mother's plate. "Give up and be happy for me. I know exactly what I'm getting in for."

Fanny gave her daughter a pained look, heaved a maternal sigh and gazed down at her clam. *"You* were probably somebody's post-adolescent daughter, too, weren't you? And look where you ended up." She slid it whole into her mouth and shot a sidelong glance at Joan, who was having trouble suppressing a smile.

"Don't get excited, dearie," she added as she chewed. "I'm not conceding that this is the greatest idea in the world. I'm not even conceding it's a good idea, but I've said all I'm going to about it. It's your life to ruin as you choose. Split another half dozen."

"It's almost lunch."

"Okay, then, here, pay the man. Now in return for my blessing, which you're getting damn cheap, you'll let me write the story on your torrid love affair."

Joan gaped at her in disbelief.

"I'm kidding. All I really want is for you to let me come visit. I've been dying to get into that—"

Fanny didn't finish her sentence. Having gathered their things, they'd just taken a step back into the sunshine when a figure darted suddenly in front of them and raised his fists to his face. They heard rather than saw the automatic shutter buzz as many as five pictures before either woman, blinded by the sunlight and confused by the event, knew what was happening. He got off another three before Joan shouted at him to stop, at which point he turned and trotted away.

Without stopping to think about what she was doing, Joan dropped the bags she was carrying and broke into a run after him. He glanced over his shoulder, saw her closing and put on an impressive burst of speed. Dodging artfully through the crowds, he sprinted up the block and disappeared down a sidestreet. Slowed just enough by the heavy foot traffic, Joan reached the corner too late to see into which store or down which alley he had ducked. She was left standing there, winded and flushed, staring down the empty street.

She found Fanny back at the bar, three littlenecks into another half dozen.

"That's the second time that's happened!" Joan said, dropping her fist loudly on the counter. Frank, behind the counter, gave her an expectant glance. "No, I didn't mean—nothing for me—"

"What, dear?"

"Someone tried to take Philip's and my picture in the damn *car* last week! I thought it was some idiot tourist thinking we were Kennedys. I can't understand it. It doesn't—what's so funny?"

To Joan's surprise, Fanny had begun to chuckle.

"You'd better get used to it, child," she said squeezing a wedge of lemon over her last clam, which visibly winced. "We *paparazzi* eat Dumases like peanuts."

8

The not altogether successful mix of eighteenth- and twentieth-century architecture that was Tony and Anika Sloan's summer home commanded the high ground of a great expanse of green lawn that overlooked Menemsha Pond and beyond it the blue haze of Vineyard Sound. The scene from the wide stone terrace that ran the length of the house looked in the sparkling end-of-summer sun like something painted by Claude Monet. Trailed about by black-aproned maids toting silver serving trays, smartly dressed guests dotted it like carefully positioned props, drifting leisurely down the steps and in and out of the broad-striped tent that billowed in the afternoon breeze. Strains of a Gershwin tune (. . . *They laughed at meeee wanting you . . . said I was reaching for the moooon . . .)* floated unevenly on the outdoor air.

The picturesque occasion was the last party of the season, which, in the crowd with which Joan had become indirectly associated, was traditionally thrown by the Sloans. It was big and usually raucous and always cost them a bundle, with elaborate bars and stretch buffets. But in his old age Tony had become obsessed with his own mortality—also not incidentally fond of drink—and by Labor Day each year he began to have premonitions of not living through the winter to see his friends again in the spring. This was at least Anika's theory. Whatever the cause, the Sloans held nothing back and this year's farewell fete was no exception. The Cooks had arrived on time and found better than fifty people already there.

They were, Fanny could tell in one delirious glance, bel mondo to a man. "Ashton the designer," she murmured excitedly to her brother as she led him forcibly into the crowd. "Her daughter just married a Dupont." "Keep your voice down, dear." "The woman talking to her is the wife of James Michener's or somebody big's agent—used to go around with the Warhol crowd—family's loaded." "Fan, please!" "Well, it's true! The money she spends on face cream alone could burn a wet elephant. . . ."

Joan watched after them for a moment with a pained look, but then turned and headed deliberately for the other end of the terrace. Collecting a large plateful of hors d'oeuvres and a glass of champagne on the way, she found a deep wicker armchair, slipped off her shoes, sat back, raised her glass to herself and took a long swallow. If her mother had come to lurk, gossip and very likely embarrass herself, she'd come to celebrate. Two months of freelance work had been lined up, her plane ticket had been paid for, her bags were packed. In three days she and Philip would be touching down in Paris, of all places. Chick and Charlotte had insisted they stay with them—"The place is so big we could have the Harlem Men's Choir upstairs, practicing, and you'd never know it"—until Philip's tenants moved out and they took his Left Bank apartment over as their own.

The romantic merits of the plan aside, Joan was ready to go. She'd miss Fanny, possibly even Uncle Eldon, but after three months in the same house, the time had definitely come to relax the familial embrace. Even as she thought this, her ears picked out the familiar voice from across the terrace. "American intellectual! Kenny Joyce is as Irish as Paddy's pig and has the IQ of a pinch of salt!"

Nor, she mused, was she going to be heartbroken at the prospect of saying good-bye to various members of the Dumas clan. Certainly not Walter, who'd not only lingered for most of the summer, but had done so with the ubiquitous quality of a cloud of black flies. But least of all Hayden, whom Joan had found as enchanting as a pit of asps. For a busy New York film producer she couldn't seem to get enough beach time on the Vineyard this year.

"It's the pimple on the face of France!" Joan heard her announce now as she strode from around the house in a flaming red gown whose slit up the leg and plunging neckline all but met in the middle. For anyone else the entrance might have crossed from high drama into comedy, but Hayden somehow carried it off. Then, Joan thought as she leaned forward to watch, if sufficiently motivated she could probably pull it off in a burlap sack.

"I mean, I personally think the Louvre as a *museum* is a disaster, but history is history. Why stop at destroying the architectural integrity of the centerpiece of French culture? With the symbol of an Egyptian tomb of all things! Why not paint Notre Dame pink? Or rewrite the *Marseillaise* to a bossa nova beat?"

"Yes, exactly!" Anika Sloan rejoined. "And haven't we all had enough I. M. Pei to last us a lifetime?"

"I rather like it," Charlotte's little-girl voice said from somewhere below Joan's line of vision.

"Oh, Charlotte, *please*," Hayden said.

"I'm quite serious. I think a glass pyramid by an Asian-American architect in the middle of the Louvre garden is a nice neat blow to French cultural chauvinism, which I for one am tired of. It's beautifully American. And so perfectly . . . mod."

"God, you're as bad as Didi, who called it a 'brilliant pinnacle of socio-architectural derring-do' or some such guano and tried to re-write our script to use it as . . ."

"A wall flower? In the nineties?"

With a jump of her shoulders, Joan whirled around to see that Walter had come up behind her. He was holding out a glass of champagne—her own was hanging upside down by its stem—and grinning. "You're hopelessly out of step, my dear."

"Jesus, Walter!" she said, having literally to catch her breath. "I'm not being a wallflower. I'm taking in the view."

"East-north-east, that'd be dead on the Eiffel Tower. Or there-abouts. Not nervous, are you?"

Joan hesitated but then, despite better judgment, took the glass from him. "What would I have to be nervous about?"

"Not a thing. The house is a bit spooky but not haunted, as far as anyone knows. Unless you count the maid, who can be a bit much but is no Mrs. Danvers. You don't have to worry about finding any *real* skeletons in the closet or Lydian gold behind the bathroom tiles—we've all searched the place a hundred times. And if you can stomach this bunch," his nod signified the party in general, "you can take the likes of Didi Devilliers and the rest of the Continent crowd. Some of 'em'll want you dead—Philip's sort of a favorite son—but I imagine you're pretty good," he glanced around and smiled suggestively, "in a corner."

"Something you'd know more about than me."

He pulled a chair up beside hers. "Just don't let anybody get you believing they're something that they're not." His gaze drifted down to the lawn. "Keep in mind that Hayden Dumas Channing, though I love her madly, is a just your average high-horse bitch. Charlotte, who carries on as if she were one of Truman Capote's swans, is just your average gold digger. Her husband, who robs in turns from the cradle and the grave, is your average slightly brilliant, slightly mad and slightly crooked scientist. And Philip—"

"I'm living with them for a few weeks, Walter, not marrying in. But I can't help wondering what *you're* doing among them if you think so little of these people." She smiled. "Or are you just an average gold digger yourself?"

"Now, I didn't say I didn't *like* them. I just see no reason for any of us to put on airs. Wealth affords one a good dry cleaner but we're all as filthy underneath." He picked up Joan's shoe and turned it slowly around in his hands as if it were a thing of beauty, or, she thought, a piece of her flesh.

"I don't believe in original sin," she said, taking it from him and putting it back on her foot.

"Not original sin. Inevitable corruptibility. The well-bred as well as the downtrodden. In fact more so as things tend to spoil faster in the sun." He nodded to the assembly below. "You'll see what I mean."

"Why don't you tell me what you mean," she said impatiently. Joan was ashamed to admit her curiosity was piqued. His answer, however, was irritatingly vague.

"Only that the human being is inherently flawed, prone to avarice, jealousy and violence, that sort of thing, and this manifests itself one way or the other. It doesn't, however, mean we're not also capable of the occasional good, breathtaking genius, even. I mean, there's Michelangelo and Mother Theresa, after all. It's just that we can better be counted on for nerve gas and," he looked back at her now and smiled, "adultery."

"What *are* you trying to tell me, Walter? That there's a sociopathic murderer among them?"

"Now that might be taking it a little far."

"Taking what a little far?"

"Ah, Phil. We were just talking about you."

"Were you?"

"No," Joan said, getting up, "I think we were just talking about Walter. Either way, we're finished. Unless there was something you wanted to add. No? Good." She slipped her arm through Philip's. "I'm feeling avaristic, darling, let's go eat."

It was late and almost everyone had gone home. The stragglers— the Dumases and the Cooks among them—were finishing their coffee in the Sloans' living room. Joan was sitting on the couch with Philip and Anika, who were deep in what should have been a fascinating discussion of a significant new archeological find in southern Africa. However, Joan was listening with only half an ear, her attention having been drawn to a conversation behind them between Chick and Tony Sloan.

Tony may have been a one-time colleague of Chick's but Joan didn't get the impression they were intimate friends. Perhaps for the same reason Chick was leaning slightly away from the man as they talked: Tony had been drinking steadily all night and was in Eldon's words as drunk as a tick. He had asked Chick about the rumored curse of the Met's East Greek Treasure and Chick was indulging his host good-naturedly.

"The first casualty was a dealer who offered too little for the goods. He had hot pepper thrown in his eyes and was blinded. The ringleader, a man named Durmush, was paralyzed by a stroke, his son was murdered in a knife fight, and his son-in-law was run over and killed by a tractor he bought with his cut of the loot. The dealer who sold it all to the Met died, too, but then he was pretty old."

"*Marvelous!*" Tony spouted with a pronounced slur. "Just deserts and all that. I love it, but, oh, Chick, it's of course our line of work, too." The man was beginning to list to one side. "Or was."

"Tony, darling, you need some coffee," his wife said coolly.

"Yes and while you're at it," Walter said from across the room, "bring a large tureen we can pour him into."

"Fuck you," Tony mumbled and, ignoring both Walter and his wife, who was trying to hand him a cup of coffee, swung back to Chick. "Ever been cursed yourself, Chick? Hear sirens singing in the night? Banshee's wail? Side-stepped any falling bricks? Missed by inches, that sort of thing?"

"Not that I'm aware of."

"I keep hearing 'bout a Curse of Croesus."

"I've heard that too, but there's no way of telling, is there? Not knowing who opened it."

"Not knowing! Right!"

"Tony, honey, take this."

Tony waved off his wife and leaned closer to Chick. Everyone else in the room had by now stopped to listen. "C'mon, Chick. Isn't it about time you came clean? Everyone knows you got it, what I wanna know is where you're keeping it? Rue St. Dominique is my bet."

"I'm afraid to disappoint you, but—"

"I always thought you had it, the way you arrived home suddenly in the middle of the Sardis thing."

"I'm sorry, Tony, I wish I had, however—"

"Just the three of you. You, Cecil and that other hooligan. All missing from the dig at the same time and all quitting early with a mysterious case of dysentery, or yellow fever, or whatever the hell you said it was."

Joan felt Philip's arm slide out from behind her head.

"Tony, honey," his wife said.

"*And* all three now in early retirement, living in—" the man reeled as he waved his arm to invoke the splendor of his own living room, "luxury. Some say you split it up three ways but I think you got the whole thing and I think it's right there in that house."

"If it ever existed, Tony," Philip said, getting to his feet, "it disappeared twenty-five centuries ago. And you know as well as anybody there hasn't even been so much as a smudge of gold dust to suggest it ever did."

Tony swayed and grinned. "Well, 'til now."

"What are you talking about?" Charlotte asked from the patio door.

"Don't you know?" he said, looking from her to Philip and finally back to Chick, who was gazing at him with a patient, bemused expression. "Where you all been? Goddamn Rawlins finally found his coin."

"What coin?" Hayden, Charlotte and, to her embarrassment, Joan, asked in unison.

"The goddamn *Croesian* coin!" Tony slurred. "For goddamn Delphi. It's her face. I saw it." Tony grinned and swayed. "It's *Mynnia.* Shwear t' God."

9

"And a bloody huge thing it was," Chick said tipping so far back in his chair Joan had a hard time concentrating on what he was saying. "That meant, of course, that there were going to be houses everywhere. There was so much pottery around you couldn't *not* step on it."

"Dad, watch your chair," Philip said.

"Von Jhering and I climbed it and after poking around called down to Mellon that it was Neolithic at the top. Nicky calls back 'it's bloody Neolithic at the bottom as well!' " Chick chuckled. "We were looking at a seventy-foot mound of Late Stone Age civilization!" To Joan's relief, the front legs of the cast-iron chair finally hit the gravel with a *crunch.* He looked at his watch and with a groan heaved himself to his feet. "Well, then, shall we, Phil? Sir George awaits."

"Why is Sir George being such a pill about this coin business?" Joan asked. "With these inner-sanctum 'appointments' and so on. I'd have expected him to publish the pictures and declare an open house. The thing supposedly vindicates his lifelong claim, doesn't it?"

Philip glanced at his father and smiled. "I imagine he has some doubts about the authenticity, but at the same time he can't resist building things up. If it ever does turn out to be what he says it is, he can be expected to try to rub Dad's nose in it first."

Joan glanced at Chick, who was gazing distractedly into the wading pool. "But why?"

"Archeologists are very competitive people," Philip went on when Chick appeared to be not going to answer. "And Rawlins is unquestionably the worst. The last search for the trove began with the ritual gentility of a lawn bowl but within a matter of weeks things were completely out of hand. All the projects going on in the same general area—his and Dad's were only about ten miles apart—all looking for the same thing got to be too much for Rawlins to bear. It started with his planting a spy in Dad's camp and the next thing we knew everybody was interfering in each other's work, lifting things, paying off local officials to harass each other. Dad got so disgusted," Philip glanced at his father, who showed no signs of having heard a word of any of this, "he finally packed up and went home in the middle of the season."

"That must have pleased Sir George," Joan said.

"Actually, I think it bugged him more than anything else—being left as he was down there on the low road. Which is why he planted the story in the local press that Dad must have found what he was looking for. As you know, the Turks leapt on it like raw meat and Dad never worked in Turkey again."

"And then Rawlins found the crypt?"

"No, no, that was later," Chick said, suddenly rousing himself.

"But of course the rumors started all over again," Philip said.

"That you'd looted it? But why you? Just because you quit your project in the middle? That's hardly a case. . . ."

"That and the fact the thing was eventually found a few hundred meters from my site."

Joan opened her mouth to say something, but closed it again.

"In any case, there's little chance Rawlins is on to anything of any value," Chick said. "I go through this with him about once a year. Speaking of which, Phil?"

Philip leaned forward to kiss Joan good-bye. As he did he glanced at the drawing on her lap, which showed the rough outline of children in tidy school uniforms sailing toy boats in a large round wading pool. "Nice," he said. "But trite."

Joan gazed at her picture and smiled. "Isn't it, though?"

Propping her feet up on the lip of the pool and tilting back her chair as Chick had done, she watched the men walk away across the park toward the street—from this angle vaguely recalling Keaton and Arbuckle—and then squinted back down at her subject. Philip had been right. Nestled like a diamond chip among the over-sized jewels of the Louvre, Place de la Concorde, Champs Elysées and L'Arc du Triomphe, it was probably the most frequently painted, drawn, filmed and photographed wading pool in the city. But it was what her editor wanted, and Joan—closing her eyes to the September sun and listening to happy children squeal in French—was not about to argue. Besides, what scene in Paris wasn't a little trite? The face of the city was as well known all over the world as a movie queen's. Its familiarity, though superficial, was one of the things Joan liked best about it. The difference was that movie queens were usually a letdown in person; Paris, from an artistic standpoint at least, delivered. From a personal standpoint, after just two and a half weeks, Joan couldn't imagine ever living anywhere else.

She could, however, imagine living in another house. Two blocks from the Seine, the Dumases' mansion—or what the French called an *hôtel particulier*—lay hidden behind a high wall that opened on Rue St. Dominique in the old and exclusive section of the Left Bank known as the Seventh Arrondissement. Built of beige stone blocks over two and a half centuries ago for a member of Louis XV's court, it looked from the outside stately and grand. Inside it was shadowy, cold as a castle and, to Joan's mind, blatantly brooding. She could see why it had occurred to Walter to assure her that the place wasn't haunted.

She also found it a bit overdone. Her bedroom was a strict period piece with a twenty-foot ceiling and fifteen-foot-high canopy bed, Louis XVI step stool, Louis XVI divan and Louis XVI chair all covered in the same rose-on-silver-figured silk. Also Chinese vases on Louis XVI mounts, Louis XVI bedside tables, a Louis XVI porcelain bidet (which she and Philip used as a waste basket) and a marble-faced fireplace with a glaring marble-eyed Roman bust on the mantle. On her first morning waking up there she'd half expected a chambermaid to come in, dress her in a crinoline petticoat and paste an artificial mole on her face.

The rest of the rooms were on the same scale, though at least not of so uniform a theme. The faux-marble dining room, which seated twenty, was done mostly in the "Return to Egypt" style but was hung at one end with a Flemish tapestry and carpeted with a nineteenth-century Persian rug bordered with surrealistic cats. The main living room, whose walls were covered in forest-green silk, ran the gamut from gilt wood Regency mirrors and gilt bronze sconces to nineteenth-century French charcoal drawings—two of which she recognized as Millets—to eighteenth-century Chinese lacquered chests, to a weird Deco coffee table supported by what looked like a bronzed sheaf of wheat.

The room she wandered into now had the most twentieth-century feel, with a billiard table that supposedly had belonged to Field Marshal Montgomery—for this it was called the "games room"—a big American rolltop desk someone had given Chick off the set of the movie *Front Page,* and a Frank Lloyd Wright lamp made of yellow and green stained glass, which she'd heard Charlotte had paid close to a million dollars for. The wall behind it was dominated by a large abstract oil painting. The single recognizable representation among the countless obscure designs that covered the canvas was a small dark urn near the center. Joan leaned forward to read the brass plaque on the frame. Painted in 1945 by Hyman Bloom, it was titled ARCHAE-OLOGICAL TREASURE.

She smiled.

"I've never liked it," a soft voice came from behind her, "I've always thought it was pointlessly obscure. . . . Sorry, dear, did I startle you?"

"No, no," Joan said, her shoulders having jerked as if they were run through by an electrical current and her hand having flown to her throat. "I just didn't hear you come in."

"It's a bad habit. Chick complains I'll give him a heart attack one day."

I don't wonder, Joan thought, glancing down to realize that Charlotte had crossed a bare floor in heels.

"Well, isn't that what archeology is all about?" Joan asked, nervously lifting a small glass box off the table as she waited for her heart rate to return to normal. Lying on a tiny red velvet cushion inside was what looked like a long sharp thorn. "Obscurity, I mean."

"Its real puzzles are never so contrived. Or so simple. That's a stingray tail. The Mayans used it for piercing their penises."

"You don't say." Joan carefully returned the box to its place. "Is that what attracted you to it in the first place?"

Charlotte's eyebrows rose slightly.

"Archeology, I mean," Joan said.

Charlotte stared at her blankly.

"Conundrums."

"Oh!" Charlotte smiled. "Not exactly. The only puzzle I was interested in at the time was how to get warm."

Fanny would have loved the sound of that, Joan thought. Joan certainly appreciated it. In the three months she had known Charlotte, the woman, while friendly enough, had rarely spoken about herself or asked a question in a manner that could be described as personal. Of course, this may have had as much to do with the fact that they'd never spent any time alone together as with Charlotte's natural reserve. Her answer seemed, for Charlotte, strikingly candid.

"In fact, by then you could almost say I was clinically obsessed," she'd gone on. "The apartment I was living in—a miserable place on the top floor over in the Eleventh—had no heat."

"What were you doing there?"

"It's a long story," she said with another smile, but this one told Joan she was not going to hear it.

Between what Philip, Walter and Fanny had told her, Joan knew some of it already. At least that Charly Jessup was raised on a dairy farm in upstate New York, ran off to the big city as a teenager, spent a few years making the Greenwich Village cafe scene, then somehow ended up with a couple of her girl friends, penniless, in Paris. For the next two and a half years they cleaned, cashiered, picked grapes, waited tables and—if Walter was to be believed—danced in a nightclub. The problem was that no matter what they did they were always poor and well before the end of it Bohemianism, for Charlotte, had gotten old.

Or, as Charlotte was putting it now:

"I've never been one of those people who could find romance or anything remotely uplifting in poverty. Poverty to me meant no heat, and I've always hated the cold. All that winter all I could think about was heat, specifically dry, searing, *permanent, desert* heat. The problem was how to get there. Then I read about a reception at the Louvre for George Rawlins and I felt as if I'd been hit by the light on the Damascus Road. As it turns out, it's where I met Chick."

Joan was impressed. There was no apology, not a shred of defensiveness for what anyone listening could have called Step One in a textbook case of social mountaineering.

"What did you know about archeology?" she asked, with a fairly good idea what the answer would be.

"Not the first thing," Charlotte said. "But I knew I could learn whatever I had to in less time than it would take whoever hired me to find me out. It's simply a matter of knowing your limits."

In spite of herself, Joan's eyes drifted back up to "Archaeological Treasure." Walter and Philip had both admitted to searching the house. How much searching, Joan wondered, had Charlotte done?

Glancing back she found Charlotte's serene green eyes on her. The slight smile on her face gave Joan the sudden, annoying feeling that she'd been reading her mind.

More quickly than she'd intended to, Joan looked away.

"This looks rare," she said, picking up a gaudy ceramic ashtray similar to the one she'd seen in the Dumas house on Martha's Vineyard, except this one had a picture of an elephant painted on it.

"Tony and Anika like to bring us gifts when they go on trips," Charlotte said. "Coffee?"

The maid Madame P., who had to have been the one to inspire Walter's reference to Daphne du Maurier's Mrs. Danvers, had just come in with a tray of cups and toast.

"Oh, no, thank you," Joan said, suddenly grateful for a natural point at which to leave.

Charlotte's half-smile deepened just a shade. "Oh, I almost forgot to tell you," she said just as Joan was reaching the door. "Chick called. Sir George's claim to have found a Mynnia coin was another false alarm . . . I thought you'd be interested to know."

10

"You really do find all this interesting, don't you?" Philip said as Joan walked him to the Louvre side of Pont Neuf after meeting him for lunch on Isle de la Cité.

"Are you kidding? It has all the ingredients of a proper mystery thriller. Academic intrigue, missing treasure, curses. . . ."

"Well, the first maybe, but the latter two are in some doubt. Now, what did you ask me?"

"What happened to Chick's partners."

"Oh, yes. Well, nothing untoward, I assure you. Cecil's living in contented retirement in Switzerland with his wife Phyllis, writing letters to scientific journals and breeding Brittany spaniels. Harry's certainly still alive, though I don't know that much about his life these days. He and Dad had a falling out."

"Let me guess—over the Croesian—"

"No, no. Sometime later. Dad has never said exactly, but I know he and Charlotte didn't like each other—in fairness to her he was a difficult man, but in fairness to him I think he felt a loyalty toward my mother. But I don't know, really, as I never got to know him that well. Not like Cecil, who for years practically lived with us. You'll meet him. He's getting old and in his words 'beginning to rot,' but only slowly. Drinking too, unfortunately, but he's still a marvelous human being. He's the one, you know, who got Dad interested in archeology in the first place."

"Chick says it was a girl."

"He would, but it was Cecil who took him on his first dig. Last question."

They'd come to the end of the bridge.

"Did he know about Rawlins's coin?"

"He thinks Sir George pressed it himself. I have to run, sweetheart, see you tonight." With that and a kiss, Philip turned and continued up Quai du Louvre. Joan stood watching after him for a moment, then strolled slowly back across the river and into the Latin Quarter to draw pictures.

Instead of carrying with it the chill of fall, the first day of October—a week and a half now since Joan's enlightening chat with Charlotte—had ushered in Indian summer. The air was thick with unseasonal humidity and the sidewalks of the Quarter were an on-going collision of strollers, shoppers, merchants and, it seemed, most of their wares. Finding it unusually difficult to get down to work, Joan browsed through shoe racks on the street, bought a straw hat from a boy on a bicycle and some flowers, figs and celery root off a wagon at the open-air market on Rue du Buci. Settling at last under the awning at Cafe Conti at the edge of the square, she ordered a glass of lemon water and five packets of sugar, and finally dragged her sketch pad out of her bag.

A minute later she found her mind had wandered back to what Philip had told her about Chick's second partner. (What was his name, Harry?) With effort, she reined her thoughts under control. If only Philip knew just *how* interesting you find it all, she chided herself. Could the entirely unoriginal suggestion of a cache of gold under your nose—the remoteness of the possibility notwithstanding!—actually be working its shop-worn spell on you? Well, whatever it's doing, she answered herself sharply, it's contributing nothing to your work, which is falling dangerously behind.

Joan drained her glass, straightened her back, ran her palm once

over the blank page staring up at her and took pencil in hand. Despite
the parade of humanity that flowed around her, however, only two
figures in the next thirty minutes managed to penetrate her day-
dreaming fog. The first was an incongruous-looking street sweeper
dressed in black overalls pushing a medieval twig broom along the
gutter across the square. The second, which appeared before Joan had
a chance to put pencil to paper, was Charlotte.

She had just stepped out of a building directly behind the sweeper.
She was too far away for Joan to have seen her face clearly but there
was no question as to who it was. Even without the familiar green silk
jacket and red leather bag, Joan would have known the distinct,
dancer-like posture and something indefinable in the manner in which
she looked around to speak to the man who had come out onto the
street behind her. And of course the Cleopatra hair.

Joan's first impulse was to call to her. It was not long-lived. Charlotte had put her hand on the back of the man's as she spoke. It was
a simple gesture but it struck Joan with some force that it was
intimate. She then took his arm and they started down the street,
climbed into a car and, after sitting—apparently talking—for a minute or two, drove off. The last glimpse Joan had of them was as the
car turned left down a side street heading toward the river.

Joan's gaze lingered a moment longer at the spot at which it had
disappeared. The man had never looked around so she couldn't have
said for sure who he was. Only that he was tall, fair-haired and
smartly dressed, and at that distance, anyway, a dead ringer for
Walter Hudson.

Which, of course, was impossible, John told herself again that night
as she and Philip sat down with Chick and Charlotte for dinner. But
only because Walter was thousands of miles away. As for the other
part of it, it hadn't occurred to Joan that Charlotte would have a lover,
but by the same token it didn't surprise her greatly to discover that
she did. In light of their little tête-á-tête in the "games room" it
certainly fit. It was just that Charlotte had never struck Joan as a
particularly sexual person. Then again—she glanced across at Chick,

who was attacking his bowl of bisque as if he were being timed—her husband didn't exactly evoke visions of connubial bliss. But, of course, one could never know for sure what went on behind a bedroom door.

"What are you doing reading a trashy thing like that?" Chick asked, waving his spoon at the issue of *Les Yeux*, a French blend of *Vanity Fair* and *The National Inquirer* that Philip had placed beside his plate.

"As a rule, Dad, I don't, but someone left it on my desk at work. It seems Sir George is on the warpath again."

"Talking to the tabloid press?" Charlotte asked. "That's a bit of a stoop, wouldn't you say, even for him?"

"They seem to have excerpted quotes from an interview he gave to the *Times* and added their own twist." He glanced at his father. "Do you care to hear it or not?"

"Why not?" Chick shrugged and continued to eat.

"The headline reads: *Sir George Points Finger at Yank Colleague in Missing Treasure*."

Joan looked at Chick, who did not so much as look up from his soup. Charlotte continued to pour the wine. "So what else is new?" she said and passed Joan a glass.

Philip went on translating:

> "*Sir George Rawlins, the British*
> *archeologist famed for—*"

"Skip ahead," Chick said.

"Let's see . . . they go on about the discovery of the coin, which . . .

> *noted archeologist Charles 'Chick'*
> *Dumas recently verified . . .*"

"That's a lie," Chick mumbled.

> "*Which means, Sir George says,*
> *the fabulous treasure in gold*
> *still exists. Just who he thinks*

> *has got it, he won't say outright*
> *but Sir George is looking . . .*

the French equivalent of 'close to home.' Now they quote Rawlins:

> *'The further you go back in time—*
> *and I'm talking about to the discovery*
> *of the cache—the less likely it is*
> *that a single piece would surface for*
> *the first time only now. The longer it's*
> *held, the greater the pressure either*
> *to reveal it or to break it up.' "*

"The man is brilliant," Chick said. "Yes, I'll take another glass, thank you."

> *" 'So barring a fluke, it is much*
> *more likely that the Hoard was*
> *discovered fairly recently. By that*
> *I mean sometime not long before my*
> *discovery of the crypt thirteen years*
> *ago. We have to assume it wasn't*
> *local looters, otherwise we would have*
> *seen evidence of this in the black*
> *market. Which means it was*
> *taken either by professionals and sold*
> *directly and intact to a collector*
> *who was willing to hold it for all*
> *these years, or by a scientific team,*
> *or element from a scientific team,*
> *working in the area, who kept it*
> *for themselves.' "*

"Subtle as dynamite, isn't he?" Charlotte said.

> *"Asked to be more specific Sir*
> *George told a reporter he is*

> *'looking close to home,' saying*
> *that Mr. Dumas himself might be able*
> *to shed some light on the subject.*
> *Reached at his palatial home*
> *here, Mr. Dumas refused to answer*
> *any questions, and hung up."*

"So, that's who that was," Chick said.

> *"He headed one of several groups*
> *working in the area shortly before*
> *the crypt was found. . . .*

They name everybody and then go back to Rawlins.

> *'In either case, the collector or*
> *archeologist stupidly seems to have*
> *decided to sell it off piece by piece,*
> *even though it is infinitely more*
> *valuable intact. One could see why*
> *a looter might do this—why loot*
> *if not for financial gain?' "*

"Well, I'm glad he cleared that up," Chick said.

Philip went on: *"But a scientist . . .* Joannie, what is it?"

Everybody looked at Joan, who suddenly seemed to have elevated several inches out of her chair. Her face had blanched unevenly in the manner of someone who had just been slapped.

"My dear . . ." Chick said.

She had reached over and was lifting the paper out of Philip's hands.

"What is it?" Philip and Charlotte asked in unison.

After a moment in which nobody spoke or moved, Joan gradually lowered the paper until it was resting on her salad and glanced around the table with a mystified expression on her face. But everyone's eyes were now on the photograph staring up from her plate. It was of two squinting women: one's face frozen in mid-speech, puckering on a word that could have been "choo-choo train"; the other in mid-blink, looking like a drunk.

"Someone you know?" Charlotte asked.

"Yes, sort of," Joan said in a voice not quite her own. "It's me."

"Let me see!" Philip said taking the newspaper from her. "God, look at that, so it is. Fanny, too. That's the clam bar in Edgartown, isn't it? I wouldn't have recognized you—I *didn't* recognize you—I flipped right by it."

"These people should be jailed for this kind of thing," Charlotte said.

"What does it say?" Chick asked.

"Chick," Charlotte said.

"Read it, Phil," Chick said.

"Actually," Philip said with a sheepish look at Joan, whose face, besides having turned quite pink, showed a complete absence of expression, "it's really pretty funny.

> HEH, MUM, LOOK WHAT I CAUGHT, SAYS
> NEW GIRL IN TOWN WHILE SOPHIE TELLS
> PALS SHE WANTS HIM BACK!
> *Insiders say New York artist*
> *Jean Cook . . .*

At least they got your name wrong . . .

> *has snagged one of the biggest catches*
> *on Martha's Vineyard this summer—man*
> *about Europe Philip Dumas, former*
> *paramour of Princess Sophia and long-time*
> *companion of arts patron Didi*
> *Devilliers. Close pals say Sophia is . . ."*

Philip started to chuckle.

> " 'crying in her chowder' (?) and
> 'wants her man back.' 'She's forgiven

him for leaving her for the widow
Devilliers,' an intimate told Les Yeux,
'but now she's ready to reconcile.
This Jane just wants him for his
dough! [SEE 'TREASURE' STORY PAGE 3]
Sophia wants him for all time.'
So if you're listening, Phil,
the Princess says she will
make you as happy as a clam."

Chick let out a guffaw. Philip looked tentatively around the table and started to laugh, too. "You know, I think we should subscribe to this."

"Great suggestion, Philip," Charlotte said, looking closely at Joan. "But I think Joan is upset by it."

"You can't be," Philip said in a tone of genuine surprise. "I thought we—"

"Can't I?" Joan said with an explosion of anger. "You may be used to living in a fish bowl, but *I'm* not!" She got to her feet. "And I don't ever intend to! There are *privacy* laws, for God's sake!"

"Welcome to the public domain," Chick said, though not unkindly.

"My dear, we've all been through this," Charlotte said. "You simply have to ignore it."

But Joan was already halfway to the door.

"What are you going to do?" Philip asked, getting uncertainly to his feet.

Between the loss of her composure and the absence of any idea herself, it was probably just as well that she never got a chance to answer. No sooner had she glanced back over her shoulder and opened her mouth to shape a reply, than she ran with all the flourish of a slapstick stunt straight into Walter.

— *11* —————————

Hayden glared down at the red satin shoes on her bony feet. What was there about them? *Something,* she sighed to herself, yanked them off and tossed them into the box in which she had brought them home the day before. Although it happened only rarely, it annoyed her to spend a lot of money on something that wasn't just right. Hayden's was an ordered and convenient world: made convenient by money, ordered by a precise and unswerving sense of what she wanted from it. And what she wanted from it generally provided. Like Walter. Although looking down at him sleeping lightly, his mouth squeezed into a little pout, his hair lying flat along his damp forehead, making it look round and childlike, she felt a twinge of annoyance. She never understood the male compulsion to sleep after sex, as if they'd accomplished some tremendous feat. For Hayden sex was energizing rather than relaxing, which is why she preferred it early in the day. She finished dressing and left the room.

She could hear voices as she neared the top of the stairs and stopped just out of sight. Her brother and Joan were in the entrance hall. She leaned forward and watched them. He was straightening her collar—an obscenely domestic gesture that fit him about as well as a pair of clown shoes. And from the look on his face he knew it, too. But she was smiling at him. That coy little sex-angel smile that turned Walter on so much. God, men were pathetic. Well, the girl may have learned a few things—hadn't she been smart enough to land a bed here?—but she was essentially still a neophyte. Even without last night's telltale tantrum, the child radiated it like a swimmer with an open wound. Which of course is probably just what Philip found so irresistible about her. After playing water boy for Didi all this time, he finally has a Galatea for his Pygmalion. But why drag her into this mess? What did he think he was doing, bringing her back here? The problem was he didn't think. He never thought. He was a dreamer, like his father. A dreamer in a pair of clown shoes. What had Walter called them? "A pair of sentimental slobs." Well, it didn't matter. Little Joannie Cook could be as delectably nubile as she wanted, but she deserved what she got. And if Philip was going to be careless, so did he.

"You're not going to blow up any buildings while you're out, are you?" she heard him ask.

"You mean *Les Yeux*?" Joan said with an embarrassed smile. "They wouldn't give me the address."

"But you *are* letting it go?"

"What choice do I have?"

"I'm sorry, sweetheart."

"I know. It's not your fault. I'll get used to it," she said with an obvious absence of feeling. Then, in another voice, "So that's the princess."

"That's her."

"Who's Didi Devilliers? God, what a name. . . ."

"A friend of Hayden's, and mine. She makes movies."

"You were, in tabloid argot, 'constant companions'?"

"At one time. Now she's more like extended family."

"Speaking of which, what are Hayden and Walter doing here?"

"What do you mean?"

"They just arrive? Out of the blue?"

"They do this from time to time. She's between projects."

"What about him?"

"He's between jobs. But they're not staying. Hayden said she has to be in Italy by the beginning of next week. And I have to go, darling, but I'll be back by noon. You'll be ready?"

"Where are you two off to?" Chick's friendly growl echoed across the hall.

"We're taking a picnic to Chantilly," Joan answered. "If our heat wave holds. Care to join us?"

"An insincere offer if ever I heard one. Of course not. I despise young couples in love."

"Joan, dear, it's not *shan-TILL-ee*." Hayden's eyes darted across the hallway like a cat's to a rustling in the brush. They followed Charlotte's slender figure as it moved lightly across the marble. "It's *shawn-tee-EE*."

"Besides, at the risk of prejudicing you," Chick went on, "it's not something I need to see again. The barn's fairly impressive but the castle itself always seemed to me to be more like someone's *idea* of a castle—someone from another planet. I'm also not wild about sausagy salon portraits, mediocre illuminated manuscripts and *l'école* de Botticelli. But I'm sure you'll have fun. Just make sure you actually *see* it."

"How can one not?"

"The first time Chick went to see it," Charlotte said, pulling her green silk jacket from the closet and handing it to her husband to hold for her. Joan recognized it. So did Hayden: It had been her mother's. "With a young lady he was trying desperately to impress—he led her as far as the 'barn,' as he calls it, showed her around and then brought her home, never having seen the castle at all."

"Why not?"

"He thought it *was* the castle," Philip said. "You'll see why. Oh, hello, Hayden. This is quite a send-off."

"I'm not here to see you off," she said and turned to her father in a manner that dismissed everyone else in the room. "I wanted to remind you about our lunch today."

"I haven't forgotten. Now, I've got to go."

There they all were again, Joan thought. If she'd been imagining the brittle atmosphere over coffee last night, there was no mistaking the wave of tension that had just rippled across the hall. It seemed to radiate out from the point of Hayden's arrival, as if she were a rock that had just been tossed into a quiet pond.

Of course, it made perfect sense, Joan mused, if Charlotte and Walter *were* carrying on and Hayden had found out. What *didn't* make sense was what—if that were true—were Hayden and Walter doing here?

Joan glanced over at Hayden, who was standing motionlessly beside her watching Chick, Philip and Charlotte climb into the back seat of Chick's limousine. The little maid Marie-Laur had come up to hover awkwardly, as if it was her job to close the door—which it may have been for all Joan knew. But Hayden seemed unaware of her presence, and for the moment Joan's. She was standing as still, and radiating about as much warmth, as a bucket of dry ice—staring out the door. *If looks could kill,* Joan thought cornily, and wasted no more time slipping quietly away.

12

"This is from the temple at Luxor," Chick said, stopping at the edge of the roaring, car-choked Place de la Concorde to gaze at the seventy-five-foot-tall obelisk rising sublimely out of its center.

"How did it get here?" Joan asked. "Napoleon's army?"

"No, later than that. A present, to Charles the Tenth from Mohammed 'Ali, a Macedonian orphan who was, archeologically speaking, if not *the* rapist of the Nile, then certainly could be said to have held her down. He was made pasha of Turkish-occupied Egypt for almost the entire first half of the nineteenth century, during which time he gave most of the country's remaining antiquities away. The man was one of history's more enduring menaces."

"You're just sorry you weren't around to get in on the plunder."

Chick made a face. "Maybe a little."

He and Joan had picked their way across the Place and were walking slowly up Cours la Reine toward the Petit Palais. A hot urban wind blew in their faces. Two weeks had gone by and the unseasonal weather was still with them. So, unfortunately, were Hayden and Walter. Joan had managed to avoid much contact with them, convincing Philip to go out most nights, and lingering away from the house when he wasn't there. (For the last three days he had been in Milan on business.) Out of sight did not mean out of mind, however, and she found her thoughts stuck on the puzzle of why Hayden and Walter would persist in staying where their welcome was mixed at best. Well, at least Hayden's was mixed. Joan had not missed how frequently in the last two weeks Charlotte had left the house alone, and how many of those times Walter was out the door by himself shortly after.

"I seem to have digressed," Chick said. "What was I saying?"

"That your father owned a South African gold mine."

Chick's cheeks were bright pink and there was a sheen of sweat on his forehead but Joan could not convince him to take a cab. He grumbled that he was feeling "vigorous" and wanted to walk. And, evidently, to talk. She'd asked him how it was that he'd first come to Paris and he had become caught up in his own life story, which after twenty minutes of tangents and background was getting to the point only now.

What he had told her so far was that by the time he was twenty he'd been to London, Barcelona, Pretoria (where his father had the mine), Shanghai, but somehow never Paris, even though his father had been born there. Charles Dumas Sr. was a wealthy man, having had some success as an industrialist but acquiring most of his fortune through inheritance. Young Chick, on the other hand, had contrived to be as poor as common sense would allow. He had by this point in the story vociferously embraced the standard political differences a young man had with his father in those days, and to drive the point home had rejected not just his money but any association with him, quit college and gone off to be an expatriate. "The fact of the matter is I was an obnoxious romantic." It had been this time of year but much colder. Chick remembered because he had been staying in an attic apartment in the Latin Quarter and almost froze to death. (Thinking of Charlotte's own, similar story, Joan wondered if a stint of poverty and cold in Paris held some secret key to success.)

"It was something right out of *La Bohème*," Chick said as he puffed along. "Except in this case, I was saved by the girl. She was an American art student at the Beaux Arts and, after feeding me, got me a job as an English tutor for the child of one of her professors."

"Was she the one you took to see Chantilly?"

"What? Oh, yes!" He looked pleased both that she'd thought to make the connection and to be reminded of the occasion. "Yes, she was."

"What happened to her?"

"Oh, well, the war. We went our separate ways. I asked her to marry me but she didn't take me very seriously. Perhaps she shouldn't have. I was a pretty dreamy twenty-five-year-old. By then she'd given up painting and was setting off to join a dig in Aswan."

"So it really was a girl who got you interested in the field."

"It was always a hobby of hers. I thought I might find her."

"You actually went looking for her?"

"Yes, but too late. She'd married a British soldier and settled in a London suburb. Or so I was told. I never really found out for certain."

"You never saw her again?"

He shook his head. They were halfway across Pont de L'Alma and had stopped to watch one of the *bateaux mouches* restaurant boats pass beneath them under the low arch of the bridge—and to let Chick catch his breath.

"I'd met Philip's mother by then and was married soon after the war. Five or so years later we inherited some money, enough at any rate to buy the house," he nodded in the general direction of 26 Rue St. Dominique, "and had the water running again in just enough time for Hayden to be born there. I'd thought of moving back to America permanently after June died, which was . . . God, already twenty-three years ago, but somehow never did."

"When did you meet Charlotte?"

"Not until 'sixty-eight. But we didn't marry for more than thirteen years, you realize." He looked over and winked. "And then it was her idea."

"That would have been *after* the search for—after you'd retired, then." Joan hated herself for being so obvious, but Chick didn't seem to notice.

"What? Oh, well, yes, it would be, wouldn't it?"

They had started to walk again and for a moment neither said anything. After about a block, Joan couldn't resist asking:

"And your children had no trouble accepting her?"

When he didn't answer right away she was afraid she'd gone too far, but before she could backtrack he finally said:

"They were very close to their mother. Especially Hayden. It was rough on her, losing June. Philip took it hard, poor kid, but with Hayden. . . . In some ways I don't think she's ever gotten over it. Watch yourself!"

A red Renault taxi had all but brushed the backs of their legs as they crossed to the other side of Rue de L'Université. "Cretin!" Chick barked as Joan glared after the cab. Whoever was in the back seat had turned around to look at them. Joan briefly entertained the urge to gesture, but her attention was drawn too quickly back to Chick. Having collected himself after their forced sprint, he'd gone on: "Happily, they've become good friends."

"Who?"

"Hayden and Charly."

Joan looked at him in amazement. "Yes, of course."

"We've been through a lot together and it's brought us all closer."

Than what? Joan wondered. "Isn't that nice," she said.

"But maybe we're just getting old. The centrifugal forces of youth seem finally to have petered out and suddenly the family's pulled together. I mean, I thought we'd lost Hayden for good—she went through a wild period—but overnight, it seems, she settled back down and wanted to be close again. I'm old-fashioned—and self-ish—and I suppose nostalgic. I prefer my house filled with family. Charly does, too. And now Phil has—Joan? What is it?"

As stunning as Chick's version of his family was to her, Joan's attention had been diverted to something else. She was standing still, looking back over her shoulder. "See that taxi?" she said. "I think it's following us."

Chick laughed.

"No, look. It's the one that almost hit us."

"How can you tell?"

"Because it's gone by twice already."

"That doesn't mean it's following us."

"Then why would it be creeping along behind us for a block and a half?"

"He's probably just looking for an address."

"Sure. Or pictures."

"Pictures? Now, Joan *dear*. . . ."

But she'd already taken his enormous arm and was leading him briskly along the sidewalk. They had only a block to go. "Come *on*," she urged as, almost immediately, he started to flag.

"Dear thing, this is as fast—"

"No, it's not," she said with a tug. Her sympathy was in short supply. Glancing over her shoulder she could see the taxi was maintaining its distance. "We're not going to give the parasites the satisfaction."

"I had no idea you were still so worked up about this."

The fact was, the one other thing that had not changed in the last two weeks was Joan's attitude about having had her picture appear in *Les Yeux*. Not only had she not been able to get used to the idea, it had grown steadily more repugnant to her over time. Far from cathartic, the irate phone conversation she'd eventually had with the tabloid's story editor had led to nothing but a follow-up article. This, combined with her apparent lack of recourse, had left her composure where this matter was concerned as stable as a gas leak.

The spark came a few yards from the gate, when Joan heard the taxi make its move. There was the roar of an engine and, as she drove her key into the lock, the screech of brakes. Someone was getting out as the bolt gave and she practically threw Chick's huge bulk through the door. "Joan, *dear one*, I don't think—" But she was already turning to face the enemy head on. Seasoned in combat now, she knew this time to go straight for the camera.

"You blood-sucking *bitch!*" she yelled as she started to charge the figure that was having some difficulty clearing the door of the cab. "*Police!*" she shrieked. "I'm going to call the pol—"

But the word caught in her throat like a chicken bone. The object of her wrath had finally erected itself now on the sidewalk in front of her and the sight of it literally choked her to silence. Appearing as it did at this particular moment, on this particular spot, it had to be a hallucination.

"And a warm welcome to you, too!" it said as it straightened its skirt and resolved into the eternally familiar face. "Charles Dumas! What on earth are you feeding my daughter? She seems to have gone stark raving mad."

13

"I don't think Hayden's at the point of cutting Charlotte's brake cables yet," Joan said in a low voice as she followed her mother around the living room, "but she's definitely come out of her hole."

"What do you mean?" Fanny asked, training an assessing gaze on the glass-enclosed bookcase at the corner of the room. "Louis XIV . . . Boulle marquetry . . . exceedingly rare."

"I mean describing their relationship as complicated would be like calling Othello moody. I somehow missed it when we were all together on the Vineyard, but now it's as obvious as a dog attack. Wait 'til dinner, you'll see. They watch each other's every move like a pair of cats before a fight."

"You're mixing your metaphors. Safawid-era Persian . . . nice. So, what do you think it's all about?"

"Beats me. I was trying to ask Chick about it when you arrived. What the hell were you doing creeping along behind us like that, anyway?"

"I got a last-minute assignment for the Rothschild wedding in Rome and left early enough for a night here on the way. I wanted to surprise you. What's above us?"

"The *premier étage*. You could've been shot."

"I've since thought of that." Fanny lowered her voice as she preceded her daughter up the stairs. "Darling, if I may be frank, you behaved like a lunatic. I've known you to be a little quirky sometimes, but I've never seen you like that. What's going on? Is Philip treating you all right?"

"Yes, of course."

"Where is he?"

"Milan. Don't look at me like that. He's wonderful. It's your brother vultures of the Fourth Estate. I've appeared in the local rags a *second* time now—you got the touching mother-daughter portrait I sent you? I'm supposed to be driving our Princess Sophia and one Diana Devilliers to sticking pins in dolls."

"Is that all, really? Well, then, just don't overreact, you'll only draw more attention to yourself. What room is this?"

Joan leaned back against the door frame and watched her mother browse the second-floor sitting room. "So I've discovered."

"Of course, it's all easy enough to understand," Fanny said. "Hayden's father goes and marries a younger woman whom he promptly installs as the chatelaine of her childhood home. Jealousy and territoriality are only natural."

"Well, I think there's more to it than that," Joan said, just above a whisper. "For one thing—Mum, I wouldn't touch that—what's Hayden doing here, at Rue St. Dominique, *now*, after all these years?"

"She's never visited before?"

"Not on this scale."

"I thought they were only passing through."

"That was two weeks ago. She's called in painters and he's leased a fax machine."

"You knew her divorce just came through. Channing took her to the cleaner's. Maybe she's broke. I imagine Walter Hudson's an expensive pet."

"I seriously doubt Hayden's here for charity from home. And it would be one thing if she had some abiding attachment to the house. However, she does nothing but complain about it. Or if she and Charlotte were moderately fond of one another, which you'll see for yourself they're not. Or if Hayden had decided finally to abdicate and play by the new rules, but I can assure you she'd sooner fly to the moon. In fact, carp as she might, she acts as if it were *her* house, ordering the servants around as if they were assembled here for her benefit exclusively, throwing parties. And all this with a kind of reckless élan that knocks everybody back on their heels. Everyone, that is, except for Charlotte. What have you found now?"

"A hidden passageway, of course. Maybe this is where the old boy stashed his coins."

"Hidden" was a slight exaggeration. The door itself was carved to resemble the rest of the panels in the room but the brass latch was clearly visible, though Joan had never noticed it before.

"That would be a little obvious," she said, reluctantly crossing the room.

"There are stairs in here. What's above us now?"

"I don't know. I've never been up there. Where do you think you're going?"

"You're not curious?" came her mother's muffled call from the darkness of what seemed to be a servants' passageway. "Come here and help me find a light."

"*Mother—*"

"It'll be your fault if I break my neck."

The stairwell was hot and smelled sharply of dust and mildew. They did not find a light switch but, just at the point Joan's skin had begun to prickle and her feet were turned to carry her back, Fanny's groping hand found a doorknob at the top. In a moment they were standing in a dimly lit bedroom. Its draperies were drawn and its furniture was shrouded in dust covers.

"Oooh," Fanny cooed with satisfaction as she began systematically to peek under each of the sheets. "Go on. Go on. What were you saying about Charlotte?"

Joan glanced unenthusiastically around the room, heaved a sigh and sat back against a windowsill. "Where was I? Oh, yes, that she endures Hayden with inhuman calm. Which is not at all to say she's ceded her position as mistress of the manor. She just refuses to be provoked, which I think is the only reason they haven't come to blows. I don't know what it would take to ruffle the woman. Maybe a missile attack."

"Didn't I say she was smooth?" Fanny said as she disappeared out the door.

Not daring to let Fanny out of her sight for a minute, Joan got quickly up, dusted off her pants and followed into the next room. It was sheeted like the first. "As a moonlit lake," she went on. "She gives absolutely nothing away. With me she's as unchanging from day to day as a portrait on the wall. Which is not to say she's insincere. I really think she likes me. She's forever asking me if I'm happy with this patterned linen, that scented soap. But the woman doesn't walk, she glides." Joan demonstrated as they crossed the hallway to another bedroom. "And speaks in that misty voice, which,"—Joan gave an exaggerated imitation—"like those hooded eyes, masks everything in an air of perfect serenity. It's impossible to imagine her ever losing her temper. You go first."

They were back where they had started, having found the door at the end of the hallway locked.

Joan was whispering as they started back down the blackened stairwell. "I can, however, imagine her finding a way to get her stepdaughter out of her house. That she hasn't must be out of deference to her husband, who for some reason remains devoted to Hayden. What's wrong, can't you find the latch?"

"No. Like an idiot, you closed the door behind you and very cleverly managed to lock it as well."

"Excuse me, but I did not close it behind me, and I'm sure it isn't *locked.* It's probably just stuck. Get out of the way, let me try." She put her shoulder to the door. *"Damn."*

"What a humiliating way to go. *Society Writer Suffocated Skulking in Socialite's Mansion.*"

"It'll serve you right," Joan said with mounting irritation. "C'mon, take my arm, let's go back upstairs. This isn't going to open and we've used up all the air in here."

Confirming Joan's worst fear, the door at the end of the third-floor hallway proved to be bolted, resolutely, from the outside. Incredibly, they were locked in. Unless, as simply had to be the case, there was a way out they'd overlooked.

"I certainly hope so," Fanny called to her daughter as they split up to make a search. "This is really very embarrassing. Will you look at this closet! You could hide a standing army in here. Man, they've got a lot of junk."

"Please don't go through it now," Joan said impatiently. "Open a window or something before I faint."

"Don't panic, sweetheart. We can always tie bed sheets together and lower ourselves into the front yard."

"I'm not panicking, I'm just feeling a little like I'm locked in an attic that's ninety degrees and smells like a tomb that hasn't been opened in a thousand years. You don't suppose the Dumases have rats. What's that door there?" They'd met again in the hall.

"A linen closet that would bring two grand a month as a studio apartment in New York. Dear heart, you're sweating. You've also managed to smear your face. C'm'ere."

"Maybe there's a phone. . . ."

Fifteen minutes later Joan and her mother were standing at the hallway door calling loudly for help. They had started with long conversational hellos but when after five minutes no one seemed to hear, resorted to banging and progressively less inhibited cries of *Help!* and *Will somebody please let us out of here!*

"Jesus, do I feel stupid," Fanny panted, pulling up a chair and wiping her face with the underside of the sheet that draped it. "Where in heavens *is* everybody?"

"We've been whispering all this time but I forgot the house was empty. Hayden and Chick went off together. Walter was due back from Zurich this morning but I haven't seen him. He's probably somewhere in the city, though. You wouldn't have noticed, but two minutes after Chick left, Charlotte was out the door like a freed bird."

"Well, what the hell are servants for?"

"What time is it?"

"Almost five."

"Philip should be back from the airport soon. Why not go down into the servants' passageway and give a call down there."

"I will *not* be found behind a panel in Chick Dumas's tea salon. I'd rather starve."

Joan started to pound and shout again. Fanny got purposely to her feet. "You're wasting your breath, darling. We're going to have to break it down."

Joan looked at her mother and started to laugh. "They made these things to keep out the masses, Mum. People like us. It's as solid as rock."

"You'd rather I scream fire out the window? Which besides being certain to generate *publicity* is most certainly against the law."

Joan had already considered it and decided that bringing out the Paris fire department was not an option. She looked dubiously at the door. "Maybe it's aged in three hundred years."

"Okay, then, hurry, I'm getting claustrophobic. In a minute I'll be on the floor blowing bubbles from my mouth." Having taken Joan by the hand she was backing up to give them a running start.

"Why do I feel like I've been here before?" Joan murmured.

"One—two—"

"There'll . . . be . . . tears . . ."

"Three—*go!*"

With a crash and a pair of startled grunts, mother and daughter bounced off the door as if it were a trampoline stood on end and landed in a heap on the floor.

"And they make it look so easy on TV," Joan said, wiping tears that were as much from hysterical laughter as from pain.

"I think I broke my collarbone," Fanny squeaked.

"I hate to tell you, but we're not going to get out of here this way."

"We're gonna die! We're gonna—" But here Fanny stopped, the laugh cut short in her throat. "Oh, my God!" she gasped. "We *did* it!"

Joan followed her mother's gaze. To her sobering amazement, the door had actually come ajar and was swinging very slowly open on a creaking hinge.

"Captain, we're saved!" Joan cried. "Now before anyone finds us—"

But halfway to her knees the look on Fanny's face told her that it was already too late. For a slow beat of ten, the two dewy-eyed, dust-smeared women gaped up from the floor at the spectacular apparition that had appeared from behind the door.

Fanny recovered first. "Who the hell are you?" she asked.

To which it replied:

"Me! Who the hell are *you?*"

14

The husky voice went perfectly with her face, which was as smooth and coldly beautiful as a portrait by Ingres. Like his portraits, it was also ageless, despite the discreet lines about her eyes that only another woman would have seen. Still, no one would have known she was forty. Diana Devilliers was one of those women who'd looked thirty-two for twenty years. Her hair, which she wore in a carefully windswept bun, was very—and unnaturally—blond. In the words that were running through Joan's mind, the color of packing-crate straw.

"We shot the interiors back at the studio, so all we've got left is a couple weeks on location," she said to the table at large as she passed her glass to Philip for more wine. "We'll be here for the week, then back to Italy, a few weeks in London and then it goes into post-production. Thanks, Phil, that's plenty. It's a great script, Hay, a great cast, it's been a great *shoot* so far and I think we've got," her eyes brightened for a split second, "a smash on our hands."

"Hallelujah, darling!" Hayden said, raising her glass. "May we both get very rich. You'll stay with us, of course."

"I couldn't," Diana said. "I mean," her glance took in the Cooks, "you're a crowd already."

"Nonsense, Didi, you know the size of this place," Charlotte said.

"Stop being coy," Chick grunted, "the girls have already made up the bed."

With far greater effort on the part of the Dumases than Joan thought was needed, the matter was settled. Diana would be a house-guest until her work in Paris was done. Fanny gave Joan a look that dripped with mischief. Joan volleyed with a warning glance and passed her own glass for more wine.

The mischief that the Cooks had been up to so far appeared for the moment to have been put behind them. After rescuing them from their well-appointed prison—Diana had been changing in a guest room directly below and heard their racket—she seemed not to have said anything to the rest of the household about her discovery. At least no one had yet mentioned it over dinner, which for the first time since Joan had been here was fully attended. Of course, with the unanticipated arrivals of both Joan's mother and Hayden's best friend and business partner within a few hours of each other—it had already occurred to Joan to wonder at the coincidence—everyone had a reason to be there.

On such short notice, it was an impressive spread. Foie gras and leek soup were followed by olive quenelles; vegetable tarts were followed by squab breasts with Germiny mousse and beet cream sauce. Later, after several bottles of wine, came meringues with red currant sorbet and poached figs filled with almond ice cream. The conversation tended to center on one of the guests of honor and her new movie, with the other content to remain on the sidelines—where, Joan knew, she was doing her best to mentally catalogue and store everything that was being said. Joan had already located her mother's foot with her own in anticipation of the point at which Fanny's questions would begin to sound like an interview. But Fanny seemed for the present happy just to listen.

"So Phil, you rogue," Diana was saying, "tell me about Maria Balsalles. She says she saw you in Genoa."

"That would be Geneva."

"Whatever. I thought you two weren't speaking."

"Have you ever known Maria not to speak? I wonder how her husband gets any sleep. . . . My, but news travels fast."

"If you read the rags." Diana's eyes darted to Joan and back. Walter coughed. Charlotte asked whether anyone wanted any more to eat.

"Oh, yes, *please*," she said. "It's criminal but I can't resist these things." Diana helped herself to another fig. "I'd be as fat as a house if I lived here," she said to no one in particular. Then, glancing at Joan, "How do you stand it, Jean?"

"Joan," said Joan, returning the woman's vacant smile.

"Right, I'm sorry. It's lucky for us thin is out these days, isn't it?"

There was a split second when they could have heard a dog scratching two blocks away. Then suddenly everyone seemed to be speaking at once.

"I was disappointed to hear that Danny Seigel has turned out to be something of an asshole," Walter said to Diana with a barely visible shake of his head.

"What? Oh, God, that's putting it nicely," she said. "He went after *every*body. Agents, writers, actors, *me*. He deserved exactly what he got."

"What was that?" Chick asked.

"They fired him," Fanny said.

"So soon?" Charlotte said. "That's too bad. I liked what he was trying to do."

"That's because you go to movies, not try to make them," Hayden said coolly. "What is it, Madame P.?"

The funereal figure had come up and was standing at Charlotte's elbow. She glanced from one woman to the other, then, turning to Chick, reported that the Monsieur was wanted on the telephone—the call, she believed, was from Zurich. Chick said he'd take it in his study and Charlotte ordered coffee for the living room.

Joan leaned back in a wing chair by an open window and looked around her. Fanny had taken advantage of the move to seat herself beside Hayden, from whom she was attempting to extract tidbits of Hollywood gossip. "So she's found another Mr. Right?" "Well, another Mr. Right Now," Hayden answered without moving her snifter more than a few inches from her lips. "Jesus, it's hot in here."

Gazing toward the door as if watching for her husband's return, Charlotte was absently smoothing the lap of her skirt. She had asked Walter whether he'd found anything in Zurich. "Nothing really," he was saying as he turned the pages of an oversized book on trekking in the Himalayas. "There are some coins floating around but I'm quite sure they're flaming hot and, as tempting as they are, I wouldn't touch them. It really isn't worth it any more, not like in Chick's day, when . . ."

Joan breathed deeply and took a big swallow of brandy. This was not exactly how she'd imagined spending Philip's first night home. She glanced over at him sitting on the piano bench tapping out the first bar of the *Moonlight Sonata* with his thumb. Diana was leaning against the piano like a lounge singer, smoothing her hair. Joan had the irritating sense that the woman knew she was looking at her, but somehow couldn't make herself look away.

"He's really very good, darling," Diana was saying in a manner that was distinctly familiar but not in the least bit hushed. "He was buying Bleckner and Fischl before anyone knew who they were. He pioneered the Italians single-handedly—Stuart bought his Clemente from him—and was *years* ahead on Robert Ryman and the minimalists. He's collecting Russians now. I wish you'd seen his house in the Zurichberg. Twenties and thirties right down to the taps. Zillionaire-Deco-kitsch—just the kind of ka-ka you hate—but the real article to the twin mermaid vases and very smartly presented. The place was worth the trip alone. I hated that you missed it."

"Josef Bieler may be a lot of things," Philip said, starting the familiar sequence of notes over, "but he knows next to nothing about art. He's just slick enough to dump recycled trash on rich widows like you. And *you* all like him because he has a pretty face, a big black car, and will say anything to get under your dress."

Diana giggled. (Joan wanted to choke.) "You're jealous."

"Not of him."

"We missed you at Gstaad."

"So you've said."

"Will you make Kia's party on the eighth? Philip?"

But Philip's eyes had suddenly flown across the room. Chick had appeared at the door but did not come immediately into the room. In a curiously uncharacteristic gesture, he placed a fat hand on the door jamb, more as if in contemplation than for support.

"Daddy, what is it?" Hayden said sharply.

"Some bad news, I'm afraid."

"What's happened?" several voices said at once.

"That was Phyllis Barnard," he said. "It seems Cecil's had a heart attack."

Charlotte set her cup and saucer down with a clatter. "Is he all right?"

"No," said Chick, reaching up to finger his little pony tail in a nervous gesture Joan had seen him make before. "As a matter of fact he's dead."

"Oh, *Daddy!* Poor Phyllis! When did it happen?"

"The day before yesterday."

Hayden's eyes flicked to Walter. "I didn't hear anything about it," he said with a slight arching of his brow. Their eyes held for a moment longer, then both turned back to Chick.

"Phyllis said it was massive and that he dropped dead, literally in his tracks, which sounds about right for Cecil."

"Was she with him?" Charlotte asked.

"Hmm? Ah, no, she was out. A friend, a former student or somebody, I didn't get it, was visiting and it happened while they were having lunch. He'd gotten up to go into the other room for something and . . ." Chick heaved his big shoulders to signify finality.

"Shall we go?"

"Not right away. Cecil didn't want a service of any kind, and Phyllis said she's holding up. She says shock's a great thing. Family's there now. Maybe in a week or so."

"I have a meeting in Lucerne tomorrow night," Diana said. "Do you want me to visit her for you?"

"Thank you, but it's not necessary. Walter, you heard nothing about this?"

"No. But the papers wouldn't have had it until after I'd left."

"Strange thing, he was strong as an ox," Chick said. "The last thing I would have expected was his heart." He looked around and smiled weakly. "Then, there are worse ways to die."

15

Chick dropped heavily into the leather wing chair that stood like a throne in the center of his library. His gaze swept over the contents of the room, which, with its tabletops and shelves buried under a pandemonium of artifacts, papers and books, had become a shrine to his life. His eyes picked out various treasures he had collected in the last fifty years: a pair of Mayan vessels from Belize; a marble *kouros* head from Arachova; a beaten-gold funeral mask from Mycenae; an *iroko* buffalo mask from Cameroon; the lyre-shaped head of a three-thousand-year-dead Greek goddess, discovered by a fisherman's wife on the Cycladic island of Naxos. The reclining, baked-clay goddess from Anatolia he'd dug up himself. Same with the pink sandstone Akkadian victory stele, though in this case more by accident than by design. But all were found, one way or another, in the uniquely satisfying company of Cecil Barnard.

Chick's gaze stopped on the photograph of three young men in safari hats, perched uncertainly on the backs of camels. The great pyramids of Khafre and Khufu could be seen in the distant background. What self-respecting archeologist didn't have the identical portrait in his library? Chick thought. But, god, were we ever really that young? Cecil's head was thrown back in a laugh. Chick couldn't imagine what he'd just said—something irreverent, something lewd, no doubt—but he could hear the laugh as if the man were in the room now.

He slipped a pair of reading glasses on and slid a sheet of onionskin paper out of the envelope he had been holding in his lap. He was smoothing it against his thigh when a noise drew his attention to the door. Joan was there, fist poised tentatively to knock. A nice girl, brainy, good-looking, a little high-strung, but Phil had been smart for a change. He smiled. Would he rather be alone? she asked before taking the seat across from him Chick was pointing to. No, no, he said, but it was late, wasn't it? Hadn't everyone gone to bed?

"Just about. Philip had some calls to make to California so I came down for a cup of tea. I saw your light . . . I just wanted to say how sorry I was—"

"I know, and thank you, but it happens and he's lucky it happened fast like that. A little rough on the living, but for the dying. . . ." He gave the gesture equivalent of "a piece of cake."

"How old was he?"

"Seventy-three, four."

"That's not that old."

Chick chuckled. "I was just looking at this picture of us in our early twenties. We may not be 'that old' but that was half a century ago. And it feels like five. I can't even remember our doing that. It would have been Cecil's idea. He was a maniac."

"You weren't the same way?"

"God, no, not like Cecil. He was daring. I mean, madman daring. I've never been daring." Just as Joan was thinking how unlikely that sounded, he added, "Well, rarely."

"Philip described him as being like family."

"Yes, well, we've kept up. In fact, I was just looking over a letter he wrote me when you came in." Chick glanced down at it. "There was something a little strange about it, as I remember," he mumbled to himself and held it up and gazed at it absently as if the paper itself, not the words typed on it, held some clue. "I probably should have paid closer attention. I think he was trying to . . ."

Joan glanced down at the wrinkled sheet that shook just percepti-
bly in his big hands. Ink had bled through what looked like grease
spots. It appeared to be typed entirely in capital letters: . . . TSAJ TA
YTIJATROM, she saw, . . . NUJ NEEB SAH, and . . . . XOB TAH
EHT FO TUO. Appalled to catch herself working on the inverted
words, she looked abruptly away and got to her feet.

Chick glanced up. "Rude of me! Rude of me! Sit back down," he
grunted, rattling the sheet dismissively. "Anyway, I'm sure I was
wrong. . . . He drank." He folded it, but, Joan noticed, did not put it
away. She turned toward the door.

"I really only came in to say good night," she said, and was not
surprised when he did not try to stop her. Glancing back over her
shoulder as she left the room, she saw that he had already slipped his
glasses back on and was spreading the letter open on his lap.

"They hated to lose you, didn't they?" Joan said, lying on her side
watching Philip undress.

"Who?"

"The women of the world. . . . Tell me, is there still something
going on between you—" Joan nodded toward the door"—and the
widow?"

"Please don't tell me you're jealous."

"She obviously wants me to be."

"Why do you think so?"

"It's a little hard to miss. You can't not have noticed that she acts
toward me as if I were a rival."

"To Didi everyone's a rival. It's an attitude that's made her rich. But
I apologize for her bad manners and I'll speak to her—"

"Don't you dare."

"Well, then, try to remember this—she's not *your* rival."

They lay in the dark, both controlling their breathing in the silence.
Wrestling with an irksome sense of dissatisfaction, Joan thought of
trying to resolve the conversation on a different note, but decided in
the end to let it go. It's boggy ground, she reminded herself, and
terrain on which you've never shown yourself off to particularly good
advan—

"What?" Philip said, having heard her open her mouth, take a breath and close it again. *The high road,* Joan admonished herself, *take the high road,* and was pleased to hear herself ask instead:

"Do you think people have premonitions about their own death?"

"How do you mean?"

"Like Sadat and Martin Luther King, for instance."

"In their case, I wouldn't call it a premonition as much as an educated guess. These were not universally well-loved men, you know. Why?"

"Cecil Barnard wrote to Chick not long before he died."

"Very possibly. They wrote a lot. And you think he told my father he thought he was about to die?"

"Not exactly. But there was something in his last letter."

"What?"

"I don't know. But Chick seemed troubled by it."

"And you think he had a premonition about his own death?"

"Sounds silly, doesn't it?"

"Completely. Especially if you knew Cecil."

Their manner with each other was easy again. Joan felt her sense of proportion return. She rolled against him and he slid his arm under her shoulder.

"Why? What was he like?"

"Practical. Fatalistic. A little reckless, but one of the few truly brilliant men I've known."

"How long has it been since you've seen him?"

"I'm ashamed to say. Hardly at all since their last expedition together."

"Which was the infamous search for the Croesian Hoard, wasn't it?" Joan propped her head on her hand. "He would have been one of the men Tony Sloan said disappeared from the site."

Philip gave a weak, sad-sounding chuckle. "Not tonight, Sherlock," he said and pulled her head back down onto his chest. "It's much too late for that."

It was too late for that in *any* case, Joan thought, as she listened enviously to Philip's breathing slow and deepen. Her brain, which was happily stewing over the events of the day, seemed to have no intention of shutting down.

"Philip," she murmured.

There was no reply.

"I love you," she whispered. "More than I've ever said." A moment later she rolled over and tried to follow him into sleep. It seemed to take forever, but eventually she must have because she was aware of being woken up, at about three o'clock, by the scream.

It was abbreviated, as if choked off, and followed almost campily by the sound of heavy footsteps. Someone was running down the stairs. There was the crash of the front door slamming shut and then silence.

"*Jesus*, did you hear that?" Joan said to Philip as she reached for the light. "It sounded—"

But the bed was empty. She hesitated a split second, then grabbed her robe and ran out into the dim light of the hall. Standing at the base of the staircase that led to the third floor, she heard someone from downstairs call out. A quieter, unidentifiable sound came to her from behind the hallway door at the top of the stairs. She flew up them and pulled it cautiously open. Light fell in a thin wedge on an unpleasantly familiar blue Oriental carpet. In the next second she made out the sheeted chair Fanny had sat in that morning. Then, with a sick feeling, a fat white foot.

Joan heard herself scream, threw the door open wide and dropped down beside her mother, who in the full light she could now see was attempting to pull her large frame to her knees. Fanny let out a little groan and collapsed again, trying desperately to catch her breath.

It seemed to Joan forever before at last she did, but finally it became evident that she was not seriously injured. By now the commotion that could be heard swelling downstairs was materializing piecemeal in the doorway behind them. The wall lamps sprang to life and the blanched faces of Chick and Charlotte were gaping at them, demanding to be told what had happened and whether Ms. Cook was all right.

"Are you in pain?" Joan asked, helping Fanny to a sitting position and wiping her hair out of her eyes. "Have you hit your head?"

"No, I don't think so," she said, drawing a long, full breath at last. "I'm all right." She took another breath. "I just . . . had the wind . . . knocked out . . . that's all."

"What happened?"

"I've no . . . idea."

"Did you fall?"

"From where?" Fanny said sourly. "No. Somebody pushed me, somebody *hit* me . . . on the back." She gingerly rotated a shoulder. "Hard."

"Did you see who it was?" Charlotte asked.

"No, he hit me from behind."

"He?"

"Well, I assume. . . ."

"I heard someone running down the stairs and then the front door slam. I think you surprised a burglar, Fanny." Joan looked up into the scowling face of Philip, who had appeared in the doorway. Over his shoulder, with a hand clutching his elbow, Diana was craning to see. It seemed everyone was now there. Except Hayden and Walter. Fanny got slowly to her feet.

"A charitable one," she said with an attempt at a smile.

"A fucking stupid one," Philip said as he bent to help her to her feet. Joan had never seen him so angry. "You're sure you're all right?"

"Positive."

"Will somebody call the police, I'm going to take Fanny back to bed."

"Oh, no," she said quickly. "I'd rather go down for a glass of something. They're going to want to question me anyway, aren't they?"

"What would a burglar be doing on the third floor," Diana asked, "with all there is to take downstairs?" Even if legitimate, the question did not have an innocent ring.

"I'm sure I don't know," Philip said. "Let's go down, shall we?"

The little group was just coming down the stairs when the front door opened and a draft of cool air swept Hayden and Walter into the foyer.

"Waiting up for us?" Hayden said as if being greeted by half a dozen pajama-clad friends and relatives at three-thirty in the morning were a common occurrence. "Aren't we all a little old for this?"

Walter was a bit less sanguine. "What's going on?" he asked sharply.

"We've decided to come down for a spot of tea," Joan said edgily.

"There's been a burglary—or an attempted one," Chick said. "We're expecting the police momentarily."

"You're joking," Hayden said.

"We're not," Joan said. "My mother came across him on the third floor. He hit her and fled."

"The *third* floor?"

"He *hit* you?" Walter asked.

"On the back. He only knocked the wind out."

"What was Ms. Cook doing on the third floor?" Hayden asked.

"Looking for Joannie," Fanny said.

"Joan, what were *you* doing on the third floor?"

"I *wasn't* on the third floor."

"Please, Hayden, save it, will you?" Philip said. "Didi, would you mind going into the kitchen and finding us some ice?"

"Did you get a look at him?" Hayden asked.

"Hayden, *please*," her brother cut her off. "If you want to wait with us, we'll be in the den. Coming everyone?" He took Fanny by the arm and led her across the hallway.

"What were you doing up there?" Joan asked quietly, taking a seat beside her mother on the couch.

"I heard a noise and thought someone might have accidently gotten themselves locked in up there, the way we—"

"Yes, yes, but you could have called someone."

"I know. But it seemed a good idea at the time. Though now," she took a long, uneven breath, "I can't imagine what I was thinking."

"I can," Hayden said as she poured herself a drink. "Where were you?" she asked her brother, although Joan couldn't see the relevance in this.

"I was in the kitchen," he said, "making myself some coffee when I heard all the crashing about."

"You didn't see anyone?"

"No."

"If he went out the front door. . . ."

"I came up the back."

"Where are you going?"

"I want to see what he was up to."

"What do you mean by that?"

"To see what's been taken."

"I'll come, too," Charlotte said.

"No, you won't, dear," said Chick, placing a large firm hand on his wife's shoulder. "And Philip, be careful."

"It's a little late for that, isn't it?" Walter said.

"We don't know that. No one actually saw him leave the house."

Within the hour, the police were satisfied that he had. They were also satisfied that he hadn't taken anything, presumably because Fanny had come across him before he had a chance to get down to business. How he got into the house remained a mystery, however, as there were no signs of forced entry on any of the doors or windows. But a more thorough investigation was planned for the morning. It also remained a matter of speculation as to why the thief, having gained entry, would bypass a veritable warehouse of priceless articles (the Frank Lloyd Wright lamp was just one that came to Joan's mind) and risk a climb of two flights of stairs. Their tentative answer was that he was most likely a professional, hired for a specific theft, probably a piece of art. An inventory of the contents of the third floor in the morning might supply the answer. In what little remained of the meantime, it was agreed that the only thing left to do was for everybody to go back to bed.

16

"I confess I have a little trouble casting you as the innocent victim in all this," Joan told her mother as soon as they were out of the house. "What *were* you doing up there?"

"Now don't you start! I told you, I heard a noise—a *loud* noise—I'm surprised it didn't wake up the whole house. And I thought—well, actually, I thought *you* might've been creeping around up there and gotten yourself locked in."

"You can do better than that. What would *I* be doing up there?"

"That's what I was wondering. What you, or *anybody*, would be up to at that hour."

"Jesus, Mum, it's not even your house."

"What does that have to do with it? Would you refuse to throw a drowning man a rope just because it wasn't your pool? Speaking of which, is this the place?"

With the idea that Fanny might try to swim off any stiffness likely to settle in her bruised shoulder, Joan had taken her mother to *La Piscine*, an open-air public pool at the edge of the Seine. Charlotte had suggested they go to her private club; however, with the temperatures back in the eighties, Fanny held out for the outdoors. Besides that, not only was it closer by—she had an afternoon plane to catch—but from Joan's description *La Piscine* offered at least one feature Charlotte's club surely lacked.

They were not, as it turned out, the only ones with this in mind. Between the Indian Summer and the national devotion to the sun, most of the city seemed to have turned out to take advantage of the weather. By noon, the scarlet decking around the pool appeared to be carpeted in live flesh, which moved in unison with the angle of the sun like blades of grass shifting with a summer breeze. The upper tiers of the coliseum-like structure were taken up mostly by men, who leaned on their elbows and gazed down at the smorgasbord of bare breasts—just as Joan had described it—below. The variety was infinite, from the tankard to the teacup.

"Much more so than male genitalia!" Fanny said with gleeful satisfaction as she spread out her rented bath towel and glanced appreciatively at the landscape around her. It was just what she had had in mind. "Given a choice of views," she said, patting the spot beside her for her daughter to assume, "I'll always take boobs."

"I thought we came here to swim," Joan said.

"I want to work up a sweat first," Fanny said, lay back and sprang her bra. Catching her daughter's surprised look as her melonous breasts surged into public, she added, "There's nothing like the language barrier for creating the illusion of anonymity. And when in Rome. . . . So, tell me, what's going on?"

Joan shook her head and sighed, but eventually sat down and slipped off the top of her suit. "Not a thing."

"I mean in that house. The atmosphere in there is murder."

"I expect it may come to that. You didn't bring any sunscreen I bet."

"Don't be silly, you can't get a tan this time of year."

"Then what are we doing lying here?"

"Taking a cure of vitamin D, and assuaging the exhibitionist in me. So what do you think, does he have it or not?"

"Chick? I really don't know. To talk to him he'd convince you he helped God draft the Ten Commandments, but if you went by the suspect behavior of everyone around him . . ."

"You'd think he had it sewn into the nearest sofa cushion."

"You don't think it was one of *them* that knocked you down last night?"

"Don't you? Heck, it *could* have been any one of them. I don't even know if it was a man or a woman, do I? All they had to do was get to the front door before anyone saw them and they could either run back upstairs dressed for bed, which half of them did, or come back in later, the picture of sympathetic innocence, which the other half did."

Joan rolled over on her stomach and studied the design of her towel. She hated to encourage her mother, but she'd been wondering about it, too. "Walter," she said.

"He'd be my guess. But think about this: It was dark up there—I never saw who hit me, but he or she might not have known it was me."

Joan glanced over. "What are you saying now?"

"Only that I don't think the ambience in that place is an especially restful one."

Joan said nothing.

"Dar-ling. . . ." Fanny's breasts stacked one on top of the other as she rolled on her side to look at her daughter. "I really think it's time for you to get into a place of your own. You can defend the Dumases up and down but I know your face like I know the alphabet and I can see the worry lines as plainly—"

Joan groaned and closed her eyes.

"Maybe so, but you can't deny it, can you?" Fanny went on. "You've seemed out of it almost since I got here. Your behavior on the street yesterday—Jesus, was it only yesterday?—was certifiable. And today you're obviously not yourself."

"My mother gets attacked in the middle of the night in a room directly over my head and I'm supposed to wake up with a smile on my face? God knows *you've* bounced back from your little adventure—I'm beginning to wonder whether you didn't secretly enjoy it—but, you know, he *could* have had a knife."

"What else?"

"What more would you want! A gun? A garrote?"

"No, no, I mean, what *else*? You're depressed."

"I'm really not. As a matter of fact—"

"It's Philip."

"No, it's not."

"Something's going on between them, isn't it?"

Joan cracked an eye. "Who?"

"Your boyfriend and Cruella Deville. She's all over him like a tree fungus."

"They're old friends."

"*She* is maybe—Christ, she's old enough to be his mother. But didn't they leave for the airport together this morning?"

"Purely by coincidence. She has a meeting in Lucerne and he has another auction and more museum business in Milan. *Don't* be trying to start something."

"*I'm* hardly the one who's starting anything. Furthermore, I sincerely doubt it's a question of *starting*—"

"Don't do this!" Joan cried suddenly, sitting up. "Philip and I are *fine!* He's not Paul Dorman and I'm not the Babe-in-Toyland who skipped and danced my way into that mess. And Diana is one of *many* long-standing friends who aren't just going to drop off the face of the earth because I've arrived on the scene."

"Okay, okay."

"The point is I *trust* Philip!"

"Absolutely."

"I've no reason not to!"

"Darling—"

"All men are *not* Arnie Hicks—"

"Joannie, honey—"

"And all women do *not* share your tortured emotional past—"

"Sweetheart—"

"So will you *please* keep your personal paranoias to *yourself!*"

"Joan!"

"*What?*"

"Why are you yelling?"

Joan glanced around. A dozen or so unfamiliar faces had popped up and were turned with interest toward hers. She took a deep breath and looked blindly up at the pristine sky.

" 'Methinks—' " her mother began.

"If you finish that sentence I'll *kill* you."

"Well, you'll admit," her mother said a wordless hour later as she followed her daughter up the steps from the pool to the bath house, "your nerves seem to be a little on edge."

If this was true—and Joan had some trouble denying it—Fanny's discovery halfway to the airport an hour and a half later did not help matters any. With Fanny taking longer to shower, dress and remake her face than Joan had planned for, they had returned from the pool in just enough time to throw Fanny's bags into the trunk of one of Chick's cars and fly out the driveway for the airport.

"I feel so rude," Fanny was muttering as Joan sped along the highway and she rummaged through her handbag. "You'll have to tell them thank you—watch that motorbike, dear—for me. I *hate* rushing like this. My stomach gets tied in knots. I'm sure I've left something. My *comb*, for starters. *God*, look at my hair. I never should have gone into the water. Chlorine is just death. Dear, may I borrow yours? Oh wait, there may be one in . . . Glory be to God will you look at this!"

Glancing over Joan saw that in her search for a comb Fanny had opened the Mercedes's glove compartment and pulled out what looked like a fancy toiletry bag.

"What have you found now?" Joan asked warily.

"The family jewels!"

"Well, then put them back. There's a comb in my purse. I don't know whose that is and you really shouldn't—"

"I mean *literally!* You won't believe what's *in* here! If you fell in the water with *half* this stuff on you'd sink like a *stone! Look!*"

Fanny opened a velvet pouch and held it out for Joan to see. In the time she was willing to look away from the road, Joan saw only a tangle of glitter, but it was enough to tell her Fanny was right.

"What would it be doing in the glove compartment of a car?" Fanny said, stabbing a diamond-and-sapphire ring with her baby finger. "Not that it's not a good place for it, with thieves roaming around the house at will. They probably wouldn't think of looking in the garage."

"That's probably exactly what it's doing here. Mother, *please* put that away. Somebody was probably taking the stuff to the bank. Or thinking about it. . . ."

"What—and then changed their mind?"

"They obviously wanted to give me the thrill of driving it to the airport and back first," Joan grumbled, glancing over at her unwanted cargo and easing off slightly on the accelerator. "You won't mind if I don't walk you to your gate."

Had Joan gotten a better look at what Fanny had uncovered, she might have been even less happy than she was to have it in the car on her dash to the airport. Unable to resist a peek into it now that it was safely returned, or just about—she'd stopped under the front-door lamp before going into the house—she saw that the satin bag held not just one but several gray velvet pouches, each evidently filled with a small fortune in jewelry. Of the two she glimpsed into, one contained what might have been a dozen heavy gold rings set with monstrous bands of diamonds, sapphires, emeralds and rubies and flashy combinations of the four. The other held bracelets—carved gold, strung stones, pearls, links of ivory—and a handful of old-looking, irregularly shaped coins—one carved or stamped with a horse, another with some fat king's effeminate profile, another with a meaningless symbol. Knowing nothing about such things, Joan would have said only that everything in the two-pound bag she was carefully resealing appeared to be the real thing, most of it heirlooms, all of it horrendously valuable. Which was why she was not going to delay getting it out of her hands a minute longer, she was just thinking, when she suddenly became aware of a human presence behind her. In the next second she felt a hand cup her flank and heard a deep, accented voice in her ear say, "Eh, bébé, whaz a nass gell lack yu. . . ."

He did not finish. Joan swung around and, before she had time to register Walter Hudson's bright hazel eyes and big friendly grin, kneed him squarely in the balls.

— 17

"I shouldn't have done that," Joan said, sitting down beside him.

"No," Walter said between short breaths, "*I* shouldn't have done that."

"You're right. What did you expect me to do?"

"I don't know," he said in a weak voice. "Not that."

"What *do* you think you were doing, by the way?"

He was sitting on the front step rubbing big slow circles on his temples. "It was a joke . . . I did say you'd be good in a corner, didn't I, but tell me . . . are your reactions always this—extreme?"

"I've been a little jumpy lately."

"The burglary?"

Joan glanced down at the satchel in her hands. "Among other things."

"Forgive me for being direct," he said lowering his voice, "but are you miserable living here, at Rue St. Dominique?"

She looked over at him. He was resting his head now on his hand—if not an innocent, he'd certainly perfected the look—and smiling at her. She might have stopped the conversation right there, but the sight of him crumpling to the ground like an empty suit two minutes before had thoroughly disarmed her.

Her own voice dropped as well. "What gave you that idea?"

"Not suffocating in the bosom embrace of—The Family?"

"Hardly."

Walter's smile broadened. "No, not hardly. It's not exactly the coziest of places, is it?"

"It wouldn't be my word."

"No, mine neither."

"Then what are you doing here?"

"It's cheaper than the Ritz."

"Yes, but drafty."

He laughed softly. "You're lovely, you know."

Walter Hudson was nothing if not resilient. "Save it, Walter," she said and started to get to her feet.

He put a hand on her arm to stop her. "I mean it."

She almost laughed. "What *is* it with you?" she said sourly, removing his lingering hand and standing up. "I would have thought Hayden and Charlotte would be enough to keep anyone busy. Or is this all some weird thing for Dumas men?"

He looked genuinely surprised. "Charlotte?" Joan had made a move toward the door, but at this he had jumped up and blocked her way.

"I must say I can't help admiring your nerve," she said, "but someone really ought to throw you out."

"For what?" This seemed to surprise him as well.

"For making passes at other men's wives."

He laughed. "I think you might have me confused with someone else. But while we're on the subject, how *is* life in a ménage à trois?"

"*You're* asking *me?*"

"Dearest, I'm afraid you don't quite cut it as the innocent. Not unless you're also incredibly stupid."

"What are you talking about?" she asked, her voice rising in anger—partly at herself for having let the conversation go this far.

"If *they* don't try to hide it, you needn't. It makes you look silly and out of step. Secondly," he reached up and brushed a lock of hair off her shoulder, "what's good for the goose can be even better for the—"

"Crawl out of the gutter and take a look around some day!" she snapped, pulling back. "It'll be good for your coat!"

She glared at him until after a last, aggravating hesitation he reached for the door.

"Well, if ever you change your mind. . . ." he said, taking his time turning the knob.

"Screw you, Walter, and the—Charlotte!"

The door had swung suddenly open—almost taking Walter with it—and Charlotte was standing before them looking as surprised by their appearance as they were by hers. Her eyes flitted from one to the other before coming finally, and firmly, to rest on Walter, and she at last opened her mouth to speak. This should be good, Joan thought, although in fairness Charlotte might only be about to express some concern: The color was still drained from his face, making the blue circles under his eyes look dramatically pronounced. Whatever she might have been going to say, however, she changed her mind. Her eyes had just fallen on the quilted bag in Joan's hands.

"Oh, good, you *do* have it," she said, but almost blandly. At least it was a far cry from the hysterical scene Joan had allowed herself to imagine ("Sweet Jesus! I've been pulling my hair out all afternoon!") as she sat in rush-hour traffic thirty minutes ago. Then, perhaps this was only a small fraction of Charlotte's jewels.

"Yes, and I'm sorry, Charlotte," Joan said, gladly handing over the bag. "They were in the glove compartment. I must say I was surprised to find them there. I opened it and looked in, I hope you don't mind. Did we take the wrong car?"

"It wasn't your fault. I didn't realize you were taking *any* car. I was going to get these into a safe deposit box. I put them in the Mercedes, went back into the house for something, got tied up with phone calls, and when I went back out the car was gone."

"I'm sorry if I gave you a fright."

"You didn't. I assumed you'd taken it."

"Are you going out?" Walter asked.

She looked at him blankly for a moment. "Oh, no," she said, backing up to let them in. "I was looking for Chick. I heard voices and thought you were them."

"Them?" Walter said.

"He and Didi went out for a walk."

"She's back already?" Joan asked with perfect mildness, feeling Walter's eyes on her.

"She got in a few hours ago."

There was a brief silence, which Walter kindly broke. "Then things must be going well," he said, cheerfully. "Why don't we go in, have a strong drink and get ready to hear all about it. I've developed a headache in the last ten minutes that I suspect nothing but vodka will cure." He turned to Joan with a loaded smile. "It may be the light out here but you look like you could stand a bracing up yourself."

"Not in the least," Joan said, and left them standing together in the hall.

She closed her bedroom door behind her, leaned hard against it and took a long deep breath. If Walter had developed a headache in the last ten minutes, Joan's mood in that time had gone from bad to worse. She crossed the room and dropped heavily onto the divan. The question was glaring. If she'd been at all sincere in her indignant rejection of his insinuations about Philip and Diana—not to mention her mother's earlier in the day—why had it come as such a nasty blow that Diana was back in the house?

Part of the answer was obvious: Joan didn't trust Didi Devilliers to mail a letter for her. (Who could trust anyone with a name like that?) She was the kind of high-handed bitch who would have thrived in the colonial crowd in Kenya in the twenties. That is, until someone shot her.

Joan toyed with the image for a moment but could not manage to find any fun in it. Rising to Diana's bait was utterly without point. The issue was obviously not whether she trusted Diana, but whether she trusted Philip. But if the answer to *this* was yes, which she reminded herself quickly and firmly that it was, why, then, had she become so easy to provoke?

Joan scowled back at the marble-eyed Roman bust. God, she hated that thing.

The answer here was no great mystery either. It wasn't Diana, who was an irritant but objectively nothing more, but the *rest* of them. The household in the aggregate. Walter flitting from flower to flower with his stinger hanging out. The rivalry between Charlotte and Hayden seeping silently like swamp gas. Madame P. and Marie-Laur lurking like Doom and Death. Chick's willful obliviousness to it all, not to mention Philip's cheerful insistence that none of this was worth paying the slightest attention to. Taken together—even without Diana's unique contribution to the atmosphere at 26 Rue St. Dominique—there was more than a kind of Happy Valley perversion about it. Joan kicked off the quilt that she discovered she'd pulled up almost over her head. She hated to admit it, but Fanny was right. It was time to get out of here. She sat up, turned around, and shrieked.

It was a short shriek, really only a loud squeak, but it reverberated in her head for several seconds after her alarm had dissolved. "Philip!" she cried when she'd caught her breath.

He was laughing. "Nervy, aren't we?"

"What are you doing here? You're a day early!"

"I thought you'd be happy. Maybe I should have called first. From downstairs."

"I just didn't hear you come in."

"What are you doing lying up here in the dark?"

Joan realized only now that the room had grown almost pitch black. "I thought that's what divans were for. What are you doing creeping around in the dark?"

"Watching you." He backed her toward the bed and tumbled with her onto it. "And wondering what sinister thoughts could possibly make you look like that."

Her smile fell away. "I was thinking I have to move out of here."

His expression changed abruptly as well. "What?"

"I can't stand it anymore. I want to go."

He glanced up at the Roman bust. He'd never really liked it much himself. "And give up all this?"

"It's time for me to get a place of my own."

He studied her soberly for a moment. "The charm's wearing a little thin, isn't it?"

"Well at least you've noticed it, too."

He said nothing for another long moment, then finally:

"Would it cheer you up if I told you I spoke to my tenants today?"

"It depends on what they said."

He smiled. "How about that they're giving in on their demand to finish out the lease and will be out by the first of December."

Joan looked at him in disbelief. It was simply too good to be true. "Why didn't you say so when you first came in!"

"I was going to wait and tell you over dinner. Let's get dressed and go out."

"I have a better idea," she said, throwing one hand behind his back and slipping a button of his shirt with the other. "Let's stay home and pack."

— 18

For Joan, the next two weeks were of as refreshingly different a cast as the weather, which with the coming of November had finally turned cold, poetically gusty and gray. Diana had left at the end of the first weekend. Joan was given a tantalizing preview of life *à deux* with Philip when Chick, Charlotte, Hayden and Walter made an excursion to carry their condolences in person to Phyllis Barnard. Hayden and Walter even threw in the added bonus of staying away an extra few days visiting friends in Bern. But mostly, the burden of an indefinite stay at Rue St. Dominique had been removed, which Joan hadn't realized was as onerous as it was until it was gone. Arriving for a half-day stopover on her way home from Italy—a pushed-up story deadline had derailed her plans for an extended visit—Fanny was relieved to find her daughter very much her old self.

"So you're finally getting out of that house," she said over lunch. "Good for you! I still think you ought to be in a place of your own, but who am I to say? When do you move?"

"In December. We can drive by it on the way to the airport. I've never seen the street myself."

"Not 'til then?"

"It's only a few weeks away."

"When did the widow finally leave?"

"Diana? She hasn't altogether yet. She's been off shooting some-where in Spain for the last ten days but they're keeping the sheets on her bed until it's completely wrapped up and she heads back to Hollywood for good."

"That'll be a happy day. And Hayden?"

"She shows no sign of leaving—ever. I've started to think the whole thing's just a test of wills between the Alpha and Beta females."

"Over *Walter*? I still find that hard to—"

"Only incidentally. I suspect what Hayden really wants is the house and she's stonewalling until Charlotte breaks down and moves out."

"You don't think *that*'ll ever happen."

"I don't know. I get the feeling Charlotte's not been all there lately. She might be showing the strain." Joan signaled the waiter for the check.

"Or plotting her stepdaughter's murder."

"Yes, well, I've thought of it a few times myself," Joan said, but without much feeling. It had all begun to seem boring and remote.

"What about Philip?"

"No, he still loves his sister, though I can't say why."

"I mean any more trips?"

"Not until this week. But only a few days. He's due back tomor-row."

"Dearie, why doesn't he ever take you with him?"

"He does. And in fact he asked me to go, but I have a big deadline on a stack of drawings I've barely begun. Speaking of which, what time is your plane?"

"So what was the story on the coins?"

"What coins?"

"In Charlotte's toil—"

"Oh, I thought I told you. I asked Charlotte about them."

"Really!"

"Well, in a roundabout way."

"They aren't from the Croesian Hoard, I take it."

"An antique shop in Poughkeepsie. She even tried to give me one. I was a little embarrassed."

"But she knew why you were asking."

"Of course. Mum, your plane?"

"Oh, yes, here, check my ticket, I don't have my glasses on."

"Jesus, Mum! It leaves at *three!*"

"I think I told you that."

"Do you have any idea what time it is?"

"Oh, hell," Fanny said, checking her watch. "And I *hate* to rush. My stomach, you know. Knots. I suppose this means we don't have time to swing by Philip's place."

"There wasn't that much to see, anyway. It's not like we could have gone in. Where's your coat?"

"Still, it would've been nice at least to see the neighborhood."

"I wouldn't worry that it's going to be a slum."

"I'm not. Here, let me pay that. No doubt it's fabulously chic."

It was a long way from being a slum, but "fabulously chic" would have been stretching it. Shaded from natural light for all but maybe twenty minutes a day and hung with the cold dampness of a cellar, Joan would have described Rue Seguier as more of an alley than a street. Certainly a far cry from Rue St. Dominique, she thought as she pulled her car onto the sidewalk. But then, so much the better.

Wasn't this how she'd always imagined Paris to be? she asked herself on finding a blue 4 glazed on a white tile over a large green door at the river end of the street. The Paris of Chick's youth. Her eyes rose up the ancient-looking facade as she tried to guess which windows belonged to Philip's apartment. Perhaps the Paris of Charlotte's youth as well.

She peered at the tags on the buzzers. Surely Philip had mentioned his tenants by name before but none of these looked familiar. Not that it would have done her much good to recognize one, as it would have been a little indelicate to ask to see the place two weeks before they were due to vacate.

At this point, which was also the point at which Joan was just turning to leave, she heard the *cl-chunk* of a bolt being thrown. She looked back to see the door swing open and, in the next moment, a short, thickset elderly woman step out. Wrapped in a series of shawls, all of them black, she could have been a Catalan peasant on her way out to milk a goat. Joan smiled: If she'd ever held any romantic picture of authentic old Paris, this had to be it.

The woman, on the other hand, was evidently less taken with the picture of Joan. After eyeing her coldly for several seconds, she asked, in brusque French, what it was she wanted. The question caught Joan by surprise. Without thinking, she answered, *"Pour l'appartement de Philip Dumas."*

It was a truthful enough but somewhat nonsensical reply—to which the woman could have been expected to respond that he did not live there. What she did in fact say, however, didn't make much sense either.

"Enfin!" was the comment, ("Finally?") and with that she took out a clutch of keys the size of her fist, unlocked the door and stepped back into the building. Joan stood on the street for a moment, not sure quite what to do. The answer came presently from inside what she could now see was a large open courtyard, which echoed the woman's shrill call of *"Venez! Venez!"* Still a bit confused, but deciding finally that this was not the time to look a gift horse in the mouth, Joan followed her in.

Crossing back and forth in front of tall leaded windows that looked out onto the cobblestone yard, she followed the woman up three flights of stairs. She missed the majority of what was muttered as the woman struggled along, but understood enough to gather that the woman managed the building. She could only assume that Philip had not only informed her of his plan to move in, but had mentioned Joan as well. The woman did seem somewhat disgruntled, however, by the fact that Joan had not telephoned first. Joan may have gotten some of this wrong, but what was clear—and it was all that mattered for the moment—was that she had managed to arrive while the tenants were away and was about to be given the grand tour.

At the third landing the woman led her to a door at the southwest end of the hall and, after fussing noisily with her keys for a moment, pushed the door ajar, said something on the order of "Close it behind you when you're through," turned and started back down the stairs. Puzzled by the unexpected show of trust, Joan nevertheless thanked her and swung the door wide. Instead of walking in, however, she stood frozen to the spot and stared.

The first thing that struck her, after the relentless dimness of the street, courtyard and stairwell, was the almost blinding abundance of light. Full afternoon sun poured in a long bank of uncurtained windows and reflected off the polished floor as if it were a pool of water. Out over a jagged horizon of gray roof tile and orange chimney stacks, she could see the lacy tip of the Eiffel Tower. Her second observation, which came a fraction of a second later and with considerably greater force, was that the apartment was empty. Not just empty: vacant. There was not a stick of furniture in the place. The kitchen drawers, she soon discovered in a bewildered turn through the place, did not yield up so much as a fork, the linen closet not so much as a towel, the bathroom cabinet not a bar of soap.

The old woman was halfway back across the courtyard when Joan, flustered from her pell-mell descent, caught up with her. Taking a moment to catch her breath, she struggled to find the words to ask when the previous tenants had moved out. Her grammar was no doubt tortured, but the woman seemed to understand. In a uniquely French expression that was as if to say "Let me think," she elongated her face and sent a column of air through pursed lips. Then she shrugged.

"*En été,*" she said. "*Oui, en août.*"

And with that she turned and shambled toward the door, leaving Joan staring speechlessly after her as if she'd sprouted wings and taken flight.

— *19* ————————————————

The first thing Joan did when she got back to Rue St. Dominique was look up the months of the year in the nearest French/English dictionary. But this only confirmed what she already knew: that *août* was August, and that her question—*Les chambres sont desertées depuis quand?*—while of dubious construction was essentially clear. It had been nearly impossible for the old woman and her to have misunderstood each other. And impossible to arrive at any other conclusion than that Philip's apartment had been vacant since before he and Joan had even arrived in France. Unless there were two Rue Seguiers in the city, and a Philip Dumas owned an apartment on each. But that, of course, was as impossible as the alternative at the other extreme: that despite what he had told her, Philip had never meant for them to live there at all.

But how much sense did *that* make? Joan asked herself as in a distracted haze she made her way up the stairs and down the hallway to their rooms. Not only had she made it amply plain how she felt about staying in this house, two weeks ago Philip had sounded every bit as ready to leave as she. What purpose could it possibly serve to delay their move? Why would he—

Joan did not finish her thought. She swung their bedroom door wide and promptly collided with the silent skeletal frame of Madame P. Coming from a preoccupied state to begin with, Joan took several seconds to regain her wits, and then to realize that she was clutching the woman's twiglike arms—probably painfully—with both hands.

Upon discovering this, Joan quickly released her. Joan did not, however, immediately step aside.

"Can I help you?" she asked, impulsively blocking the woman's way. The madame's skin appeared as white as chalk in the dim light, making her eyes look like two bits of black ice. Her deathly composure was, as always, intact. But Joan could not help noticing that there was, for her, an almost animated set to the lipless mouth.

"Non," the maid said, raising her pencil-line brows a fraction of an inch. *"Pardon."*

If the look was intended to make Joan feel foolish, it worked. After an awkward, meaningless pause, during which Joan was forced to ask herself what she thought she could possibly accomplish, she stood sheepishly aside to let the woman glide smugly by.

Joan watched her disappear around the bend in the hall and then turned back to her room. Whatever it was the woman had been doing—perhaps she *had* only come to bring the pile of laundry Joan now noticed stacked neatly on her bed—it was finally trivial in the face of her more immediate concern. It was five-thirty in Geneva. Philip was unlikely to be at the hotel, but she could leave a message for him to call.

As she looked for the number, she realized suddenly that what she really wanted was just to hear his voice. He would have an explanation about the apartment, but she didn't really need to hear it. If anyone needed to keep their tortured emotional past in perspective and their personal paranoias to herself, it was she. Could she really be turning slowly but inexorably into her own mother? Joan wondered with a sinking feeling as she listened to the call make its arduous journey through. Although the appeal of it seemed safely distant now, she would not want to have to count up the hours she'd spent musing over the various mysteries surrounding Philip's family. Add to that now these essentially unfounded fears of infidelity and deceit and it appeared the sins of the mother were indeed being visited on—

"Ambassador Hotel," a distant voice said across the static.

Joan opened her mouth to answer, but nothing came out.

"Ambassador Hotel," he said again. But she had already returned the receiver to its cradle.

Hidden as it was by the bundle of folded clothing, Joan had not noticed it when she first came in. But in toppling the stack when she sat down to make the call, she'd exposed it. Whether it was Madame P. who had left it for her to find, it certainly explained the woman's amusement. *Les Yeux* had outdone themselves this time. The picture was not so good of Joan's face, which was downcast and slightly out of focus, but it was *great* of her breasts, to which the lower two-thirds of the frame was lovingly devoted. They gleamed with moisture; their two big brown nipples pointed cheerfully toward the sky.

From the floor, leaning against the side of the bed, Joan gradually took in the details of the larger display, which comprised a group of smaller photos laid out around the *coup de grâce*, the torso shot at *La Piscine*. The headline said something in the French rhyming equivalent of "tears"—Joan's presumably, as with the perspiration she did appear to be weeping—and "cheers"—judging from the subhead, Diana's. The smaller pictures showed Joan and Philip on Martha's Vineyard; Joan looking dowdy at a function at the Louvre; Princess Sophia, at Longchamps, looking as if her horse had just won; Diana, on the deck of the *Finisterre*, looking like Bouguereau's if not quite Botticelli's *Venus*; Philip with much longer hair skiing with Diana somewhere in the Alps; Philip more recently at the door of a restaurant called Elenora's. In this last one his face was partly shielded by his hand, which he was thrusting up into the view of the camera, but it was definitely him. The woman on his arm was also obviously Diana. To his credit, Joan thought, he appeared angry. To hers, she noted inconsequentially, the hat went perfectly with the dress.

Joan could not have said for how long she sat there before the rude sensation of hitting bottom replaced the relatively painless suspense of falling down the well. But the full force of the insult finally sank in. She got to her feet and snatched up the phone.

At this point, however, a second jolt registered. Not from anything on so grand a scale as having her bare breasts plastered all over Europe. Rather from a small detail she'd been looking at without really seeing all along. It was in the picture of Philip and Diana at the restaurant, the one in which Diana's hat went so smashingly with her dress. The one in which Philip was wearing the tie that Joan had picked out for him *barely three weeks ago.* She hung up the phone once again, picked up the magazine and turned it to the light. There was no mistaking it—it was the tie she had given him before he had left for Milan.

The explanation, Joan quickly told herself, was that the picture had to have been taken in Paris: Philip and Diana had certainly met for lunch while she was in town, and he would not have seen her outside the city in the last three weeks without mentioning it to Joan. But if Joan was so confident of this, why then were her eyes desperately searching the background of the photo for clues as to where it had been taken?

Whatever the reason, it hardly mattered now. She hadn't had to look very far. The evidence littered the picture as if in mockery. Five street signs were clearly visible. And every one of them was in Italian.

Joan dialed the Ambassador again and asked the desk to put her through to Philip Dumas's room. It seemed like an eternity before the ringing stopped, but finally the receiver was raised. It was a better connection this time. She heard Didi Devilliers's smoky voice as clear as a bell.

"Hello . . . Hello . . . who's there?"

—PART TWO—

— 20 ————————————

Looking like an aging WAC in her khakis and heavy-soled shoes,
Veronica Filmore marched as far as the Victoria Grand sign, pivoted,
pressed two fingers against the side of her Adam's apple and started
back down the white stone driveway that wound through a cover of
mango trees and flowering shrubs. Not breaking stride as she reached
the hotel's wide marble steps, she surged up them, across the spacious
lobby and into a waiting elevator, where she finally stopped, put her
fingers back to her throat and looked down at her watch. Barely
fifteen minutes later the lift doors parted again and out she marched,
back across the lobby and out the door. The only difference was that
she had changed into a paisley dress, pearls and a yellow straw hat.
At the top of the steps she paused for the first time, inhaled deeply
and glanced with satisfaction around her.

Rocky, as everyone knew her, had lived at the Victoria Grand hotel
for the last eight years. After almost fifty years in the Queen's
colonies and ex-colonies—which accounted for the chipped Briticisms
in her manner of speech—she had drifted down to Zambia in search
of a setting for another of her best-selling Betsy Blair mystery novels,
which she published under the pseudonym Mary Lord. *Zambezi* broke

Mary Lord's previous record of twenty weeks on *The New York Times*
best-seller list by two weeks. It was her twelfth and, according to her,
her last. Having reached retirement age, she was settling down, she
told her agent, publisher, and friends, to write a "serious" work of
southern African history in "dignified obscurity." Seven and a half
years later, the history was still unfinished and Rocky was still here.

Rocky was certainly a dignified woman, if also a little eccentric,
which, as the Vic Grand's old-style artist in residence, was her due. As
for obscure, her five-room suite on the sixth floor of the majestic,
baby-pink hotel was a long way from Park Avenue, but it was not
exactly the bush. Having run down during the fifties and sixties, the
seventy-three-year-old landmark had finally been purchased and re-
stored to the splendor of colonial days. With fresh paint, its grounds
hacked back to putting-green lawns and its staff built back up to two
hundred, including a three-star kitchen and house marimba band, it
was once again one of the finest old hotels in southern Africa. Shun-
ning publicity and determined to keep Mary Lord a famous but
faceless name, Rocky's African hideout was thus designed to remove
her from the press of humankind in general but only to a point. A
ten-year sag in the price of copper and Zambia's resulting economic
troubles had put a never-booming tourist industry into a slump.
However, Victoria Falls, and once again the Vic Grand, remained a
traditional stop-over for that adventuring slice of Society that found
romance in brief, expensive and well-padded forays into the Animal
Kingdom and the Third World. Photographic expeditions were a
favorite and Robert Mbo's photographic safaris outfit did a decent if
not exactly brisk business out of the lobby. More recently, the
Karanga burial mound discovery had brought in a steady stream of
clients in the form of scholars, academics, journalists and assorted
fusty types from the art world's institutional side.

In other words, Rocky's obscurity could best be described as
selective, as she picked and chose among these—her fellow guests—
from whom she extracted information about the goings-on in Europe
and America and against whom she sharpened her "rusting intellectual blades," in her words, and exercised "flabbing social muscles."
Combined with the wealth of fresh historical information coming out

of the Njoko dig, Rocky Filmore realized her goal in life of having the best of all possible worlds.

She was just reviewing this fortunate state of affairs when she was jolted back into action by a salutory beep on the horn of a mud-encrusted Landrover, which was pulling up to the hotel. The legend, ZAMBIAN PHOTOGRAPHIC TOURS, was barely visible on its door.

"My *dears*, what happened to *you?*" she exclaimed as she bounced—it was the only word—down the steps toward it. A handsome African man in a badly soiled Wimbledon T-shirt was leaning out of the driver's window toward her. From the passenger's side, a woman with short dark hair and a dirty, boyish face climbed stiffly out in a small cloud of dust. "Good God, you look as if you just crossed the Kalahari. On your hands and knees."

"We bogged down," the man said with a weary grin.

"What fun," Rocky said, "I can't wait to hear all about it, but I have *tea*"—she raised her penciled eyebrows and stuck out a plumpish pinky finger when she said this—"with the Ambassador's Wife at their twenty-room hideaway, then a stop in town. So why not dinner at, say, seven o'clock, that way you two have a chance to clean up. No offense, sweethearts, but ten days in the bush—Juanita, you look particularly disgusting. All right then? I'm off to hear the cover story on how it is our cultural affairs attaché got caught with a crate of Uzis in the boot of his Mercedes. Tad Appleton has got to be the dumbest spook we've had in years. I've never trusted a man who'd wear a bow tie if his mother didn't absolutely insist—it's a sure sign of a superiority complex. Well, I'll be late." She had been looking into her straw handbag and now closed it with a satisfied pat. "Juanita, you have mail. Robert, tell Alfred he's welcome, too, if he's up to it. Where did I leave my car? Oh, there it is. *Ciao.*"

The girl she had addressed as Juanita gazed after the bobbing figure a moment longer. Then, shaking her head slightly, exchanged a smile with the man behind the wheel, slung a camera, binoculars and pack over her shoulder, turned, and limped into the lobby. She ordered a double whiskey soda from the bar and took the elevator to her room.

Through the latticed glass doors that opened onto a private balcony, she could hear the muffled roar of the great Falls. It was as constant as the hum of a highway or hiss of the sea against a rocky shore. She paused at the railing for a moment to sip her drink and watch the thickening rays of the sun slant over the tops of the trees of Zambia and, on the other side of the river, which was marked only by plumes of mist, those forming the hazy green carpet of Zimbabwe. A puff of warm, humid air touched her skin. It carried the wild, gull-like cry of an African fish eagle hunting over the river. From nearby came the *trip trip trip tee tee tee* and flute-like whistle of a greenbul. She drew in a deep breath of the distinctly African evening, gazed a moment longer, then turned and went indoors to fill the tub with hot water and bath oil. With a long low groan, she lowered herself gingerly in. When she emerged a hour and a half later, sunburned but clean-scrubbed and revived, she was almost recognizable as Joan Cook. But not quite.

Quite a bit more about Joan than her name had changed in the eight months since she'd abandoned Paris. The new name—adopted temporarily on a briefly considered whim under circumstances that made it almost irresistible—was the least of it. Like the quasi-British accent that now colored her speech, the metamorphosis had started the day she met Veronica Filmore. Which was also the day she packed her bags and without another word stormed out of 26 Rue St. Dominique for good.

Joan had not been sure just what she was going to do in Cologne. Besides the fact that she didn't speak a word of German, the friend she had remembered on her way to the Paris train station in the middle of the night might not even have lived there anymore. But at that point all she had wanted to do was put some credible distance between herself and Philip Dumas—and the photo staff of *Les Yeux* while she was at it. At about six that morning, the train she was riding on derailed, fell over on its side, slid for a quarter of a mile and crashed. Joan woke up in the hospital with her nose bandaged and her head partially shaved, but not seriously hurt. Besides the fact that she'd lost her money, her passport and her bags, and had no idea where she was or what anybody around her was saying. She stared silently at the ceiling for about thirty minutes, then burst into tears. After about five minutes of this, the apple-cheeked lady with the broken foot in the next bed said to her in British-sounding English, "*Honestly*, it can't be as bad as all *that!*" To which Joan replied "Yes, it could!" and in the course of the next five days told the woman in gratifying detail how.

By the end of that time, Rocky had in turn not only told Joan about her life in Africa, but invited the younger woman to come back to Livingstone with her to serve as nurse/companion until Rocky's foot healed or Joan's interest failed, whichever came first. Joan accepted immediately and Rocky made a call—to whom, Joan never got straight—and secured a Zambian passport for one Juanita Castlerosse, a name they deliberated over at great length and finally chose for its "mystery, symbolism and comic value." The idea had been to erase any trail that *Les Yeux* or Philip might have been tempted to follow. If sensational in retrospect, the notion had appealed enormously to Joan's current frame of mind. Joan called Fanny to tell her what had happened and three days later got her first unforgettable glimpse of Victoria Falls. Standing in its drenching mist, she felt, appropriately enough, as if she were baptizing a new life.

As for her old one, there remained, to this day, lingering details to attend to. There was still the letter she had intended to send to Philip explaining finally why she left. She'd also always wanted to use the line "I'll send for my things," but somehow she never seemed to get around to it. That chapter in her life was now closed, she told Rocky whenever the woman asked. The question of how things with Philip had spun so ruinously out of control, she said, like all the unresolved mysteries of 26 Rue St. Dominique, no longer interested her. As for the name Juanita Castlerosse, visions of baying tabloid hounds had faded quickly enough, but for reasons Rocky never pressed her on, Joan continued to use it, and with it the harmless fiction with everyone but Rocky that that brief and disagreeable period in her life had never taken place.

Within a month of moving to Zambia, Joan's duties as nurse were no longer needed and she went to work for Robert Mbo, an Oxford-educated Zambian conservationist whose interest in making a living from a job "for which I do not have to change my clothes" had been the seed for the inception of Zambian Photographic Tours. Juan, as Rocky liked to call her, continued to share the Filmore suite, running errands and doing her best to maintain some semblance of order in the older woman's life. From time to time she suggested moving to an apartment in town, but Rocky, having grown attached to her, insisted she stay.

In the meantime, Joan's nose had healed but not exactly in its original shape. What had been a delicate and polite if characterless feature was now almost aquiline and somewhat crooked, although interestingly so. Combined with the emergence of thick dark eyebrows, which like her now closely cropped hair she had let go back to their original color, it gave her face an arresting strength. Add to this a loss of almost fifteen pounds and for the first time in her life her face was also now angular, with visible cheekbones and a clearly defined jaw. Whereas she'd always been pretty in a safe, predictable sort of way that owed nothing to nuance, she had in the last half year developed an exotic, somewhat androgynous beauty. It was the kind of face described alternately as that of a handsome woman or beautiful man.

There was, however, no question as to her sex tonight as she sauntered across the dining room in a red sundress to join the others on the veranda for drinks. The dress seemed to flow rather than fall from her slender neck and bare brown shoulders. Her hair was wet and combed back off her face. She'd painted her lips bright red. Robert grinned appreciatively and stood as she crossed the porch to where he and Rocky were sitting. "Do I know you?" he asked as he made room for her to sit down. Smiling, she dropped into the cushions beside him and leaned back to look out over the verdant grounds. The setting sun was a corpulent orange ball and the air was full of the fragrance of heavy blossoms and the first sounds of the night.

"Rocky was just telling me about her tea"—Robert raised a long brown baby finger—"with the Ambassador's Wife."

"Oh, no, I can't abide that woman," Joan said. "What a pretentious nit."

"My dear girl, to call Lily Timberman a nitwit is like calling Ghengis Khan antisocial—it hardly covers it," Rocky said in her breathless manner. Even lounging over cocktails she managed to convey the air of someone in a rush. "She's a *menace*. All these little plans she has for the 'brown babies,' which she habitually refers to in the possessive. I wonder if all missionaries come back as ambassadors' wives. Wouldn't that be a fun story to write?"

"Of course, you'd have to find a way to excuse your frequent association with her."

"Couldn't be done. It's inexcusable and I should be ashamed. However, beside being a ninny, she's an inveterate gossip and half of what pours out of that flapping maw is classified information. The stuff's just too good to waste."

"So what's the official word on—"

"Oh, heavens, yes, Our Man in Lusaka! I'd almost forgot. He's been bundled home in disgrace! For *running guns*, no less! You know, they *have* people for that. He didn't need to go and do it himself. And to get caught! She didn't seem to know who they were for—I can't imagine UNITA—I mean with the settlement and so on. Besides, the movement has been getting *plenty* of U.S. arms through much more efficient channels than the trunk of Tad Appleton's car. But then these things aren't supposed to make sense. What time is it? Here, let's move to the table and I'll tell you the rest. It's really rather a riot."

It was a funny story, even if it did not make sense, but the three of them enjoyed it for what it was. After agreeing there was either quite a bit more or quite a bit less to the real story, they went on to other things.

"So, Bwana," Joan asked Robert as two hours later the last plates were cleared, "when do we have to go out again?"

"You'll be happy to hear the Wesleys have postponed yet again so we've nothing major until they show up three weeks from yesterday."

"The Wesleys. That'd be the reg'lar folk from Ayun-toe-nee-o, Tay-ack-suss?"

"They're all right, really. I've had them before. He'll call you little lady and she'll tell tasteless jokes but they're easy. Variety means nothing to them. The world begins and ends with elephants. If we don't see another thing it won't matter so long as we find them an elephant."

"Speaking of elephants," Rocky said, "there's one about the size of

Brazil in a mud hole on the river track about a mile up river. What he was doing down there by himself, I haven't the foggiest. Pity I didn't have my camera. Who wants more coffee?"

"I can't," Joan said, getting up. "I told Sidney I'd meet him at the George."

"He's back from Harare?" Robert asked. "Good, that means I'll have my new lens for the weekend."

"Yes, and hopefully my copy of Wenders's *Ancient Civilizations*," Rocky said, "which certainly should have been in by now."

"I thought Wenders didn't study Africa, at least not southern Africa," Joan said.

"No, he didn't, you clever thing, but he's very good on prehistory and archeology in general, and though I'm loath to admit, there are"—she tapped her forehead—"gaps."

"Only to let the machinery breathe."

21

Sidney Cleese was one of a special breed of white men in post-colonial Africa whose most outstanding talent, besides a knack for making money, was always to end up on the right side of historical events. This had less to do with political convictions or ideology than with being able to recognize when to abandon this ship or that, and then to which side to jump. Sidney was not only one of the few European (by way of South Africa) expatriates whose businesses had survived the colonial cleanup in the early days of independence, but his enterprises, which, besides the Vic Grand, included a newspaper, hotel in Lusaka, contracting firm and sundry other concerns not all so obviously connected with him, continued unmolested. There were ~e schools of thought as to the nature of his survivability. The first was that he was protected by his unusual friendship with the Zambian president; second, in keeping with the first, was that he was a consummate politician who kept his connections well-greased. The third, which was held by Rocky and Joan if not by Robert, was that, after almost thirty years in Zambia, he was widely held to be a fair and honest "white African" who genuinely held his adopted country's interests close to heart.

He was, at any rate, a charming and attractive man, at forty-four the picture of health. Perpetually tanned from frequent forays into the bush, he had sandy brown hair that was graying with good taste at the temples. His eyes were muted green and he had slightly crooked but very white teeth, which one saw often, as he had a facile smile. Besides showing off his nice teeth, it also carved deep lines at the sides of his mouth, which Joan found sexy. She was thinking so now as he grinned at her through the sweltering dimness of the James, the quaint-to-run-down pub about half a mile up the road from the Victoria Grand favored by locals and expatriates of lesser means than Veronica Filmore.

"I don't want to talk about Harare," he said, "I want to hear about your trip. Alfred tells me the German was a bit of a Nazi."

"Yes, a bit. What else did he tell you?"

"Let's see, that you broke an axle on the second Jeep and had a rather dicey run-in with poachers." His smile had dissolved into an exaggerated paternal frown that Joan found sexy as well. "I can't say I much like the sound of that. Where was this?"

"Practically inside the Nanzhila Camp."

"What were they doing?"

"Carving a hippo into steaks."

"Come on, Juanita, what *happened?*"

"Well, you know how Alfred is, he started abusing them."

"How many of them were there?"

"Only two. Mashasha, I think. But they had rifles. So did Alfred and Robert, but as our side was less inclined to use them, they had a distinct advantage."

"I don't know how disinclined Albert is to shoot a poacher."

"Enough at least that Robert was able to talk him back into the car and back down the track."

"And the German?"

"Much tougher before and after the incident," she said with a chuckle that made her dark eyes gleam. "During, I thought he would—as you say—sod his pants."

He laughed with her and touched the back of her hand with a long forefinger. "I'm glad you're back," he said. His hand was large and strong-looking, the skin deeply tanned, the hairs bleached gold. A thick vein bulged on its back and there was a whitened scar that drew a half-circle around the first knuckle. "Me too," she said tracing it with her finger. "Now tell me about Harare."

"Not here."

Halfway between the James and the Victoria Grand, whose lights were just appearing up ahead, Sidney stopped her and put his mouth to her ear.

"Shhh . . . do you hear it?" Joan turned her head. "There it is again," he whispered.

The night was black, moist and airless. What sounded like the wind was the roar of the Falls in the distance. Joan heard a faint *hoo hoo hoo.* "A spotted eagle owl," she said.

"A scops." They listened a little longer in silence until he took her hand by the wrist and went to press it against his cheek.

"Agh! How can your hands be *cold?*"

"They're always cold," she said and touched the back of her fingers against his neck. He cocked his head, pinning them there and, reaching around to place his hands on her buttocks, pulled her pelvis into his.

"Come with me to Nairobi this weekend."

"What's in Nairobi?"

"Noise. Nightlife."

"Street crime. I thought you didn't like big cities."

"I don't like medium-size cities. I think big cities are bloody miracles.

"*Do* you?"

"Oh, yes. I *love* New York."

"I'd never have guessed. . . . Then what—besides molesting girls half your age—are you doing out here?"

"Freedom," he said softly. He pressed his nose against her hair. "If I could have it in the heart of Manhattan, I'd live there. Mmm, nice pheromones. You didn't like it?"

"What?"

"New York."

"No."

"And Paris?"

She said, after only a slight hesitation, "I've never been to Paris."

"You're *serious*? Forget Nairobi! We'll go to Paris!" He released her and, taking her arm, started them walking again. "I grant you the Seine would be a cleaner stream if the city had never been built, but then the world would be incomplete."

"No berets."

"No Camembert, no Mouton-Rothschild, no *Tour Eiffel*. My God, no Marc Lefevre, which would be a great loss to womankind. But didn't I hear you speaking French with him tonight?"

"Barely. I took enough in college to say things like 'how are you' and 'I have a yellow pencil.' "

"*J'ai un crayon vert.*"

"*Jaune.*"

"*Jaune.* He's in love with you, you know."

"You always say that."

"It's because I worry that you'll run off with him some day."

"With Marc?" She laughed. "You should know me better than that."

"But I don't. Even after . . ."

"Six months."

"Is that all?"

"I was here for over a month before we met. You were away."

"Whenever it was I remember the very day. It was hot as Hades and you were half-naked on my veranda and covered with sweat. It looked like lacquer. You were laughing at something. Your big nose was wrinkled and your head was thrown back like this" (he demonstrated, "ha ha ha"). "I couldn't tell whether you were a girl or a boy—"

"In a bikini?"

"You had a T-shirt on. Really, I felt like Gustave Aschenbach—"

"Who?"

"*Death in Venice*—facing a sudden homosexual urge after all these years." She couldn't see but could hear the spreading smile in his voice. "And like poor Gustave, I've been pursuing you ever since."

Joan laughed. "Not very seriously."

"For me, seriously."

She slid an arm through his and started them again down the path. "Well, don't strain yourself."

"Sometimes I think I should ask you to marry me."

"I'd say no."

"Just so you don't go off and marry someone else. It would be a real blow to the ego, which in my case needs a lot of stroking, particularly when it comes to such well-turned-out rivals as Marc Lefevre and the strapping and arcane Robert Mbo—What do you mean you'd say no? Why would you say no?"

"I make it a policy not to get serious about international playboys. They never give you a moment's peace."

"What would you know about that?"

"I read a lot."

He stopped her again just beyond the globe of light that illuminated the door of the silent hotel and turned her around to face him. "What I find most irresistible about you, my tempting Tadzio, is that you're too innocent to know what you're talking about." With that, and a quick look into the empty lobby, he took her face in his hands and slipped his tongue into her mouth.

"Oh, before I forget," he whispered as several minutes later he was leading her by the hand up the grandly curving steps to the first floor where he kept a suite, "there's a message for you at the desk. The Texans moved their reservations back again, now to mid-June—God pity their travel agent—"

"I heard."

"But a group coming in next week called to make arrangements for a trip out to the site. They'll be here on the fourth, I think it was, and want to go out starting the sixth."

"I'd better call Robert."

He tightened his grip on her hand. "In the morning."

22

Rocky was already at the Zambian Photographic Tours office. Joan found her and Robert leaning back in swivel chairs on opposite sides of an old wooden desk like a sheriff and his deputy in a Wild West town. Except that Rocky was filing her nails. Indeed, with its scarred hardwood furniture, inevitable slow-turning ceiling fan and cage of rifles and handguns, the bare-floored ZPT headquarters had the feel of a sheriff's office. In fact, Livingstone's main drag, which comprised a strip of run-down, understocked stores, had the feel of a frontier town. Joan half expected to see a bottle of corn whisky and two shot glasses on the desk between them.

"What is it, my dear? You look like you've just had a session with the Ghost of Christmas to Come," Rocky said at first sight of Joan. On second sight, she added: "Or Igwe the Rain God. You're dripping all over the floor."

"Our Njoko party, Robert," Joan said almost breathlessly, "have they checked in yet?"

"Not that I know of. But they're due today or tomorrow. Why?"

"What's the name?" Joan's attempt at nonchalance had obviously failed as both Rocky and Robert were gazing at her with interest.

"Let's see," Robert finally said, opening the book on his desk. "Philip . . ."

"Dumas," Joan and Rocky said in unison. Robert looked at the two women looking at each other: Rocky with eyebrows raised; Joan with a pallid absence of expression.

"How did you know?" Joan asked her.

"Sidney mentioned it to me. How did *you* know?"

"I just ran into him down at the Falls."

"So that's why you're all wet." Rocky resumed filing her nails. "How did it go?"

"What do you mean, *how did it go?*"

"What am I missing?" Robert asked.

"It *didn't* go," Joan said. "We didn't speak."

"I was just wondering," Rocky explained to Robert, "what the man was like." She added, with a dusting tap of her file against the edge of the desk, "Juan knows him."

Joan looked at her sharply.

"Well, she knows *of* him," Rocky went on. "So do you, Robert. He's Charles Dumas's son." Getting no response, she raised her eyes to Robert, with a glance at Joan on the way. "The *archeologist?* Sardis? The lost treasure of Croesus? *Life* magazine? Or was it *National Geographic.* . . . Whatever, haven't you ever read a society column? The family's been the fodder of choice for years. After the Royals, of course. God, there's been all *sorts* of nasty stuff, starting with the Croesian Hoard, which the father was supposed to have pinched. A *most* intriguing story."

"What story is that?"

"Oh, hello, Mr. Cleese. How are you, dear? We were just gossiping about your newest arrivals."

"The Andreottis?"

"No. The Dumases."

"Ah. Juanita, dear, you're all wet."

"I read about them not long ago." Robert's partner Alfred Mapoma, a tall, thin Totela with a broad-boned mahogany-colored face, had emerged from the sunlight behind Sidney. "What was it? He stole some big treasure in Egypt, didn't he?"

Joan shook her head slowly. As if the conversation hadn't become ludicrous enough, Alfred's participation gave it a distinct sense of the unreal. One of the best trackers in the business, the man rarely spoke of anything less immediate than where a particular bull elephant might feed, a leopard was sleeping, a pride of lions had knocked off for the afternoon. In fact, between his abiding respect for animals and overall contempt for humankind, he rarely spoke of anything at all, which is why when teamed with him, especially on trips to the Njoko dig, it was a big part of Joan's job to work the crowd. Hearing Chick's Sardis fiasco discussed now in Alfred's crisp consonants, rolling r's and lyrical accents ("I *seem* to *rrre*-mem-ba, the *old* man *dis*tubbed an ancient *cuss*"), Joan could only stare in disbelief.

"And his partner died recently of mysterious causes, I believe."

"Well, not too," Rocky said. "It was a heart attack."

Sidney glanced at Rocky. "My, my," he grinned. "Someone's been taking a little time from ancient Shona civilization. . . . Is that from *The Sun* or Lily Timberman?"

"Did Juan tell you she ran into him?" Rocky asked. "The son, that is."

"I remember reading something about him, too," Alfred said.

"Yes, he's supposed to have killed his girlfriend."

Everyone swung around to look at Robert. Rocky let go a hoarse laugh. "Robert Mbo! You *shock* me! Now *here's* a man who reads the gossip page! What are you talking about?"

"He was going around with some sad little ingenue, who mysteriously disappeared."

"Sad little ingenue!" Alfred laughed. "She was a topless dancer!"

"Well, she did disappear rather abruptly, as I recall," Rocky said, with a mild look at Joan. "However, I missed the part about his supposedly having had a hand in it. Then, my sources"—she looked from Robert to Alfred and back—"are not so up to date."

Joan, who hadn't spoken a word until now, leaned across the desk to Robert and asked in a low voice: "How badly do you need me on this trip?"

"Why?"

"Can Alfred go in my place?"

"He's already going in my place."

"Since when?"

"After the Wesleys canceled I loaned myself to Marty for two weeks. Tomorrow we're leaving for Chobe to resurrect his jeep then driving down to Gabarone to take a BBC camera crew out to the Kalahari. What's wrong, are you sick? I must say you don't look well at all. . . ."

"I'm fine," she murmured, glancing over her shoulder at Rocky, Sidney and Alfred, who were absorbed in tabloid gossip. "It's just that I really don't like these people."

"You just finished saying you'd never met them."

"Well, I've *read* and believe me I *know* what they're like. They're arrogant, pretentious, narcissistic society snobs—"

Robert laughed loudly. "Our kind of people, dah-ling. We could hardly run a business without them."

"What's the trouble, dear?" Rocky cut in. "You don't really believe the man's a murderer, do you?"

"Well, who's to say, Rocky," Joan said curtly.

"Then lie back and enjoy it," Rocky said, returning to her nails. "It sounds like all sorts of fun to me."

" 'Lie back and enjoy it'!" Joan growled as they walked up the street to Rocky's car. "Are you out of your mind?"

"Not at all, Juan, dear. You said he didn't recognize you, didn't you? You don't have to give yourself away. And nobody here knows that you know them—although Robert should have an idea by now—lord, you're indiscreet. But he'd never guess that you're Joan Cook, even if he'd seen the pictures. No one would. If I hadn't seen you in the hospital that first day, I'd not have believed it on a bet. So who's going to tell him? Unless you do." She added in a slightly different tone, "And have you thought of that?"

"Of what, telling him? Forget it!"

"Why not?"

"What would be the point?" Joan said snatching a large white blossom off a flowering shrub that was growing at the edge of the road and almost immediately beginning to tear it apart. "I don't want anything from him. I'm not interested in apologies or explanations—hearing it now would be so . . . insulting. It's why I left like that in the first place."

"Eight months ago."

Joan gave Rocky a quick look. "What's that supposed to mean?"

"Only that it's been a while. And that perhaps it's begun to appear differently now. Perspective has a way of changing over time."

"Yes, and often growing clearer," Joan said testily. "What's your point?"

"I have none, other than if you're going to lie, even by omission, you'd better be fully committed to the task or risk looking stupid. That's all."

"It's less of a lie than you make it sound. On balance I'd say I'm more Juanita Castlerosse than I ever was Joan Cook."

"Perhaps. Just as long as you know what you're doing."

Joan tossed the tattered remnants of the bloom aside, briskly dusted the pollen off her hands and tried to sound convincing. "I do."

"Then, it's perfect."

Joan looked over. The woman's tone had changed again. "For what? The whole idea was to avoid any involvement."

"You mean to say you're not the slightest bit curious?"

"About what?"

"Mr. and Mrs. Dumas senior? Maybe the sister has finally done her stepmother in, or perhaps the other way around. And what about the treasure business. Something's bound to have come of that in all this time."

Joan gave a short laugh of amazement. "You can barely contain yourself! What's *your* interest in all this? Obviously not my emotional welfare."

"My dear child, *you* got me interested. I feel like I know these people. The way you iced the whole affair in mystery, you should consider taking up the pen."

"You know, I never realized what a resemblance you bore to my mother. You two really will have to meet. I wonder, though, what does that say about me, associating with people like you?"

"Aren't you the least bit interested in hearing what happened after you left?"

Rocky's faded red Citroen was parked behind Sidney's big black Mercedes, which gleamed like polished onyx. Of all the symbols of success, Joan could think of none that had had such longevity or such universal appeal. It was certainly the case in this impoverished country. In keeping with his own fastidious appearance, Sidney's had not so much as a nick on it, even after ten years. How, she wondered irrelevantly, had he kept it so black under this sun?

"No!" she said firmly. "And please don't *you* make this any more difficult than it has to be. I'm not going to take Philip Dumas or whoever else he's traveling with to Njoko or anywhere else and that's all there is to it."

23

Rocky Filmore was like a bulldog when it came to detail. It showed in her books, which were acclaimed not just for the intricacy of her plots but the textures of the scenes through which the story line moved. Without being overburdened with facts, the reader knew the thickness of the carpet, the carats of her diamond, the brand of his pipe tobacco. The way some people looked like their dogs, Veronica Filmore, with her lingering gaze and quick, incisive tongue, looked and acted exactly like the kind of person who would write a Betsy Blair novel. Her most valuable asset, however, was a less obvious ingredient: the kind of keen personal interest that made people want to talk about themselves. What had a kindly, almost a maternal face, had the predatory impulse of a shark, and the appetite and digestive capacity of a swarm of locusts. In Sidney's words, "Rocky ate people for lunch." Knowing this about her, Joan should not have been surprised that evening when she went out to join her for drinks on the patio to find her sitting with Philip. Given what she knew of the Dumases, she shouldn't have been surprised either to find Charlotte, Hayden, and Diana Devilliers there, too, only that Chick and Walter were not nestled in among them.

"And here is Juan," Rocky said with cheerfully false innocence, waved her over and performed the introductions.

Rocky watched Philip shake Joan's hand and each of the women nod cordially in turn. If there was any sign of recognition on Philip's part, she failed to see it. Nor did any of the women show any special interest beyond the ritual once-over unacquainted females accorded one another. Philip's gaze might have lingered somewhat; then Joan looked particularly striking tonight. She had a radiant flush of pink in her cheeks. Was it powder or an authentic blush? Rocky wondered. And was it apprehension that made her eyes look that big and black, or had she been upstairs all this time working on the effect with an eye-liner pencil? With Philip wandering about the hotel, she hadn't been about to come down looking like the village goatherd, regardless of how she felt about him. She was a woman after all. . . . Rocky had a sudden protective urge—accompanied by a pang of guilt—toward Joan, though she couldn't be sure yet whether it was called for or not. It wasn't until they had moved to the dining room that she heard them finally speak. However, this put the question to rest: The very picture of *sang-froid*, Juanita Castlerosse could've been interviewing a new butler.

"Is this your first trip to Africa?" she asked as Philip pulled out a chair for her between Diana and his sister.

"Sub-Saharan, yes."

Joan lowered herself gracefully into their midst and ordered a second drink. "And what's your interest in the excavation?"

"Well, it's potentially an important find, isn't it?"

"I meant is this a business trip?"

"In part. The Louvre is fairly good in African antiquities. It's not a specialty of mine, exactly, but I was happy to find the excuse to come."

"Do you plan to tour a bit while you're here?" she asked, turning now to Hayden.

"We'll have to see what time allows. I've always wanted to go on a game safari but somehow have never gotten around to it."

"Zambia has some good parks. Kafue, which we're nearest to, is one of the biggest. South Luangwa is one of the richest in game.

Lochinvar is good if you like birds. Chobe, just over the border in Botswana, has the biggest population of elephants in Africa."

"You seem to know a lot about it," Diana said.

Joan took a leisurely sip of her drink before turning her head to answer. "It's my job."

Diana blinked once and looked away.

Didi Devilliers was virtually as Rocky had imagined. Heralded for statuesque beauty, she found her prosaically overdone: the hair too blond, the bosoms too big, a face with the kind of monotonous perfection that had cosmetic surgery written all over it. The only thing she found vaguely entertaining was the saving glimmer of crudeness in her manner. Rocky enjoyed the way she absently licked the olive that came in her martini, for instance, before pressing it into her mouth. Her skin was better tanned than a day and a half in Livingstone would allow: No doubt she'd been on the Mediterranean before landing here. For just an instant, Rocky imagined Diana copulating on the bloodstained deck of a fishing caïque—with a teenage member of the crew.

Hayden came as more of a surprise. An interesting-looking woman but more severe than glamorous, with something carelessly inelegant about her in person. She was witty certainly and not without charm, but, if provoked, Rocky could easily imagine her throwing her drink, glass included, in someone's face.

As for Charlotte, she was least of all the way Rocky had guessed. Unlike the other two, her china-doll skin appeared to have been barely touched by the sun. The woman was obviously scrupulous about such things, and would look remarkably the same twenty years from now: striking but never quite beautiful. Between the air of control and the shape and color of her eyes, she brought to mind a cat: soft and delicate looking, but essentially secretive, survivable and remote.

Rocky sat back and glanced around at the little assembly. Joan was right. Taken together, it was more than an unlikely group. It made no sense at all.

"Your husband, Charlotte, will he be joining you?" she asked.

"No. He's not been well."

"Oh, I'm sorry."

"Is it serious?" Joan asked casually.

"No, but he decided at the last moment to stay at home. The rest will do him good." She added, as if feeling an explanation was called for, "He insisted I come anyway."

"He'll be sorry to hear he could have met Mary Lord," Hayden said. "He's a great fan of yours."

"Perhaps another other time."

"Do you ever travel to Europe or the States?"

"Occasionally."

"Then you must come stay with us."

"I'd be delighted."

"You, too, Juanita. And you, Sidney, you're welcome any time."

"Though I think you might find it a little mundane," Philip said, "after this." He moved his hand to indicate their surroundings. Because of the slope of the grounds, the dining room was at tree level and their table was positioned in front of a tall set of French doors that opened onto a painterly panorama of dense floodlit foliage. The air was heavy with mingled fragrances from the blossoms of Sidney's potted gardenias and orange trees that grew against the walls of the hotel.

"I do sort of feel like I'm in a Stewart Granger movie," Hayden said.

Diana, who was absently turning her crystal wineglass in her hand, said, "Yes, I could see getting used to the hardships of life on the Dark Continent."

"Oh, don't let our three-inch pile fool you," Sidney said. "The Vic Grand isn't the real Africa."

"Oh! What, then," she asked with flirtatious deliberateness, "is the real Africa?"

"For a lot of people—the immigrants who spend their nights drinking and throwing darts up the road, for example—it's a network of outposts like the James, islands in the stream that look only just enough like home to make them miss it all the more. But they don't *go* home because they failed at something back there, even if just at fitting in."

"What is it for you?" Charlotte asked.

"For me, possibility. The way most people will tell you anything can happen in New York City, say," he glanced sheepishly at Joan, "I feel the same way here. Zambia's a poor but young country that's scarcely begun to grow. And in its youth, or 'underdevelopment,' as some see it, it remains closer to Eden, which surely had to be a mix of savanna, veldt and jungle, with its own set of possibilities. I find it personally invigorating and on the grand scale rather hopeful that there are still places in the world where you can be mauled by lion."

Rocky started to laugh. "My dear boy, you sound like Bror Blixen striding in from the hunt. Technically I suppose you're correct, but isn't that a little overdrawn? You'll have them listening for drums in the night."

Diana looked disappointed. "So, there's *none* of Karen Blixen's or Beryl Markham's Africa left?"

"Happily less of Karen Blixen's," Joan said, tossing her linen napkin onto the table.

"Why happily?"

"Hers, remember, was a colonial Africa. She used to refer to the Kikuyu who lived on her farm as 'her people.' The colonialists really saw them that way—as children, although of course not deserving of the privileges of white children—and an ocean of blood had to be shed to remove the yoke of that parentage. There is, of course, a legacy, but not one you'd recognize. Speaking for myself I've never found much romance in repression or exploitation. As for Markham's Africa, the African bush, 'wild' Africa is still here," she nodded toward Sidney, "though in rapidly diminishing form. Population growth and development needs have put tremendous pressure on it."

Diana looked at her a moment, then turning the dull platinum back of her head to Joan again, asked Sidney, "Do you think we'll see a lion?"

"That depends. Which way are you going, Juanita?"

Diana's face swung back quickly. "*You're* our guide?"

There was a long count of three before Joan said, "One of them, yes."

24

"So what made you change your mind?" Sidney asked, coming up behind Joan and resting his chin on her shoulder.

"About what?"

"About taking the dreaded Dumases to Njoko."

They were standing on the balcony of her room. There was no moon and the night sky seemed clamped down, its stars so dense they looked like stationary wisps of fog, clear down to the horizon.

"It's like Robert said—where would Zambian Photographic Tours be without them? Someone has to buy our debt. All this clean air does nothing for sunsets but it sure is an astronomer's dream. It's no wonder the ancients imagined themselves enclosed inside an oyster."

"You did rather make it plain you're less than enchanted with them," Sidney pressed.

"I wasn't uncivil, was I?"

"No, but you weren't exactly a chatterbox, either."

"You missed my lecture on African history? I'll have to get out my three-by-five cards and give it again."

"It's just that you didn't say one word after that."

"I thought I'd said enough."

"Which I confess surprised me just a little, as I find them a rather attractive group. They were certainly taken with you. At least Philip was. He seemed to be staring at you most of the night. Didn't you notice?"

"And you, my dear Sidney, seemed quite taken with his stepmother. As I recall, you stared at her most of the evening."

Sidney smiled. "You'll admit she's an extraordinary looking woman. In fact, I seem to remember you were staring at her yourself. Rocky, too, as a matter of fact. Is this some kind of female thing or simple character study?"

"Maybe she's auditioning for a murderer, though I'd be rather more inclined to give the part to the woman's stepdaughter."

"Hayden? Oh, I liked her. There's something a little racy about her. Why not Philip? He would seem a perfect antivillain: boyishly handsome, charmingly uneasy, Rod Taylor eyes, Laurence Harvey smile. . . ."

"Tell me, Sidney, don't you think it odd that it's just the four of them? Wouldn't you find it a little dull to travel with your brother and stepmother? How interested in Shona civilization can *she* be? And what about Charlotte? How much fun can it be to travel with your stepchildren?"

"Perhaps they're all keeping an eye on one another," Rocky said in a stage whisper from the door.

"If anybody should know," Sidney said with a laugh, "it would be our own Mary Lord! Tell us, in your expert opinion, who's the most likely scoundrel among our infamous guests. Juanita's choice is Hayden, but I'm partial to Philip myself."

"The crime being murder or theft of ancient treasure?"

"I think we have to assume Charles took care of the latter. But who murdered the partner?"

"You mean the one who died of the heart attack?"

"And the topless dancer, while you're at it," Joan said.

"The dancer," Rocky said turning back inside. "Double suicide. Sorry, dears, I'm too tired for original thought. We'll have to take this up in the morning."

"I think I'll say good night, too," Sidney said, following her in.

"Well, I'm sure you two'll have it all figured out by the time you get back."

"*We two?*" Joan said as soon as Sidney had left.

"Yes," Rocky called over her shoulder as she disappeared into her bedroom. "I thought I might tag along."

"This is awfully sudden, isn't it?" Joan said, following her. "When were you going to tell *me?*"

"I didn't think you were going yourself, now did I?"

"You voyeur!"

"No more than you. I thought you didn't want to have any more to do with them."

"Robert asked me to go."

"Of course, and I promised Werner I'd bring him some books."

"Which I could take for you—"

"*And* I'd like to see Margot. I'd like to see the gold *horns,* Alfred said you've got the *space,* I doubt very much the Dumases will *mind,* and I'm in the *mood to go to Njoko.* So," the little woman gave a grunt and hiked herself onto the bed. "I'm going to Njoko."

"You know we're going to be in camp for five days."

"My, my, I'll have to bring a net for my hair! Look, if it's too much for you to deal with, just say so. But I can't see why you'd mind so terribly."

"It's just that I can tell when you're not telling me something."

Joan sat down on the edge of the bed and looked hard at the older woman, who stared defiantly back. Joan wanted to laugh. Clad in a frilly pink nightgown laced with a white satin ribbon up to her throat, she was the picture of frailty and innocence. Like a polar bear in a tutu, Joan thought.

"What's your interest in them?" she asked.

"You have to ask?"

"You're not coming all that way just to see if I slip up." Rocky said nothing. But in the next moment a smile began to spread across Joan's face. "I know you so well, Mrs. Filmore, I scare myself."

"Well, you're beginning to scare me, Ms. Castlerosse. Has Sidney put you on another one of his herb cures again? You're acting very strange."

"And you've been keeping secrets again. You're not coming to *spy* on the Dumases. You're coming to *study* them."

"Why would I do that?"

"Because you're writing another novel."

Rocky looked at Joan expressionlessly for a long minute. "You weren't like this when I first met you," she said acidly. But then, slowly, she began to smile herself. "All right! I'm *thinking* about it."

"Bull's-eye! I'm so smart! But why didn't you tell me?"

"Because I haven't told anybody. I've only been *toying* with the idea."

"For a Betsy Blair? Based on the *Dumases*? This is too much. Since when?"

"Well, actually, *years* ago I roughed out an outline for a story that involved the exploits of an archeologist but never got round to doing anything with it. I came across it again a few months ago and, all things considered, I think it has possibilities."

"So you decided to retool it around *Chick*?"

"It's not as remarkable as it sounds. The Sardis business is, after all, choice stuff. I'll be surprised if somebody else hasn't used it already. Especially now, with the dead partner, and—" she patted Joan on the knee "—missing topless dancer. It's a little obvious, but what the heck, with some work. . . . I thought I'd throw in another death or two and either play up the curse idea or bring in a murderer. Either way, everybody'll be falling over each other looking for the gold."

"And slipping into each other's bed. What are you going to call it, *Death Among the Ruins*?"

"That's a little obvious. I rather liked *The King's Cook*."

"I don't have to warn you to leave me out of it."

"I was thinking of Mynnia."

"So you're taking advantage of the Njoko excursion to conduct a little field research."

"As source material it's difficult to pass up."

"The whole thing sounds unethical to me."

"My dear girl, where *do* you think novelists get their ideas?"

"Well, I know where you got the idea for this one, don't I?"

"I'll dedicate it to you—if and when it's ever done. In the meantime, pull the door on the way out."

Joan got up and crossed the room. Flicking out the lights, she hesitated at the door. She whispered into the darkness:

"So which is it?"

"Which is what?"

"Curse or murder?"

"Oh . . . I haven't decided."

"You'll let me know."

"Of course."

"Good night."

"Juan?"

"What?"

"Why *did* you change your mind about going?"

"I don't know," Joan said truthfully, adding, for want of a more credible explanation, "morbid curiosity, I guess."

25

There had never been any question that Diana Devilliers might have come to Africa out of some genuine interest in archeology. But Joan was impressed that at least she had the good taste to inquire about the find she'd traveled thousands of miles to see—even if the extent of what she wanted to know she could have read in the single-column blurb in last month's *Time* magazine. "So exactly what's the big deal out here?" is how she put it, then yawned.

They had just passed Lumombuzi, the halfway point between Livingstone and Njoko. The rolling scrub flashed by the Landrover's windows in what seemed from the dirt track like featureless repetition. This was the *miombo* of Zambia's ridgeland. In the lowlands between, scrub would give way to open grassy stretches, sometimes cut by a stream, called *dambo*. Such had been their drive, under a blank blue sky: a hypnotic two-note arrangement of *dambo, miombo, dambo, miombo*. It was no wonder the woman looked tired and bored.

"Well, first of all, this is farther north than the Karanga—if it *is* a Karanga site—had previously been believed to have settled," Philip called over the engine's high-pitched whine. "Furthermore, it may be the first undisturbed burial ruins of its size to be discovered since the thirties. The level of artistry in what's been found already is supposed to be unusually advanced, and—"

"Who was Monomotopa?"

"Mono*mata*pa, also Mwenemutapa, is what they called the chief of the Karanga, who ruled the kingdom of Zimbabwe, to the south, for several centuries."

"Why isn't he buried down there?"

"The tribe is thought to have deserted the region when the area's supplies of salt ran down." He glanced across at Joan. "That's the theory, isn't it?"

"What? Oh!" Joan had forgotten for a moment that she was actually there. "Another is that he was driven out by the Rozwi . . . no one knows for sure."

This last bit of information did the trick and Diana moved on to items of obviously greater interest, among them an affair at the weekend villa of some Italian publishing giant that she and Hayden had attended but that Philip seemed to have missed. "It's across the harbor from where we stayed," she said to the back of Philip's head. "I'd as soon spend a week in Punta Arenas as another night in that horrible little town, but I'd give anything for that house."

"Your friend *Jan* was there," Hayden said drowsily, "wearing the national debt of Mexico around her fat neck and a haircut like the Mayor of Munchkin Land on her fat head."

Given her self-proclaimed boredom with antiquity—and the lengths to which they were going to study it—Hayden's presence in the group made less sense than Diana's. The two women took obvious pleasure in each other's company but that Hayden would come this distance for something she got in ample supply at home was stretching it. Joan glanced in the rearview mirror. With enormous sunglasses covering half her face, earrings dangling and designer scarf wound around her head like a turban, Hayden looked like she belonged anywhere but bobbing miserably in the backseat of a lurching Landrover, fanning dust and flies. A pale face appeared and faded like an apparition through breaks in the red cloud behind them: especially, Joan thought, with her stepmother bouncing along in the vehicle behind.

For her part Charlotte was obviously no stranger to excavation sites and it was not impossible to see how her and Chick's inclusion might have been part of the original plan. It might even have been their plan in the first place. But, if plausible, it certainly didn't feel right. Then, it had never felt right. Even as Joan glanced back again through their billowing tail of dust to wonder what theories were hatching in the mind of Mary Lord, she was already thinking that whatever they were, it was too weird. She dragged her focus back to the dirt track ahead. It was *all* too weird. That she would be driving Philip Dumas, not to mention his sister and girlfriend, into the Zambian hinterland—flimsily disguised as someone else, no less—was nothing short of absurd. Deciding to come along, Joan had long since concluded, had to have been one the worst ideas she'd ever had.

"Kia had some knuckle-dragging meat-pile with her," Diana was saying. "You know, shirt open to the navel, doesn't know a word of English, or any other language I've ever heard, wears sunglasses indoors. Someone said he was a dock attendant."

"She's completely redone her hair," Hayden said. "You wouldn't recognize her. Perm, weave, twenty bottles of bleach."

"You know who she looks like now?" Diana said. "Like that girl— what's her name—Joan. *Whoa!*"

"Sorry," Joan murmured, pulling the Landrover back out of a skid that had been less dramatic than it felt. "A pile of dried elephant dung can rip an oil pan open."

For the next few minutes nobody said anything. When a few stretched into many, Joan glanced back and was not surprised to see that Hayden and Diana had slumped in their seats and were on the verge of dozing off. The day was warming up and they had been on the road for almost four hours. If Philip felt it too, he had unfortunately not succumbed. Joan saw in a sidelong glance that he was gazing contentedly out the passenger window.

They had just passed a group of tiny gray birds clustered in the branches of a msasa tree, whose blazing spring leaves had cooled to a tender green. Beside it a ten-foot-high termite mound rose impressively out of the ground.

"What's that?" he asked.

"An African penduline tit," she murmured.

"Funny, looks more like an erect phallus to me."

Joan looked at him. "Oh! You mean the *ant* hill."

"What were you talking about?"

"The little bird on top."

They were crossing *dambo* now and the sun, which had climbed high in the sky, glinted harshly off the silvery grasses. A solitary baobab tree rose in the distance, gray and baggy like an elephant. A marabou stork watched them go by with the unaffected calm of a road sign. Its swordlike beak was dirtied with dried blood.

"Is it true you can still be eaten by a wild animal out here?" Philip asked.

"More Zambians are killed each year by crocodiles than in car accidents."

"Is that a lot?"

"There are probably more car accidents per capita in Zambia than anywhere else in the world." She added, after a moment, "I've also heard that more people die in hippo attacks than by crocodiles."

A family of red-necked spur fowl darted across the road ahead, disappearing into the confused green-on-gray tapestry of combretum and thorn bush. Farther along, a troop of long-faced baboons glanced over their shoulders from across a sun-blistered clearing. They appeared to Joan to be looking at them with mild amusement. And no wonder, she thought.

"Which is the deadliest on land?" Philip asked.

"Pardon me?"

"Which predator."

"Oh. Including snakes and insects?"

"No."

"Well, lion, first. After that leopard, elephant, rhino, buffalo."

"Have you ever had to shoot anything?"

"An impala once," Joan said, "but it didn't take a great deal of skill."

"Why's that?"

"Its back was broken."

There was a short silence. If Joan had intended this to be a conversation-ender, however, Philip didn't seem to catch on.

"Have you been running safaris for very long?"

"I don't run them. I cook for them. And change an occasional tire." She decided not to mention that she also illustrated Robert's brochures. "Why?"

She looked over to see that he was smiling ambiguously at her.

"I'm just curious about you," he said.

"What about me?"

"Your life here. It's a little unusual."

"You *don't* mean 'What's a pretty girl like you . . . ?' "

"I suppose I do. Not that pretty girls—or beautiful women, as the case may be—don't belong in the bush. It's just that one doesn't often find them here."

"Beryl Markham was singularly beautiful."

"Yes, and singular in many other respects. She was also born here. How is it that someone—like you—*comes* here?"

Joan looked sharply at him. His smile had broadened. It was not in the least like Laurence Harvey's. Who, she wondered with a sudden wave of panic, was kidding whom? Joan turned her eyes quickly back to the track. To her immense relief, the von Jherings' outpost was just coming into sight.

For now, the scale of the dig was small. Word—still unpublished—had by design been spread only far enough for the project to have received a fresh infusion of funds and a handful of volunteer students to support a second season. Evidence of the steady trickle of visitors from the scientific community that had begun as soon as the rains stopped and the digging resumed was a trampled clearing in the paltry shade of a mopani tree that recalled a departed circus. Joan and Alfred pulled the Landrovers up here.

A pair of yelping Jack Russell terriers were the first to greet the stiff-legged party that emerged from the cloud of dust. The von Jherings and an assortment of students had been eating lunch under a canvas canopy in the center of the little compound when their visitors arrived. Werner, tall, caved-in and properly bald at seventy-six, gave them a broad smile, a Queen Elizabeth wave and made no visible move to get up. His snowy-headed wife, by contrast, had already bounded to her feet. Like Rocky Filmore, the woman was not appreciably less spry than she had been twenty years earlier. Like Rocky, too, she was not much over five feet and every bit as robust. The two women looked like long-separated sisters as they bounced up against one another in a vigorous embrace.

Joan was next ("Darling,"—she pronounced it *darlink*—"look at *you!*"). Then Alfred ("He*llo*, dear!") and back to Rocky, who handed her a bag of books.

"Oh, you sweet *thing!*"—sweet *ting*—"Oh, *Werner!*" she exclaimed to her husband, who had managed to intercept the group a few feet from the table. The students looked phlegmatically on—some stood up but none moved away from his plate. "Look what Veronica has brought you!"

"Yes, I see. Great thanks, madame," he said, extending Rocky a large, slightly shaking hand, drawing her to him and bending, cautiously, to kiss her on the cheek. *"And* the Dumases! This *is* a treat. Hello, hello! Philip! You couldn't look less like your father! Come, come, everyone sit down." He took Charlotte's hand and led her toward the table.

Joan stood for a moment and just stared, a crooked smile frozen on her face. As logical as it was—and as obvious—it hadn't occurred to her that of course the von Jherings and Dumases would know each other.

"I first met your husband," Werner was saying to Charlotte, "at a symposium on . . . something or other, in Paris. Nineteen-fifty or so. Long before the Sardis expedition. Terrible business, wasn't that? Academics are such jealous people, especially in the aggregate. We were supposed to have made off with a treasure in gold ingots ourselves. Ask Margot about it. It was a terrible business. *I* doubt they ever existed. If they did, someone else evidently got them. It certainly wasn't us. But a pity he couldn't come. Illness, you say. I'm really awfully sorry about that. We uncovered a wonderful soapstone bird this morning. Just on the other side of this little rise. . . ."

— 26 —————————————

Werner and Margot von Jhering had come to Africa more than fifty years ago on a visit to Margot's Boer uncle on a farm in the Transvaal and never left. Newlyweds not out of their teens, they became enthralled with the rugged but graceful beauty of the land and its people, and then by an idea they would spend the rest of their lives pursuing. In 1932, an acquaintance of Margot's uncle, a man named van Graan, convinced an African to show him the location of a long-secret burial place on a hill called Mapungubwe. Van Graan found skeletons and gold and the traces of a once great iron-age civilization. The significance of the find was just coming to light when the von Jherings first visited the site. Although it was a big leap at the time for most Europeans to attribute these remnants of an ancient society of such wealth and advancement to a black African people (that the Phoenicians were responsible was much the more popular view), the notion of a great southern African empire captivated the young Germans. They joined on in the excavation and for the next five years took turns going to school and crawling around in the midden of Mapungubwe.

The next five decades were devoted to sifting through the ocherous dirt of what was then Southern Rhodesia in an effort to trace the shadows of the lost empire of Zimbabwe, of which Mapungubwe was theorized to have been in some way a part. By a mix of good fortune and the persistence of only true fanatics, the disappearing trail led them a hundred and fifty miles north of the Zambezi, to a field near Njoko, where they stumbled, almost literally, across what was beginning to look like the undisturbed burial ground of an ancient African king. What they had pulled from the soil so far was unmatched in splendor and craftsmanship by—but bearing a basic resemblance to—artifacts found at Great Zimbabwe, Khami, Dhlo-Dhlo, and, significantly, Mapungubwe. There was, in short, some basis in reason to believe that the possibly gold-laden skeleton they hoped to find lying at the site's center would be the great Monomatapa himself. If it was the chief, and if any two people deserved to find him, it was probably Margot and Werner.

It was twilight. The sky overhead was a deep-water blue fringed with yellow on the western horizon, black in the east. A fingernail moon had appeared and the stars were beginning to poke through. At 4,500 feet, the seventeenth parallel usually cooled off dramatically at night, but the Dumases' arrival in Njoko had ushered in what was going to be a late, week-long heat wave and at seven P.M. the air was still warm. The group was pressed in at two collapsible tables joined end to end. Chairs were shoved back and plates pushed away showing the remains of a dinner of jugged warthog, Cape buffalo tongue and mealie pup. The table was littered with half a dozen mostly empty bottles of wine. After the long day of work or travel in the heat, nobody seemed to be in any hurry to move. The conversation revolved mainly around the archeological trenches, to which Joan listened with only half an ear as she marveled at the tenebrous tableau of lantern-lit faces, all familiar but half of them insanely out of context, like some tasteless mix of Caravaggio and Dali. Someone had just mentioned Cecil Barnard and she had just poured herself another glass of wine.

"Cecil Barnard! Good god!" Werner exclaimed. "What a madman *he* was. Damn near got us killed! If Winston Churchill's greatest thrill in life was to be shot at and missed, it's only because he never went antiquing with Cecil."

"What happened?" Rocky asked, pressing for details as she had all night.

"Oh, let's see. Cecil had been digging at Beycesultan and things were disappearing from the site."

"It was a real problem," Margot said, "and still is—your own workers palming pieces and selling them to dealers. Oh, well, *you* know." The pair had a habit of taking turns in the telling of a story like relay runners trading off a baton, though they did not always carry it in a perfectly straight line. More cooperative than competitive, it probably grew out of Werner's infirmity, which had the earmarks of emphysema.

"Cecil was piping mad about it," Werner went on, "and decided to try to track the stuff down. He was also, that night, bleeding drunk on some terrible raki we'd been into. Anyway, we drive to the house of a man everyone knows sells on the 'informal' market, as you say. After drinking quite a bit more and dickering over a mediocre collection of store-front pieces, the man takes us into the back and pulls some rather nice pieces out. I mean really good, really old stuff, obviously from Hacilar—"

"Mellon's dig," Margot said.

"But Cecil kept mumbling to me that they were fakes and the next thing I know he's telling our *host* he thinks they are. The man may have been a hood, but he took it all rather well, I thought. Until Cecil decided he had to prove his point and took a perfectly beautiful little goddess in his two hands"—he demonstrated with a half-eaten roll—"and snapped it in half. I thought our man was going to have a heart attack. I thought *I* was going to have a heart attack. You see," Werner laughed and drew as deep a breath as his lungs would allow, "it was quite obviously—at that point—not a fake at all."

"Sounds like Cecil," someone said.

"Without blinking he said, 'You were asking fourteen thousand pounds for it?' (This was back in the sixties, remember.) 'Well, you'll never get that much for it now, I'll give you seven hundred.' "

"How did you get out of there alive?" Rocky asked.

"They walked," Margot said, "rather quickly. If they'd stayed a moment longer the shock would have worn off and they would most certainly have been cut into little pieces."

"Who has the goddess?"

"Oh, I imagine Cecil still has it," Werner said. "Unless he managed to sell it himself. But I doubt he would. He tended to keep things—he loved the stuff so much. How *is* he, I wonder."

Nobody said anything for a moment. It was Philip who said, gently:

"He died, Werner."

Werner looked at him blankly.

"You remember, dear," Margot said.

Everyone watched as the old man's face gradually fell.

"Oh," he said finally. "Yes."

In the little silence that followed, in which most of the people at the table were apparently remembering various attributes of Cecil Barnard, Joan found herself back in the green living room at Rue St. Dominique just before Chick came in with the news of his old friend's death. How ironically similar that moment was to this one, she thought. Nearly everyone accounted for—Fanny even had a stand-in of sorts in Rocky—and each acting according to script. Hayden looking overdressed and vaguely put out, as if she'd been forcibly carried rather than traveled here of her own free will; Charlotte flattering her hosts with her winning blend of informality and Emily Post manners; Philip and Diana rubbing shoulders—in this case literally.

It had also, Joan recalled, been the day she'd first laid eyes on Diana.

This last memory was one in a long series that Joan had been trying to digest all night. Like shots of retsina, they were like broken glass going down, but had the effect of heating the innards and, in moderation, clearing the brain. She had spent the first part of the day convinced that trying to keep up the Juanita Castlerosse charade, and then throwing herself onto the tracks by agreeing to come, had been the sure sign of a feeble personality, if not a deranged mind. By this point, however, it had all finally begun to make some, if not perfect, sense: Though morbid curiosity may have played a small part, Joan understood now that she'd come along to make absolutely sure that leaving Philip had been the right thing to do. Which, as she watched him take the bottle out of Diana's hands to pour her another glass of wine, she could say with steely resolve that it was. As for the way she'd left him—wordlessly, literally under the cover of darkness—she had done it, she knew as she watched Diana pick a piece of grass out of Philip's hair, for the very reasons she'd often told Rocky: There was nothing Philip could say to her about what had happened between them that she had the least desire to hear. Then or now. Her only task was to hang on as Juanita Castlerosse for four more days. She turned her head away from the table and listened to the reassuring sounds of the African night: clicking insects, the *tok, tok, tok, tok, tok* of a Gaboon nightjar, the yip of a jackal. A spotted hyena let go a series of woops.

Diana wiggled her shoulders in a theatrical shiver. "Oh, God, is that one of those . . ."

"Hyena," Philip said.

"They make my skin crawl just thinking about them."

"Oh, but they shouldn't," Joan said mildly. "They're really quite impressive when you stop and think about it. They're highly successful scavengers with one of the best survival records of all land mammals."

"Maybe so, but I think they're foul looking," Diana said.

"Well, they're not Irish Setters, if that's what you mean."

"Never mind that they're known to start eating their prey before it's dead," Philip said.

Joan glanced at him. "Haven't we all?"

"So, you were in Turkey, then, too," Rocky said with a cough and turning pointedly to Werner. "I never thought you ventured that far from Africa."

"Mmm? Oh. Yes, it was off-season. Margot and I spent a few weeks at the Bosphorus visiting friends. You know them, I think, Philip—Nicky and Arlene Mellon?"

"Of course."

"Nicky had wanted to get down to see what Sir George was up to," Margot said. "Of course, Chick was down there then, too."

"*That* was a memorable encounter," Werner said. "I found him—Chick, that is—all alone in the middle of a big open plain about ten kilometers outside of Usák. I've no idea how he got there but here he was with his ratty tennies—Does he still wear that silly ponytail?—a knapsack full of obsidian arrow heads and a pocketful of rocks he carried to throw at growling dogs. He was standing perfectly still, staring. Anyone might have thought he'd stopped to see the sun go down—in the middle of a deserted Central Anatolian plain. What he was doing, of course, was watching for the slight rises and depressions you can see only when the sun is low on the horizon."

"And if any man could see one," Margot said, "he read the land like a diviner."

"Anyway, I gave him a ride back into town," said Werner. "That was just before all this nonsense about. . . ." His voice trailed off as an unexpected sound rose over the other noises of the *dambo*. Heads turned in unison to listen to the whine of a car engine fade and then grow louder. It grew steadily stronger until it was covered up entirely by the yowling of the von Jherings' dogs.

The Landrover's lights swept the table as it swung into the compound. They died with the engine. Two doors slammed and, in a hail of yaps, two figures started in the direction of the table. Joan immediately recognized the stride of the first as Sidney's. The second was oddly familiar but harder to place. Then, just before he stepped into the light, she knew who he was. It was all she could do not to laugh.

— 27

"Walter! What are you doing here?" several people said at once.

"What a romantic looking little party this is!" he called gaily. "You should see yourselves, really. You're a scene right out of Livingstone's *African Journals*."

"But I thought you weren't coming in until Monday." Hayden was on her feet and giving him as warm an embrace as she could without coming away smeared with dust.

"Change of plans. I tried to call, but you'd left, so I thought I'd catch you up. Cleese here was nice enough to bring me out. Phil. Didi." He shook Philip's hand and nodded to the women. "Charlotte."

"Darling, this is Juanita Castlerosse," Hayden said. "Juanita, Walter Hudson."

"Nice to meet you. Oh! But we've met before—somewhere . . . haven't we?"

"No."

"Really. I could swear—"

"And Veronica Filmore, also known as Mary Lord."

"Really! Enchanted!"

"Alfred Mapoma. And of course Werner and Margot vo Jhering. . . ."

By now Sidney had squeezed in beside Joan and was beginning to inspect the leftovers on her plate.

"Dear *boy*," Margot scolded. "Let us get you a plate of your own. There's plenty left."

"Don't you move," Sidney ordered, stabbing something dark and oily looking and putting it in his mouth. "I'm not hungry in the least. How are you and the good doctor making out?"

"We've had an interesting week. We'll show you in the morning. Here, dear, have a warm beer."

"Lovely, thanks. And you had an uneventful trip out?" he asked Joan.

"Completely. What, by the way, *are* you doing here?"

"I couldn't stand the separation."

"I'm so glad," she said. Her tone was sarcastic but in truth she couldn't have been happier to see him.

"Hudson showed up about thirty minutes after you left and, after plying me with gin over lunch, convinced me to take a weekend in the bush."

"This is a lie," Walter said. "It was you who offered."

The two men were obviously in very good spirits.

"Well, I hardly expected you to take me up on it. At any rate, here we both are. Well-fed, but, I must admit, a bit parched. Oh, good, my beer. Margot, you're a saint. Ah, and body temperature. Just as I like it."

Something like a festival air settled over the table as Walter slid in beside Hayden and more bottles were opened. Joan, who was fast closing in on a state of pleasant numbness, if not yet insouciance, took another large swallow of wine and dropped a clammy hand on Sidney's bare thigh.

He jumped. "Agh!"

"What is it?" Hayden asked.

"Nothing. Forgive me. What were you saying?"

"Oh—just that he was then blamed for the supposed disappearance of this royal trove. I'm surprised you never read—"

"I remember hearing something about it, but I thought that was just a squabble among friends. I'd no idea the Turks got in on it."

"As a matter of fact they were pretty quick to act," Walter said.

"You may or may not have heard about the Marmora affair, involving a Yortan treasure that disappeared. Nicky Mellon was supposed to have found it. It's similar to the Sardis business, except in this case, according to Nicky at any rate, it really *did* exist. In Chick's case, it never did. At least not in our time. But, stung by the Marmora business, the government was feeling particularly sensitive and rejected his permit requests out of hand—'in perpetuity.' He couldn't, after all, prove he hadn't taken it, and the press went into a feeding frenzy over it."

"Well, you can't blame them," Sidney said. "The press, I mean. After how many years of suppression they're finally given a free rein? Growing pains are only natural."

"Yes, but in this case, they went berserk," Philip said stiffly. "Suggesting he smuggled *how* many pounds of gold out of the country? Now how was he going to do that with everybody lurking about looking over his shoulder? Everyone for miles in all directions knows about any given project."

"That's true, but only up to a point," Sidney said. "If you're working on something over a series of days, and *during* the day, yes. But if you find something, get in and get out in one night, and are quiet about it, it can be done."

Philip gazed evenly at Sidney. There was a moment of silence during which Joan, in another frame of mind, might have noticed something crackle in the air between the two men. "You sound like you know quite a bit about it," Philip said finally.

"Enough to know that smuggling in Turkey in those days was child's play. You could've shipped the bloody Elgin Marbles out through the U.S. Army post office with no questions asked. Parcels mailed that way didn't even go through customs."

"Well, the sad fact *is*," Charlotte said softly, but effectively bringing the conversation to a close, "he didn't take any treasure out because there was no treasure there."

Everyone had gone to bed. The air had cooled and Rocky and Joan were sitting outside Rocky's tent, both mildly drunk, finishing a rum.

The sky was a blizzard of stars. Something had disturbed a troop of monkeys somewhere nearby and the screeching was just dying down.

"Well, I certainly didn't know they knew the von Jherings," Rocky said. "You might have said something."

"I didn't know myself . . . though I should have. Chick even mentioned Werner once." Joan laughed sourly. "But how about Walter's movie-moment arrival for isn't-it-a-small-world?"

"He recognized you for an instant, could you tell?" Rocky said. Joan shrugged. "And speaking of which, dear, I really think Philip knows who you are."

Joan glanced over. "Why do you think so?"

"You don't?"

It was a moment before she answered. She had certainly wondered herself earlier in the day. Tonight, however, he'd ignored her almost completely. At least he'd scarcely spoken to her, though more than once she had thought she felt his eyes on her. But that, of course, could be anything. . . .

"No," she murmured at last. "But tell me what else you saw tonight."

"Was I obvious?"

"Only to me."

"Well, I'd say first that you were quite right about Charlotte and Hayden. They're like a pair of card sharks grinning at each other across a green velvet table."

"Hmm. What else?"

"Walter Hudson may fancy himself a Lothario, but I don't see him sleeping with both women."

"Why not?"

"I can't imagine him having the wit to pull it off, for one thing. Certainly neither of those two are dim enough not to notice."

"You'd be amazed how easy it is to miss," Joan said, finished her glass, yawned, and, after a moment's thought, reached again for the bottle. "Besides, maybe they know."

"And put up with it? Doubtful."

"I suppose. What else?"

"It's not a science, you know."

"What about Philip and Didi?"

Rocky gave her a look. "What about them, I thought you didn't—Oh, are you still up? Come join us in a drink."

Sidney had appeared from around the corner of the tent. "Lovely idea. What are you two conspirators hatching back here?"

"I'm trying to get Ms. Lord to tell me what's she learned so far from her spying mission," Joan said.

"It's early yet," Rocky said, pouring Sidney a drink. "What do *you* think?"

"Well, I don't think *Charlotte's* the murdering sort."

"I'd have to agree," Joan said. "Not with a voice like that."

"No?" Rocky said. "*I* wouldn't want her as an enemy."

Joan chuckled. "Or Hayden."

"For that matter, Didi Devilliers is no shrinking violet herself," Sidney said.

"The three of them should form a rock and roll group," Joan said with another yawn, "and call themselves The Amazons."

"Is it true they cut their right breasts off so as to be able to draw a bow farther back?" Sidney asked. He was obviously as tired, and possibly as drunk, as Joan.

"I didn't notice," Rocky said.

"No, he means the *Amazons. The* Amazons."

"I don't recall. But what does that say about Chick, Walter and Philip? The latter two don't strike me as male slaves, exactly."

"Yes, and wasn't *he* the testy little bastard!" Sidney said.

"Philip? He did seem a little tightly wound," said Rocky.

"I still think he's your man, Madame Lord."

"Yes, and you would."

Sidney was quick on the uptake. "For a male slave, he was rather straining at the leash."

Joan looked up to see the other two were looking at her. "What's the matter with you?"

"Well, I'm sorry, darling," Rocky answered, "but the burst of static electricity was hard to miss."

Joan gave Rocky a sharp look. "Save it for your novel."

"Are you writing another novel?"

"No, I'm not, Sidney. She was speaking figuratively. But then what *was* all that ridiculous nonsense about hyenas? I mean, *dear* girl, *hyenas?* I thought Alfred would fall off his chair. It *was* about hyenas, wasn't it?"

"I gather I missed something," Sidney said.

"No, you didn't," Joan said.

"I also gather you're not going to reconstruct the scene for me," Sidney said, watching the two women exchange some wordless communication. "I thought not. Well, then, Rocky, does this mean your murderer is a woman?"

"Perhaps," Rocky said, getting to her feet. "But I don't think an epiphany is coming tonight."

"So that's it. You're leaving us at the edge of our seats."

"Yes, I'm fagged. So, as they used to say at the Princess Theater: You don't have to go home now, but you can't stay here."

"She's right, Juanita," Sidney said as he walked Joan back to her tent. "He couldn't keep his eyes off you."

"My, my, aren't we turning into quite the *attentive* international playboy, Mr. Cleese. Don't you know what jealousy does for a reputation like yours? No one will ever take you seriously again."

"So, I'm weak. . . . Tell me, don't you think I'm better looking than he is?" he asked, stopping in front of her tent.

Joan grinned. "Yes, as a matter of fact, you are."

"Taller too."

"By at least an inch."

"Richer," he murmured in her ear.

"And stronger, I'm sure."

"Are you sure you won't marry me?" he said and backed her through the flaps.

Much later there was a *hoo, hoo, hoo* in the dark.

"A scops," Joan whispered.

"A spotted eagle owl," Sidney whispered back. "Tell me, dear—are you always like this when you get out in the bush?"

"I just like these cots."

"That's because you're on top."

"Where else can I go?"

"At the risk of being practical in the middle of a love scene, I think one of us has to sleep in another bed."

"Agreed."

"Good, then you won't mind if I spend the rest of the night in my own tent—this is definitely too small."

"Not in the least."

"Sweet dreams then," he said, kissed her and was gone.

Joan's dreams were a lot of things that night, but something short of sweet.

— 28

Sidney stayed Saturday night as well but was expected back at the hotel Sunday afternoon, so shortly after breakfast Sunday morning he packed his Jeep and left Njoko for Livingstone. The scientists and students, accompanied by Philip, Rocky and Charlotte, had already taken advantage of the comfortable coolness of first light to get out to the site, leaving Hayden sleeping in, Walter and Diana lingering over the eggs Joan had prepared, and Alfred lingering over coffee, playing country western tunes on his *likembe*, a Zairian lamellophone, or kalimba, with his thumbs. *(". . . Don't flatter yourself, I'm over you. . . .")*

"So tell me about yourself, Juanita," Walter said when Joan finally sat down to eat. "Philip tells me you've been out here quite a while."

"No. Less than a year."

"I'd ask what's a pretty girl like you doing in a place like this, but I hear it's been used."

Alfred struck a sour note and winked at Joan, who glared back.

"To death," she said.

"I can see it. You have that look. No doubt you were a tomboy growing up."

"I had a Chatty Cathy."

"And a box of bird skulls, too, I bet, and terrorized all the boys in the neighborhood. We had a girl like you on our block. We feared and absolutely adored her. I still have fantasies about her. She married a Coca-Cola distributor, settled in Athens, Ohio, and had three sets of twins, but back then she was The Stallion."

Joan shook her head. Walter certainly hadn't changed a great deal since last they'd met.

"I still think you look like someone I know," he went on, narrowing his eyes as if reading fine print. "Though a little less so in daylight. Not nearly as interesting-looking as you, but not exactly an eyesore either."

"In other words," Diana said, "Walter had a thing for her."

"I did, actually. Besides being sexy, she was treated somewhat shabbily by my dear friends here—"

"Don't blame me!" Diana protested.

Walter smiled. "I was thinking of Charlotte and Hayden. And Philip."

"You're being a little disloyal, aren't you?"

"Not at all. Hayden knows she's a bitch. And Philip must know he was stupid."

"Oh, Walter, *please*," Diana said, giving Joan a men-can-be-such-idiots look. "This girl was right out of your worst nightmare. You know the type—fuck-me body, make-mine-milk sort of face. Not to mention exhaustively blond. They invariably show up for a few months at a certain stage in a man like Philip's life."

"You mean like Fay Wray and King Kong?" Joan said, getting up from the table.

"Come on, Didi, she wasn't exactly a calf-eyed waif out of a Keane painting," Walter said.

"No, but she was no Josephine Baker either, and then to go off and *die*. The perfect exit—it immortalized her."

Joan stopped and turned around. "She actually died?"

"Oh, I don't know, but she may as well have."

"What do you mean?" Joan could not stop herself asking, but did not get a reply. All heads had turned suddenly to the other side of the compound where Philip and one of the students had just appeared. They were carrying Charlotte.

"She's twisted her ankle," Philip said as they eased her into a chair.

"I don't think it's serious," Charlotte said, "but I must say it hurts like hell."

"Let me see." Alfred bent over the raised foot. It was creamy white and perfectly shaped. (How like Charlotte not to swell, Joan thought.) "I doubt it's too bad a sprain if it hasn't started to puff up yet. Can you wiggle it about?"

"A bit," she said and moved it cautiously to one side, but winced. "I really don't think it's anything to worry about. I just need to walk it out."

"That may not be such a good idea," he said as the woman got deliberately to her feet. She took a step and promptly crumpled into his waiting arms. "If it is a sprain, you oughtn't to walk on it for at least a week." He returned her to her chair and went to get his first-aid kit.

"Silly me to have forgotten to pack my crutches," Charlotte said sourly.

"We'll come up with something, dear," Margot said.

But in the end, it was decided that the trip would be cut short. Charlotte might have stayed; however, Diana, obviously looking for an excuse to get back to the hotel, insisted Charlotte could not take proper care of it short of going back. Hayden, who had also apparently seen enough, did not particularly want to stay without Diana, and Walter did not want to stay without Hayden—or Charlotte—or both, or whatever the case might be. It came as no surprise to Joan that Rocky wanted to go where the action went, and Alfred, hearing that Hayden and Walter would rather spend the rest of their time down in Chobe seeing animals, had already trotted off to tear down the tents.

This left Philip, who stated clearly that he preferred to stay, however, had little choice given that one vehicle could not hold everyone who wanted to leave. Unable to convince Diana to change her mind, Joan was relieved to hear him consent and see him join the others in gathering their things.

At this point, in a cloud of dust, Sidney's Landrover reappeared. "What's going on here? You look like you've had news of The Flood."

"What are you doing back here?" Joan said, leaning into his window.

"I couldn't stand the separation. *And* I left my damn case. In *your* tent. I was only thirty minutes along. I thought it'd be worth it, considering my wallet's in it. Where are you all off to?"

"Charlotte's turned an ankle and the rest want to go back. Do you want to wait for us or go on ahead?"

"I'd just as soon get started—I was supposed to be back by one—but I'll take your injured party with me, if it'd help."

"It would. Why not go and ask her."

If she'd thought about it a minute longer, however, Joan might not have been so quick to say this. After offering Charlotte the opportunity to join him, Sidney then agreed to take Rocky as well, which, because it solved the earlier problem of space, meant it was no longer necessary for the entire group to leave *ensemble.* Meaning, with one vehicle still free, Philip could stay the extra two days.

As to which vehicle would stay behind, it was never open to debate—not since Diana and Hayden had spoken of Chobe. Alfred was not staying behind to watch a pair of old Germans pick through bones, not if there was game to be spotted, and one look from his quick black eyes told Joan she could save her breath.

Joan sat down beside the Landrover, took out a book and tried—in vain—to read. Rocky came to say good-bye, gave her an irritating wink and told her not to pout. An hour later, the second vehicle drove off, leaving Joan and Philip, from opposite ends of the compound, gazing after its cloud of dust.

If the comings and finally goings of their visitors had something of the air of a circus, the von Jherings had a particularly productive day. Margot found a gold H-shaped ingot, and Werner unearthed a beautifully carved soapstone bowl, twenty inches in diameter, intact. Not only did it bear convincing resemblance to stone bowls uncovered at

Great Zimbabwe, but it was unusually detailed in the decoration of its rim, showing handsomely stylized pictures of cattle with lyre-shaped horns and great vulture-like birds. Even more interesting were the bands of geometrical patterns that echoed the complex brickwork of the Naletali ruins in western Zimbabwe. As for Margot's ingot, cross- and H-shaped iron ingot molds—believed to have served as money—had been found in several places in Africa, most significantly for the von Jherings at Great Zimbabwe. Evidence, in the form of gold flecks stuck to the small clay crucibles used in casting, had been found to indicate that gold ingots were once made; however, no one had ever found one at the site. The discovery of a gold ingot at Njoko, though no one was going to come right out and say so, could not help but raise the vision of a cache of gold buried somewhere nearby. As always, possibly right under their feet. Werner and Margot took turns in the excited telling of all this to Joan and Philip that night over supper. Philip encouraged them with intelligent questions. Joan nodded her head and missed most of what they said. Alcohol was doing nothing for her tonight. After half a bottle of wine, she was strung tighter than piano wire.

In fact, the later it got, and the longer she sat there beside Philip, who seemed content to spend the rest of his life at the von Jherings' table, the more agitated she felt. The day she had spent more or less in his company—though, thankfully, none of it alone—had taken a heavy toll on any idea that "hanging on" for the rest of the four days was going to be easy. *Or* that the fact that she *could* would prove a thing.

It was not that Philip had been overly solicitous. If anything, ever since their car ride out together, he'd been polite to the point of formality. If he *had* showed undue attention that first night, as Rocky and Sidney had insisted, his interest, clearly, had flagged. It had been her intent, of course, to keep him at a safe distance, but his impersonal conviviality was working on her like slow torture. That and trying to decide whether he knew full well who she was or really hadn't recognized her after all. She didn't know which idea upset her more. Either way, she was furious with him for effectively marooning her here and putting her through it, but even angrier with herself, having come full circle on the basic question: *Why* had she come?

Particularly when his light bright unreadable eyes touched casually on hers, as they did again now.

The conversation had swung around to looting. "In '71 my father was digging at a site near Çatal Hüjük," he was saying, "and ran out of money. There'd been a coup of sorts at the Institute and his funding was suddenly up in the air. It was very aggravating. Anyway, he knew he had only enough time either to finish the town, which was incomplete, or try to find the graveyard. So you can imagine. . . ."

"No doubt a lot of Rolex watches came out of that little mixup," Werner said.

"What do you mean?" one of the students asked.

"Artifacts found in the ruins of a village or town are for everyday use," Philip explained, his attention moving democratically around the table, resting only fleetingly on Joan before continuing on, "and usually broken, whereas things deliberately buried in a grave site are generally the finer examples of a society's artistry and craftsmanship and usually intact. They're equally important from a purely scientific point of view, but from a collector's the burial pieces are of much greater value. As a scientist, my father would have been obligated to finish the excavation of the town, even with the promise of an undisturbed burial site probably only a matter of meters away. Which he did, and within a week of his packing up, the tombs were found, broken into and emptied. Everyone for miles around knew what he was doing and that the graves had to be somewhere nearby so they just waited for him to leave. It was quite a boon for the local economy. Or part of it."

"I wonder what happened to the stuff they took," Margot said.

"It's probably in a major museum somewhere other than Turkey," Werner said.

"Probably," Philip said with a smile. "But I've checked the Louvre—it's not there."

"People are so greedy," Margot said.

"Well, Turkey's a very poor country," Philip said.

"The United States, England and France, on the other hand," Joan heard herself say, "are not."

Something flickered in Philip's eyes. Of course, it might only have been surprise: She had, after all, contributed virtually nothing to the dinner conversation so far.

"Which is to say the museums of those countries should keep their hands off other peoples' things?" he asked.

"They've been rather avid over the years, wouldn't you say?" Joan answered. "I understand they don't even display a tenth of what they've taken."

Philip smiled. "So, you don't think of history as communal property?"

"It's a nice-sounding idea, but a bit self-serving," she said, digging the hole a little deeper. "If a Turkish team found Charlemagne's war chest under a farm in Avallon, would you mind seeing it go on permanent display in Ankara?"

She smiled, wondering what on earth she thought she was doing. A glance at Werner and Margot told her they were probably wondering the same thing. A glance at Philip told her it hardly mattered now. He was leaning back in his chair, cradling his wineglass, looking at her with exactly the kind of expression she'd told herself she never wanted to see again. She got to her feet.

"I'd have to agree with you," Margot said awkwardly, "it *is* just another form of looting, if you take the long view. God knows there's so little still left here. . . . So you're turning in, then, dear. Is it that late already?"

"No, but I'm tired."

"I'll walk you to your tent," Philip said.

Which is just what I deserve, Joan thought. "You needn't," she said quickly.

"I'd rather," he said, got to his feet and followed her across the compound.

"Let me ask you something," he said as soon as they were out of earshot of the von Jherings.

"No, let me ask *you* something," Joan said, rounding on him with such vigor he actually took a step back. "Why did you insist on staying?"

He looked at her speechlessly for a moment. "Where?"

"Here! At Njoko!"

He glanced around with a confused expression. "Why do you think?"

"I think to be with me!"

His eyebrows arched. He said, slowly: "As you remember, I wanted to stay *before* Charlotte hurt herself, and even if I had shoved her down the scree myself, I couldn't have known it would be just you and me. Orchestrating that would have meant getting the whole group to act in concert, or at least the principals—Cleese to leave his wallet—in *your* tent—and, of course, Didi had been bored and want—"

"I'm not *her*, Philip."

His eyes widened slightly. "Not who?"

"What do you *want* from me?"

He looked puzzled. "Not a thing."

"I have nothing to give you."

Showing his palms, Philip leaned slightly away, as he might from a lunatic with a loaded gun. "I—haven't asked for anything."

"Good," she said, even as it dawned on her that he was quite right, he hadn't, and that there was a very good chance he had no idea what she was talking about. Then, why should he? At this point she hardly knew herself. She finished, with a miserable sinking feeling, "Don't."

"Don't worry," he said, almost apologetically. "I won't."

29

When Philip broke his promise over lunch the next day, Joan barely noticed. She'd woken to lambent rays sparkling in the dew, thoroughly depressed. Not only was she embarrassed about her outburst—what had Rocky said? If you're going to lie be up to the task or risk looking foolish—and quite sure Philip had been thoroughly mystified, and probably equally embarrassed, by it. She also had to own up to the irrational, arguably neurotic, sense of humiliation that not only had he indeed *not* recognized her after all, but that he hadn't even been going to make a pass at her—her bristly behavior toward him since his arrival, of course, notwithstanding.

Whether any of this made sense or not—very little of what Joan had been thinking or feeling in the last few days made much sense—the wind had been sucked out of her sails. When he asked her to take him on a walk into the surrounding bush, ("Oh, yes," Margot chimed in, "there's a *wonderful* view from the top of that hill!") she was not happy with the idea but could mount only a token struggle, suggesting lamely that he might find his own way.

"What about snakes?" he said.

"Watch where you step."

"What about lions?"

"There aren't any around."

"What about hyenas? It is true, isn't it, that they eat their prey alive?"

"Not in every instance."

"Juanita!" Margot exclaimed. "For crying out loud! Take the poor man on his walk! Isn't that what he's paying you for? He's obviously a little nervous and he has every right to be. . . ."

"You're not nervous in the least," she said sullenly as soon as they were out of camp.

"I'm not a big animal person," he said. "What kind of gun is that?"

"A .375 H&H."

"Do you think we'll need it?"

Yesterday she might have said, You never know. "No."

"Can you do anything about these tsetse flies?"

"Sorry."

"One got me on my toe."

"Keep your shoes on."

"It was through my boot."

She led him into the thickets. A pair of crimson African fire finches trilled excitedly from the branch of a sausage tree, whose seed pods hung heavily like the meat for which it was named. A permanent audience of tsetses followed them through the scrub and into the broken shade, where the two eventually began their climb.

It was perhaps only because her own mood was so morose, but Philip seemed more garrulous today than he had since arriving in Zambia.

"When I was a boy," he was saying cheerfully, "I used to play out in the wilds—well, to me they were wilds—of Chappaquiddick—in Martha's Vineyard. Have you ever been there?"

"No."

"It was deserted then. You could go for miles and not see anyone. Wampanoag Indians now and again. Anyway, I used to imagine I was in Africa. Although—oh, you *bastard!*"—Philip slapped a tsetse fly on his shoulder—"not quite in a place like this." His palm left a splotch of blood the size of a silver dollar on his shirt. "I guess I was thinking of something with slightly larger game."

As if on cue, a noise between a bark and a screech rang out and echoed like a shot from somewhere up above.

"What was that?" Philip said sharply.

"Baboon."

"Where?"

"There." She pointed to the ledge above them. "A male."

"Oh, yes. Jesus, he's big. Do they bite?"

Joan glanced around at Philip, who had taken a nervous step toward her. He'd run a hand across his brow and smeared it with blood. Also a little dirt. The man looked as if he'd been out in the bush for a month instead of an hour. Under any other circumstances, Joan might have laughed. The sight at this particular point only depressed her more.

"Yes, as a matter of fact," she murmured. "We'll go this way."

Further on they stopped on an overhang to catch their breath.

"What was Margot saying about the Ancient Ruins Company?" Philip asked.

"It was a concern formed in 1895 to exploit ancient ruins," she answered without much feeling. "They did a lot of damage, as they were after only gold. Destroyed most everything else, though most of the gold was probably already gone by then."

"Why?"

"King Solomon's mines."

"What do you mean?" Philip should have known the answer to this already, but Joan was not going to make anything of it.

"Let's see," she said with a sigh, "as Werner explained it to me, word went around Europe in the 1890s that the legendary Ophir was not in Arabia at all but located in southern Africa. Specifically Matabeleland and Mashonaland. By 1900 something like a hundred thousand gold claims were registered, most on ruin sites. If they didn't find gold—or even if they did—they carried off any carvings and artifacts they came across. And all the while believing it was not really *African*, of course—not possibly belonging to the 'primitive' black people they were shooting on site. I mean, if you're going to ransack, at least give credit where it's due. . . ."

She took a deep breath. He was gazing at her intently, but seemed to have nothing to say. "Shall we?" she said.

They continued their climb. Malachite sunbirds chased each other like tiny attack helicopters just over their heads. Sweat bees buzzed in their ears. In another hour they were at the top.

"Tell me about Mrs. Filmore," Philip said, sitting down beside her on a smooth lip of ledge and holding his water bag out to her. "What's she doing here?"

"Researching a never-ending history of the Shona people. Thanks."

"She's a character."

"I suppose."

"How did you meet?"

"Completely by chance, in a hosp—hotel in Milan. She likes to pick people up. It's like a tick."

"What were you doing there?"

"Visiting a friend."

"How about Sidney Cleese?"

"What about him?"

"Where's he from originally?"

"Cape Town."

"An immigrant, as you call them."

"Well, his case is a little different. After all these years, this is really home to him. He's always supported the right side—handsomely— and it's won him a certain acceptance."

"Are you in love with him?"

Joan gave him a surprised look. "That's none of your business."

"Sorry," he said with a quick smile, and turned to look out over the tops of the trees, which rattled and swayed slightly in the hot afternoon breeze.

"It's a shame this can't all be preserved," he said.

Joan said nothing. She had begun absently to rattle a scoopful of pebbles in her closed fist.

"You don't agree."

"I do. It's just what most people mean when they say that. . . . Now that the industrialized world has created a kind of permanent poverty here that makes poaching and, in so many places, deforestation an economic necessity, we want to 'preserve' it."

"But surely deforestation is not an economic necessity, it's economic suicide."

"In the long term, of course, but your children's health, in a lot of cases their lives, is a matter for the short term."

"You know, I'm not the capitalist running dog you think I am."

The rattling stopped. "I never said you were a running dog."

"But you think of me as—"

"I don't think of you as anything," she said quickly. "I don't think of you."

"I think you do."

She got to her feet. "That's your conceit."

He was on his feet as well, and, whether intentionally or not, standing between her and the entrance to the path back. "Will you stay here?" he asked.

The rattling started again, in earnest. "Yes, I think so."

"Why?"

"Why not?"

"What about your friends?"

"My friends are here."

"Your family?"

She said nothing.

"It isn't also a hideout?" he asked.

"From what?"

"From life."

"If this isn't life," she said, tossing the stones and heading deliberately for the path, "I don't know—"

She didn't finish. Before she knew what had happened, Philip had reached out, taken hold of her and pulled her into his arms. He looked her in the eye for a count of two, then kissed her solidly on the mouth.

When the initial shock had passed—there had not, after all, been much of a buildup—she drew vigorously back. She stopped short of breaking entirely free, however. For several seconds they stood like this, staring at each other.

Happily, she never had to decide how to resolve the scene. At this point something startled a family of turkey-sized ground hornbills that had evidently been foraging nearby and, with an outburst of grunts that sounded convincingly like a full pride of lions, they crashed toward them through the brush. Philip dropped Joan as if she'd struck him—one of the options she had been considering—and whirled around. When he turned back to her, she'd already disappeared back down the hill.

They arrived back at camp just as the sun was setting and the von Jherings were pouring their first round of drinks.

"We were hoping we wouldn't have to come looking for you two," Margot said cheerily. "I for one am much too pooped. Come look at what we found after you left. . . ."

30

Balabala. Filabusi. Shabani. Mashaba. Joan turned the names over in her mind as they drove east through the Matopo Hills toward the ruins of Great Zimbabwe. She and Rocky had decided to take the southern route to the modern Zimbabwean capital of Harare. As Joan had never seen the ruins, they planned to have a picnic lunch there, which was more or less on their way. More intent than ever on the idea for a new Betsy Blair novel, Rocky had set up a meeting with an archeologist in Harare from whom she said she hoped to elicit color, background and scientific gossip. Joan was invited to come along to share the drive.

The ancient ruins, the seat of an empire that had stretched between the Zambezi and Limpopo Rivers from the Indian Ocean almost to the Kalahari Desert, were deserted and eerily silent when the two women approached it down the dusty path that led in from the road.

"The last time I was here was during the war," Rocky puffed as the smooth, ten-foot-thick, thirty-foot-high brick wall that enclosed the ruins came into view. "Sam Buti, a reporter for one of the wire services, and I came down on our way to Johannesburg. The area was what Sam called 'very hot,' as you'll see by the bullet-sprayed walls of gas stations and huts farther along. In fact there had been fighting in and around the ruins themselves."

"What were you doing here?"

"Why are you whispering?"

"Why are you?"

"Oh! I suppose I am. This place does it to you. It's like Stonehenge, don't you find?"

They'd entered the enclosure, which was shaded by tall trees. A huge, windowless conical tower stood largely intact at one side. Enormous succulent plants, with sharp curved leaves growing like spiked dreadlocks atop long neck-like stalks, poked up from behind piles of rock, giving Joan the distinct impression of being watched. "I don't know," she murmured. "I've never been there."

"Are you quite all right?"

"Quite. Why?"

"Because you don't seem 'quite' at all. You haven't seemed 'quite' since you got back from Njoko."

"You mean, 'So when are you finally going to tell me what happened with Philip?' "

"I was trying to be delicate. But as you mention it . . ."

"*Nothing* happened with Philip. He asked me to visit him in Martha's Vineyard this summer. I told him no."

"You never told him who you were?"

"No."

"Did he ever ask?"

"In a manner of speaking."

"I gather you denied it."

"After a fashion."

"Did he believe you?"

It was a good count of five before Joan answered. "I've no idea."

"So that bland good-bye you staged in the lobby two days ago was it?"

"It wasn't staged and yes, that was it."

"Why?"

"Because nothing's changed," she said heading briskly out of the enclosure. "It's over."

They climbed the acropolis on a nearby hill and perched on a ledge that overlooked the great kraal. Behind them a bright blue corner of Lake Kyle was just visible in the east. Rocky pulled out her pocket knife and began to carve a mango into slices.

"Why am I not convinced you're convinced?" she said.

"Rocky, *please*," Joan said testily. "Just let it go."

They had started back down the hill when Rocky asked, "So, you're not going to see him again?"

Joan sighed. "Certainly not before you do."

Rocky left it at that.

Percy (he pronounced it "Pessie") Cekisani was still a reporter with the *Harare Evening Star*. A compact dapper man with a smile that engraved every inch of his face, he was waiting for them in a sunken bar—it reminded Joan of an airport lounge—off the lobby of the Monomatapa Hotel, a sleek dark tower in the heart of the modern city.

"Oh, yes, we go back," he told her with a quick grin and a deep-throated laugh. "We were *gassed* together. Who wants another drink?"

"Yes, that's how we met!" Rocky said. "In Rufaro Stadium—that's the football arena I pointed out on the way in. My God what a night! I'll never forget it. *Everyone* was there. Indira Gandhi, Prince Charles, Bob Marley and the Whalers. I had a wonderful conversation with Averell Harriman about mulch."

"The entire stadium was packed with people invited to attend the ceremony," Percy said, "which was supposed to take place on the stroke of midnight, at which time the British flag would come down and Zimbabwean independence would be officially granted."

"Percy and I were both with the press in the middle of the field. It must have been close to midnight. The hottest most humid night in memory. And for some reason—I suppose there were riots or something outside—there was the sound of gunfire and then a cloud of tear gas poured into the stadium. People were running every which way and Percy rescued me from being trampled."

"The truth is I offered her my handkerchief, but you can interpret the gesture as you wish."

"We spent so many hours in this place," Rocky said with a sigh, taking in the whole of the hotel in an abbreviated sweep of her hand, which came to rest on the back of Percy's. "Those were such heady, hopeful days, Percy. They seem like such a long time ago."

"It has been a rough time, though they're not doing such a bad job, considering. However, this you know, Vera. Tell me, what is it you're doing here and how long are you going to stay?"

"Just a couple of days. Juan is here as my chaperon and I'm here mostly for research. I'm meeting with a man—knowing you, you will have heard of him—in my latest field"—she wiggled her eyebrows—"of study."

"Tell me the name and perhaps I can guess"—he tried to wiggle his eyebrows—"the field."

Joan and Rocky both laughed. "He's a Yank," Rocky said. "Henry Gilbert."

Percy laughed too. "Ha! I should have known! For what other reason would Mary Lord come all this way if not for hom-i-cide." He drew out this last word with the satisfaction of a cheating dieter ordering "hot apple pie."

Joan and Rocky exchanged a glance.

"You told him?" Joan said.

"Told me what?"

"About doing another Betsy Blair," Joan said to Percy.

"No!" Rocky said, looking hard at Percy.

"Well, I just assumed," Percy said, beginning to look confused himself. "Then why do you want to know about Gilbert?"

"Because he's an archeologist."

"Yes, I know."

"*That's* what I've come to talk to him about. I have an interview scheduled with him at ten tomorrow morning."

Percy looked from Rocky to Joan to Rocky, his eyebrows slowly rising to little peaks. "Well, I doubt you'll get much out of him, dear," he said patiently. "The chap was found dead as a post just two days ago."

31

Someone had washed the blood away. All that was left was a brown stain on the cement between the bricks in the hearth and a discoloration of the camel-colored carpet that underlay the living room's large Oriental rug.

Henry Gilbert had not lived in material splendor. He could, however, be said to have lived in material clutter. His apartment was dark and stuffy, due probably to being sealed for the three days since his body was found. The furniture was old and fine, but the size and shape of his rooms were obscured by the thorough sprawl of his collection of artifacts. Many had been knocked on the floor, but by their sheer numbers every inch of level surface had to have been covered by icons and artifacts from Roman Cybeles to Maori bird snares to Dogon masks. His bookshelves were filled with magazines, scientific bulletins and reference books, and his walls were covered by photographs, many evidently dating back to the forties and fifties.

"It looks like a museum," Joan said, following Rocky and Percy into the living room.

"Fantastic, isn't it?" Percy said.

"Is everything just as it was when he was found?" Rocky asked.

"More or less." He picked up a squat clay figurine from the floor and placed it on a littered tabletop. "Not much finesse."

"Any fingerprints?"

"His. The housemaid's."

"What was taken, besides his wallet?"

"It's almost impossible to tell. As you can see, things have obviously been disturbed but the housekeeper was not much good for an accounting. She remembered a small metal plate of some kind that was on this stand, she thinks it was gold, and coins in a case on the mantel, but nothing else for certain. She did say he used to go on sometimes about a secret cache he kept hidden somewhere in here, but she didn't take him very seriously. Apparently"—Percy brought a cupped hand to his face and took a puff on an imaginary pipe—"the old boy indulged."

Gilbert lived alone, Percy had already told them on their way out to number One-Ten in the exclusive Mafeking Gardens complex on the outskirts of Harare. Percy had not reported the original story but was a friend of one of the police detectives involved in the investigation, which is both how he knew what the police knew by the time Rocky and Joan arrived in town and how he was able to gain them entry to the apartment the next morning. According to his source, no one in the building or anyone else the police had talked to saw Gilbert in the week between the time the maid last saw him alive and found the body. This, however, was not so unusual. His neighbors said that after his wife of twenty years, an Ndebele woman with whom he'd had no children, died some years before, he'd gone into virtual seclusion and saw only the housekeeper, who cooked and cleaned for him once a week. When she let herself in Sunday morning, she found the old man lying in his pajamas in his own blood on his living room floor. He'd suffered a blow to the back of his head.

"The weapon?" Rocky asked, standing, hands on her hips, surveying the general mayhem.

"Not found," Percy said. "Very possibly the fireplace hearth. That's where most of the blood was."

"You mean he could have fallen. Was an autopsy done?"

"Yes, but I don't know what the report says beyond an initial finding of traces of alcohol in the blood."

"Time of death?"

"They couldn't be certain. The place was closed and with the heat
. . . Early estimate was between four and six, possibly even the full
seven days before the body was found." He chuckled. "These boys
are known for their caution."

Rocky picked up an obsidian arrowhead and fingered the roughly
scalloped edge. "So, what do you think? Accidental death during
robbery, or the appearance of it to cover murder?"

"Without knowing whether he knew his assailant, Vera, impossible
to say for certain. However, there's reason to suspect he did. Besides
there being no sign of forced entry, there was the blood-alcohol
count. The housekeeper said he liked weed—the police found a
couple of ounces in the freezer—but she'd never known him to drink,
at least never alone."

"Contents of the stomach?"

Percy shrugged. "Haven't heard. There's the bottle."

"Fingerprints?"

"Smudges."

"A glass?"

"Everything washed and put away."

"Where's the kitchen?"

"Through there."

Rocky disappeared down a hallway and Joan slipped in behind a
grand piano for a better look at the gallery of photographs on the
walls. They appeared to be about evenly split between family portraits, the majority of which were in color, and expeditions, largely
black-and-white. They showed Henry Gilbert as a slight man with
small black eyes, a pencil-line mustache and prematurely receding
airline. His wife was a delicate brown-skinned woman with a wide,
entle face who appeared to have been several years younger than
r husband. It also appeared from the pictures that he either had not
t known her or did not as a practice take her with him on his digs.
t of great quality, these photos showed him exclusively in the
pany of men, posing at the walls of Jericho, at the Ziggurat at Ur,
r the Lion Gate in Anatolia, in the Valley of the Kings. There was
evitable camel-mount shot before the Great Pyramids of Gizeh.
That is it, Juan?" Rocky asked, having just come into the room

and catching the look on Joan's face. "You've flushed like a beet. Is this all a little too much for you? Or perhaps it's the air in here. Percy, open that other window, would you mind?"

"No, no, I'm fine," Joan said quickly. "But I think I will go get some air. I'll wait for you downstairs."

"What is it, dear?" Rocky asked again as soon as Percy's car rounded the corner and was out of sight. He'd had to return to the newspaper but agreed to meet them later for dinner. He had dropped them in front of a coffee shop a few blocks from where they were staying. "What did you—?"

"Why the hell didn't you tell me Henry Gilbert was the third partner?"

"The third . . . ? Oh, you mean with Cecil and Chick! But why would I, darling? I mean, you knew. *Didn't* you? Of course you knew. What did you think we were doing here?"

"Interviewing an archeologist."

"Yes, but—" Rocky put up a hand to shield her eyes from the sun and peered closely at Joan. "You can't be saying you didn't *know.* How could you not? You knew the man's name, for heaven's sake."

"Harry! Philip called him *Harry!* And I don't think he ever mentioned his last name, and if he did . . . I forgot it." She was shaking her head. "I can't believe this."

"You thought we came all this way just to talk to an archeologist? *Any* archeologist? Crimminy, child, we had Werner for that!"

32

"So which picture was it?" Rocky asked. "The three of them on the camels? Yes, I liked that one. It would make a perfect jacket cover for *The King's Cook*, don't you think? The three partners in crime. . . ."

"Chick has a copy of it in his study," Joan said.

"Cecil Barnard had one too, no doubt."

"No doubt."

An oncoming rain had turned the eastern sky a steely blue as they descended the Hunyani Range of northern Zimbabwe on their way down to the Zambezi. It was five o'clock. In another couple of hours they would be at the Timbermans' in Lusaka, where they planned to spend the night.

"So, did you find out everything you wanted to know?" Joan asked.

"Hardly—the man's dead, after all. It's a damn shame, too, having had him right under our noses all this time and missing the chance to meet him in the flesh—and by a matter of days, God rest his—"

"I mean at the scene of the crime."

"No. The copy of the police report Percy brought me was essentially worthless. I wish we could have taken more time in the apartment. Not that that would have told us much either. . . ."

Joan swerved to avoid a dead animal on the road. Rocky glanced over. "Listen, dear, are you sure you're all right? You've been uncharacteristically quiet ever since the apartment. There *was* something a little much about that big dark stain, but I've never known you to be squeamish."

"You've never known me at the scene of a murder. *I've* never known me at the scene of a murder. And of someone I almost knew, no less. It's a lot less engaging than one would gather from your books."

"You think so?" Rocky seemed genuinely surprised. After a moment of contemplation, she added, "You don't actually feel ill?"

"No, no. So you knew Gilbert was here all the time?"

"No. Lily Timberman said something about him to me only a month or so ago—before I knew the Dumases were due to arrive. I could have sworn I mentioned it to you. Anyway, *that's* what made me think about the idea for the novel. I'd meant to go down earlier, but never got around to it. What's so funny?"

Joan had started to laugh. "Just listen to what you're saying! First you come up with the idea for a murder mystery based on the exploits of Charles Dumas. A few months later you discover the man's long-lost partner has been living barely a day's drive away. Only a matter of weeks after that, your protagonist's entire family shows up—in the flesh—in *Livingstone*, of *all* places. (And this is without mentioning *my* connection with all of this!) And while they're here, the aforementioned partner is *murdered?*" A plaintive noise came out with her long sigh. "It's all a little much, don't you find?"

"I think it's even more of a coincidence that I was planning to kill Gilbert off myself. Literarily speaking, that is."

"You were," Joan said mildly.

"It's a bit clichéd, but there's no getting around it—not if you've got a treasure, which at this point I'm quite convinced we do."

"Are we talking fiction or reality now?"

"You mean *where's the line?*" She wiggled her grandmotherly eyebrows much as she had done with Percy.

"Speaking of which, what is this *Vera* business?"

"It's a nickname. Short for Veronica—sort of."

Joan raised her eyebrows. "How come I've never heard it before?"

"Because it's only used by my lovers. Are you ever told you have a suspicious mind?"

"Not nearly enough."

They had pulled off at a three-sided roadside cafe and ordered grilled chicken and what turned out to be not very good gin. Rain splashed the hot orange dirt beyond the reach of the canopy.

"Alright, how were you going to do it?" Joan asked. "Or should I say, *who* were you going to *have* do it?"

"Well, that's where the creativity comes in. You have the curse option, as we've discussed, but which I think for our purposes ought to be ruled out."

"Agreed."

"Which leaves foul play, and here there are a number of choices. He could have stung a Turkish smuggler—they're a notoriously tough crowd—and been menaced, if not finally chopped with a scimitar."

"That would be diced?"

"Whatever. He could have been about to give his share of the gold back to the Turkish government, and the unaccounted-for Dumas could have murdered him to keep him silent, and while he was at it secure his share of the Hoard."

"Was there any sign of its having been there? Empty safes, secret panels ajar?"

"No, and nothing was indicated on the police report. But remember the housekeeper's story about a 'cache.' "

"How big would it have to be?"

"Unknown. It depends entirely on what it is."

"Well, anyway, isn't Chick a little . . . fat for that?"

"He's gotten fat?"

"*Phew.*"

"Okay, which leaves a member of his family, the principal hangers on—Walter and Didi—or some combination of the above."

"You could borrow from Agatha Christie, give everyone a motive and bring them all down to Harare to kill Gilbert off together. Half of them were here at the time of his death, for all we know. Come to think of it, all of them were."

"Or you could have an outsider trying to find and steal the Hoard," Joan suggested.

"He or she stalks each of the three men in turn and kills them off, one at a time."

"The Turkish smuggler scenario again."

"Or someone closer to home."

"George Rawlins."

"Who?"

"Never mind."

They drove for a moment in silence.

"Chick's in danger, isn't he?" Joan said in a different voice. "In *real* life."

"It would appear so."

They were on the outskirts of Lusaka when Rocky asked:

"If they'd embraced you, would you have left the way you did?"

Joan looked at her with surprise. "Whatever do you mean?"

"If you'd felt at home there, at Rue St. Dominique, and then found out that Philip was having an affair, would you have at least tried to talk to him? Most couples go through rough waters—"

"You make it sound like I caught him smoking cigarettes in the bathroom."

"Couldn't there have been circumstances—"

"The circumstances were that we'd only been living together a matter of *weeks*, which for me is still a little early for setting the precedent of self-indulgence and deceit."

"But is Philip really that kind of a man?"

Joan hesitated before answering. "Frankly, I don't know what kind of man he is."

"Thinking in the broadest strokes, do you think he's the kind who could have killed Henry Gilbert and Cecil Barnard?"

"God, no!"

"He certainly had means, potential motive and opportunity. . . ."
But before Joan could respond, Rocky said: "Oh, my, here we are already! Juan, dear, I think the less said about any of this to the

Timbermans the better. Telling Lilian Timberman that I've been researching a character based on a freshly murdered American scientist
would be like doing a spot on the evening news." She grinned and
waved at Lilian, who could be seen waving excitedly from the front
door.

"So what's our plan? Send Chick a letter warning him that his life
is in grave peril?"

"That might work," Rocky said doubtfully.

"You have a better idea."

"I do, in fact."

"Go to the police."

"And be treated politely and ignored? A man falls and hits his head
in a burglary; another one, *age seventy-five*, dies of heart failure. I
wouldn't call out Scotland Yard. *Hi, hi, Lilian!*"

Rocky had climbed out of the car. Sticking her head back in to reach
for her handbag, she said, "No, my dear, the only way to protect the
old fool is for you to somehow convince him to give up his share of
the Hoard."

—PART THREE—

— 33

The unlikeliness of their plan became more and more obvious the closer to Martha's Vineyard Joan and Rocky got. They had flown to London less than a week after returning to Livingstone, and from there to Boston, a day later. At three o'clock on the last Thursday in June, they checked into a room at the Ritz Carlton, changed their clothes and traipsed wearily downstairs for a drink.

"What," Joan asked, any sense of heroism and mission having long been replaced by dread, "are we doing here?"

Theirs had not been the operation of secret agents. Their hurried departure from Livingstone had been lamely explained by the "sudden illness" of an old and dear friend of Rocky's. Juanita was accompanying the older woman as a traveling companion and for support. Mrs. Filmore's need for either was easily the most conspicuous part of the lie. But they had together judged that until Joan was willing to publicly embrace her alternate identity—something which neither felt was advised at least until their little adventure had played itself out—it was just as well they find a way not to mention their intended visit to the Dumases. ("You have, after all, rather gone *on* about them, my dear.") At least this was the story as told to Alfred and Robert.

Sidney had proved to be another matter. Joan decided to finally come clean on the Castlerosse business and tried to explain to him why she'd kept up the charade for so long, first in his case, then in Philip's. He sat quietly, let her talk and at the end had mercifully little to say of a judgmental nature. If anything, he seemed amused. His reaction was so mild, in fact, Joan suspected he might have known already. Or at least had guessed, just as he had about the nature of their trip to Harare. On that score, their conversation in the Vic Grand's dining room their first night back from Zimbabwe had gone something like this:

"So how's your little investigation going?" he had asked.

"Why do you think we've been investigating anything?"

"I know you too well. And I read the papers. Henry Gilbert worked with Charles Dumas at one time, didn't he?"

Thus he was told of their discovery, and their theories on the event, although not that they were planning to make an appeal to Chick directly: The fewer opinions registered at this stage of their harebrained scheme the better.

Rocky did, however, own up to her plan for a new Betsy Blair novel. "I'd appreciate a little discretion if you don't mind," she'd said in conclusion.

Sidney had smiled. "Oh, of course. But that's quite a coincidence, isn't it?"

"Life is full of them," she had chirped and ordered another round.

Boston, a week into summer, bustled brightly beyond the glass. Rocky signaled the waiter for the check. "We're here to try to save a life, I thought. It may prove to be as simple as pie."

"It doesn't appear so simple to me."

They gazed at each other wordlessly, each occupied with a different series of preposterous mental images, then drank up and went back to bed. The next day they took a bus to Woods Hole and joined a seething throng of holidayers waiting on the dock for the afternoon ferries.

The Fourth of July was almost a week off but the annual invasion of Nantucket and Martha's Vineyard had begun. The only clouds in the sky were of the benign cotton ball variety blown by a warm southwest wind. The green Sound glittered cheerfully, a gentle chop reflecting the sun in a million beams of light. The *Islander*'s stentorian steam whistle sounded, startling Joan half out of her skin. A moment later they were underway.

"I think we've been going at this from the wrong direction," Rocky said, pulling up a deck chair to join Joan in the lee of one of the ferry's lifeboats. Herring gulls looking for handouts hovered above them like kites on short strings. "It's very possible Joan Cook knows more than she thinks."

"You're suggesting I unknowingly glimpsed the secret plans, overheard some scheme, saw a crime disguised as simple fun? I think you've been reading too many of your own books."

"The supposed 'burglar,' who knocked you down, for instance, could easily be tied in with all of this."

"He didn't knock me down, he knocked my mother down, and she couldn't even tell you his—or her—sex."

"And didn't you tell me someone once locked you in the attic?"

"Fanny was probably the one who locked us in the attic, and how could that possibly be relevant?"

"Well, we've got to start somewhere. Try to be helpful."

Joan heaved a sigh. "The only thing that stands out as even remotely clue-like—if you discount the hours of generally suspicious family behavior—is the letter Chick got from Cecil Barnard a few weeks before he was—had his heart attack. Chick himself said there was something strange about it, but I never actually saw the thing. Well, I saw it, but with the exception of one or two words that bled through the back, I certainly didn't read it. Rocky, I don't think this is going to get us anywhere. Admittedly, the atmosphere in that house was less than cozy, and there were members who I'm sure were glad to see me go, but I can't quite see it as a conspiracy designed simply to get rid of me. What possible threat could I have been to any one of them?"

Rocky said nothing for several minutes, but then asked:

"I can understand why you felt like cutting off even the chance of contact with Philip, though I think you might have taken it a little far, but what about Chick?"

Joan reached over and gave the old woman's chubby knee a reassuring pat. "That's why I'm here. But I must say I'm beginning to wonder about you. Are you always this zealous in your research? One might think you had some personal stake in all this."

"I do. Do you have any idea how much money a best-seller can make?"

Joan might have pressed her on the point, given the obvious evasion, but in the next instant the *Islander*'s whistle sounded again as Vineyard Haven came into view. The two women jumped as if their chairs had been electrified. Joan laughed. Rocky was silent. Also, it seemed suddenly to Joan, a little pale.

Indeed, the closer to their destination they got, the paler Rocky became. It was not until five o'clock that night, having rolled off the *On Time* and driven ten minutes east on Chappaquiddick Road, that Joan finally realized why.

In the last hour they had picked up their rental car, driven through the preholiday chaos of Vineyard Haven to the preholiday chaos of Edgartown Harbor—where by some miracle they'd been able to book a room—and telephoned Fanny, to whom Joan had told much of their plan, to say she'd arrived. In the course of their drive, Joan had been forced to remember the last day she had been on the island, now ten months ago: She had been on her way to Paris, half deranged with passion and the intoxicating sense of adventure. The memory, while carrying with it a combination punch of humiliation and rage, had had a positive effect: By the time they were turning down the Dumases's driveway Joan's flagging determination and courage had been salvaged, if not entirely galvanized. If she'd made mistakes in her dealings with the Dumases—perhaps she *had* overplayed the disappearance of Joan Cook—coming here to see Chick was not one of them. She was ready for whatever waited behind the big white door that was just now coming into view.

The one thing she was *not* ready for, however, was what seemed to be happening to Rocky. Joan hoped it was her imagination, but virtually at the moment she was ringing the doorbell it became staggeringly clear to her that the woman had suddenly lost her nerve.

"Maybe this wasn't such a grand idea after all," Rocky said in a voice Joan barely recognized. The younger woman gaped at her in disbelief. If the timing was not bad enough, it was the first time she had ever seen Veronica Filmore less than recklessly courageous. The sight chilled the blood in her veins.

"It's a little late for that!" Joan said in a ferocious whisper. "Rocky, what's *wrong* with you?"

"Nothing, I just suddenly don't feel as if I can go through with this."

Joan stared at her aghast, reached out and grabbed her by the elbow. "I'm so terribly sorry, but you don't have any choice!" They could hear the sound of footsteps nearing them from inside the house. " 'When weak feign strength, when strong feign weakness'," she said desperately. "Sun-tzu *The Art of War* . . . Besides," she added as the blood rushed to her face, "Philip's expression will be worth the trip."

Then the door opened. It almost was.

"I changed my mind," Joan said cheerfully breaking the whooshing silence that had swept over the threesome. "But perhaps we should have called."

Philip may have been momentarily overcome by their unexpected arrival, but the rest of the household, which Joan was sorry but by now not in the least surprised to see included the entire cast, received their presence with remarkable equanimity. If there was a murdering thief among them, their reactions did little to give him or her away. Charlotte was as gracious as ever, Hayden as blasé, Diana as breezy and Walter as amused. The only participant acting out of character seemed to be Rocky, who to Joan's immense discomfort had yet to recover her poise.

Chick, of course, had not yet seen Juanita, although judging from his manner he had been warned of the similarity between Ms. Castlerosse and Joan Cook. "They said you looked like someone we all knew," he grunted at one point. "You do." Joan was immediately struck by how *in*vulnerable the huge man appeared, but he was in every other way quite as she remembered: burly, crude, brusque, obese, charming. He was particularly attentive to Rocky, being delighted for the chance to meet Mary Lord after all, and then to find their mutual acquaintance of Margot and Werner von Jhering. He also showed great interest in her work-in-progress on Shona civilization, though, for whatever reason, Rocky was much less at ease with all this than the situation should have called for. Catching her eye at one point, Joan was struck suddenly with an unfamiliar surge of protectiveness, as if the small, gray-haired woman smiling stiffly across the terrace had abruptly given in to her years.

Aside from this unexpected feature, their entrance went fairly smoothly. There was no opportunity to speak to Chick alone, which they had not expected to find, but Philip insisted they move from the hotel to rooms in the house as their guests for as long as they intended to stay. Rocky's protest, particularly in light of the fact she and Joan had anticipated the invitation and agreed ahead of time to accept it, was in Joan's view too vigorous by half, and took Chick's help to put down. After another round of cocktails, Joan drove them back into town with the promise they would return the following day in time for lunch.

On the way Rocky refused to acknowledge her change of heart, insisting that she was *fine*, a little undone by their three days of travel, but had every intention of holding up. The saltiness with which she brushed off Joan's concern was at least reassuring.

"This whole thing is *rather* out of the ordinary, you'll agree," she said fussily as they drove slowly through the congested town.

"I, for one, think it's insane. But there's no point in backing out now."

"I assure you I have no intention of doing so. But one is permitted a little *pause*, isn't one?"

"I think a nap is a great idea."

"Not *that* kind of pause," Rocky huffed. "I mean a moment of wonderment. I find our situation intensely strange."

Stranger still than she might have gone on to say. Waiting for them with a drink in hand in a rocking chair on the veranda of their hotel was yet another familiar face.

"*Sidney!*" Rocky cried out her window as their car pulled up.

"Ahoy!"

"What in the name of the great good *God* are *you* doing here?"

"What else, in the name of the great good God, *would* I be doing here? Looking for you two."

"Sidney!" Rocky demanded more sharply now as he offered her a hand getting out of the car. *"This* is not a coincidence."

"No," he said, taking each women's arm and leading them up the hotel steps. "This is quite intentional. I hope you don't mind, but I knew you'd never stand for it if I told you ahead of time."

"Stand for what?"

"For protection."

"You're right! You're ridiculous!"

"Perhaps. However, I know what you're up to and, as admirable as your intentions might be, the plan is also foolhardy and dangerous. You've come eight thousand miles to place yourselves in the path of a murderer and I couldn't very well sit by and see either of you get hurt. Do what you will, but I'm afraid I'm going to be here to keep an eye on you."

They all stared at each other for a moment with raised eyebrows.

"Well, you're a dear boy," Rocky said at last, sounding very much like her old self. "Welcome aboard our ship of utter fools."

34

"So what do you think they're doing here?" Hayden asked Diana as she passed her a bloody Mary.

"Beats me."

Hayden dropped into a lawn chair. "Something's not right."

"Why do you think that?" Diana said sleepily.

"Let me remind you that a week ago Safari Sue was trotting barefoot around the bush with an attitude the size of this house. I would have thought it beneath her to put on shoes, let alone fly in an airplane—and fly in an airplane to *Martha's Vineyard? To see us?* Who's she kidding?"

"Mmm. I wonder if she got her hunting rifle through customs."

"What the hell could she want?"

"Maybe she came across a back issue of *National Geographic* and read about the Hoard."

"I don't doubt it."

Diana opened her eyes, rolled her head and smiled slyly at Hayden. "You're being a little hard on her, aren't you? Has Walter been going on about her or something?"

"Yes, as a matter of fact. It seems that sinewy girls with butch haircuts and dirt under their fingernails turn him on."

"I thought he liked overweight blondes."

Hayden glared at her. "I don't know what the matter is with *you*—she's obviously here because of Philip."

"Maybe, but sinewy girls with butch haircuts *don't* turn *him* on."

Hayden took a swallow of her drink, glanced at the blue-green sea, then closed her eyes and tilted her face toward the midmorning sun. "Besides the fact it's presumptuous as hell to arrive at someone's door unannounced."

"You didn't have to invite them to stay here."

"*I* didn't. Philip did. Christ, I thought Charlotte would have a heart attack."

"What do you mean, 'what could they be up to?' Why do they have to be *up* to anything?"

"C'mon, Charly, you weren't surprised to see them standing there?"

Charlotte, chest-high in the flower bed on the south side of the house, sat back on her haunches and wiped her forehead with the back of her arm. Walter was lying on the grass a few feet away. "Of course I was surprised. And the only reason I didn't jump for joy, as you put it, is because (Jesus) we just spent the last month either moving or traveling and I didn't want to see *anybody* for a while. Pass me that basket, will you. Thanks, dear. But people do this constantly. And I did tell them they were welcome any time. Although"—Charlotte gave a mirthless little laugh—"I wouldn't have expected them quite so soon."

Walter rolled over on his back, plucked idly at the lawn and squinted up at the sky. "And you find nothing strange about it?"

"No, Walter, I don't. I have too many other things to think about to spend time working up a conspiracy theory with you."

"What is it, Dad?" Philip asked. "What's troubling you?"

"What? Oh, nothing, Phil."

Chick and Philip had stopped for a breather at the side of the court and had somehow never gotten started again. Chick was gazing absently at his clay-dusted sneakers. Philip was watching his father.

"Is it Juanita?"

"She seems like a nice girl."

"No, I mean, her looking like Joan. Has it made you . . ."

"She does a little, I suppose. But not that much."

"Dad!"

Chick looked over. "*What*, Philip. What's *bothering* you?"

"What's bothering *me*? What's bothering *you*? You seem completely out to lunch."

To Philip's annoyance, Chick began to chuckle. "I assure you I'm all here. But you, son, seem a little tense yourself. Why don't you go for a swim?"

Of course as soon as the Dumases learned that Sidney Cleese was afoot, Charlotte promptly insisted he join them as well. This was seconded quickly enough by Diana, Hayden and Walter, all of whom remembered him for his nice looks and good taste. Philip was conspicuously silent on the subject, showing joy only in the news that he had already taken over Rocky and Juanita's room at the inn and would not be sleeping under the same roof with all of them.

Arriving at half past eleven the next morning, Sidney was taken out to the terrace, where coffee was still being served, and Juanita and Rocky were shown their rooms. Rocky was given a large sunroom on the first floor and Juanita was led upstairs and down a long hallway to the last room on the wing. It was a cozy, beachy room with white walls hung with botanical prints, scatter rugs and a view of the lighthouse Joan knew by heart. The door was closed behind her, she sat down on the brass bed in which she and Philip had made love on rare afternoons when the house was empty, and felt as if she were going to choke.

Answering a light knock on the door a few minutes later, she found Philip standing there. Would she come with him for a sail? It was the last thing she wanted to do. Why, yes, of course, I'd love to, she said.

"So why did you change your mind?"

She had known he was going to ask, but could not at the moment remember what she had decided to tell him. She said airily, "I don't know," and for a minute let him take her hand.

He didn't press. "Well, I'm glad you did."

Philip also seemed ready to accept the story Joan and Rocky concocted to explain why Sidney had appeared only after the fact—that he hadn't been sure he would be able to get away (business in New York) to join them until the last minute. He asked only, "Are you traveling with Sidney Cleese?"—to which she truthfully answered, "We are now,"—and left it at that. She was also relieved that no mention was made of his long-missing girlfriend, although it was a safe bet that their huddling together on the ocean-sprayed gunwale of the red Laser, racing over the waters of Edgartown Harbor, held some degree of poignancy.

It did, at any rate, for her. Simply put, it had not been a good idea to come. As they neared the mouth of Caleb Pond, she remembered finally the line that she had rehearsed: "No, thank you, I don't like to sail." But she also devised a way to make up for her mistake. Pressed by Philip to take over the helm, she chocked the mainsheet, waited for a gust, headed off and capsized the boat.

"What have you done with her?" Sidney demanded, catching sight of them trailing soggily across the driveway. "Juanita, darling, you're all wet!"

"Brilliant observation," Philip said and swept the disheveled girl by his guest without another word and led her into the house. As for Joan, Sidney could have been the Aga Khan for all she cared. Nothing in the world mattered for the moment but a hot bath. It wasn't until she had soaked herself pink that she could function socially again. When Sidney rapped on the door forty-five minutes later, she was just beginning to revive.

"I came to see if you'd drowned," he said cheerily, poking his head around the bathroom door.

"The drowning part was back in the harbor." She took a glass of wine from him but made no move to emerge from the tub. With a wrinkled toe she eased open the hot-water tap.

"Joan," he said, taking a sponge and running it slowly over her calf, "why don't you come back with me tonight to the inn?"

"I can't."

"Why not?"

"I've got to talk to Chick. I don't know when I'll get the chance and I have to be here."

"I doubt there'll be much opportunity between the hours of twelve and eight A.M." She refused with an apologetic smile. But it faded as he added: "Or any at all if you're off with his son."

"It's by his son's invitation that I'm here."

"Tell me, have you been sleeping with me to prove to yourself you're not still in love with Philip, or is it the other way around?"

She might have been angry had he not come up with such a convincingly wounded look. And before she had to decide how to answer, he let her off the hook. His handsomely weathered face creased in a smile.

"I'd infinitely prefer it was the latter," he said as he handed back the sponge, adding on his way out, "It's time for you to get out of the tub. You're pruning up."

From the outside looking in, the next twenty-four hours passed like yet more scenes out of impressionist paintings. Family and guests mingling with summery haphazardness in small, handsome groups at the beach, on the tennis court, on the terrace, at the edge of the lawn . . . drawing together for meals, eddying off again in new combinations, gossiping, laughing, watching each other. . . . Everyone seeming to enjoy himself against a sun-dappled backdrop of green grass, blue sea and blue sky.

These idyllic hours, however, passed without affording Joan so much as three minutes alone with Chick and by the second day she was beginning to show the strain. Rocky, on the other hand—to Joan's annoyance—had begun to relax.

"You needn't get so worked up, my dear, there's still plenty of time," the older woman said as they walked along the sand together before Sunday lunch was served. The day was brilliant and the mouth of the harbor was jammed with boats.

"Who's to say *how* much time we have?" Joan shot back.

Rocky gave her a studious frown. "Is being back here, with Philip, getting to be too much for you?"

"Yes. I mean no. I mean he's making it hard to get to Chick. Between him and Charlotte—and Walter—and Sidney—it's impossible. It's as if they're in league!"

"You sound paranoid. You also sound overwrought, dear. What's troubling you?"

"You *do* remember why we're here, don't you? You're beginning to sound like you're on holiday!"

"It's called backstopping a legend."

"What?"

"Trying to lend a little authenticity to our charade."

"Well, lend a little support and get Charlotte and Philip off my back. If you can tear yourself away from Chick for a moment yourself. You two certainly are the chummy pair. In fact, why don't *you* tell him?"

"Do you want me to?"

"No," she said after a hesitation. "But if I don't get to him by tonight, I'm going to make a general announcement. I don't care who knows who I am. I can't take this another day. You can spend the rest of the summer here, if you want, but by this time tomorrow, I will be gone."

The announcement, as it turned out, would not be necessary.

35

If the occasion for Anika and Tony Sloan's Canada Day party was something new, the form had not noticeably changed. The tent, caterers and orchestra appeared to be the same, as was the guest list, judging from Joan's initial sweep of the crowd. In her first glance she recognized James Michener's agent, this year in a suit made out of blue Tuareg cloth; "Ashton the designer," in a dress made out of a Palestinian kaffiyeh; and Eldon Cook, having yet to catch on to Third World chic, in madras. He stepped directly on Joan's foot before she was halfway through the door.

"Sorry! Sorry! Sorry!" he exclaimed, pulling off a ridiculous looking Panama hat and staring her straight in the eye. "Did I break anything? Lemme look. Oh, good. I hope not. Eldon Cook, nice to meet you. Juanita Castlerosse, hmm, interesting name, Spanish, you say. Great party, isn't it? Can I get you a drink? No? Well, nice to meet you."

Joan started breathing again after she got into the tent where she joined Sidney and Rocky at the bar.

"There you are, what can I get you?" Sidney asked above the music and slipped a comforting arm around her waist. "Are you feeling well, darling? You look a little green."

"So do you. It's the tent."

"Then you'll dance with me."

"Not till I have a drink."

"Feeling a little jumpy?" Rocky asked.

Joan mimicked her tone. "Whatever for?"

Joan was dancing not with Sidney but with Philip when she first saw Fanny. The band was playing "How Long Has This Been Going On?" (". . . I could cryyy salty tears . . .") He was holding her as diplomatically as a teenager on his first date. His questions, however, were more direct.

"Juanita," he asked matter-of-factly, "why are you here?"

"You invited me."

He leaned back to look at her, with an ironic smile on his lips. "Well, I may have, my dear, but it's fairly obvious you didn't accept my invitation in the spirit in which it was given."

"And what spirit was that?"

"Well, for one thing, I didn't expect you to bring your boyfriend."

"He's not my boyfriend. And I didn't bring him. He came on his own."

"I see. Then he's not the reason I haven't been able to have one honest, relaxed conversation with you."

"I've been honest," she said. "And—" Here she stopped. To say she was relaxed would be too big a lie, even for her.

He smiled his acknowledgment. "Juanita," he said again as if he enjoyed the sound of the name, "you didn't come to see me at all, did you? Tell me," he said this almost gently, "who *did* you come to see?"

Joan looked helplessly over his shoulder. She noticed that several pairs of eyes were on them. One pair were faded hazel and full of tears.

"What is it?" Philip asked. He had felt her catch her breath.

"It's nothing," she said, but pulled herself free. "You're right, Philip, and I'm sorry. It was a mistake to come. I honestly don't know what I was thinking. You were very nice to invite me and I appreciate all you've done. But I'll be leaving in the morning."

She turned before he could say anything and walked quickly out of the tent. By the time she reached the driveway she was running.

In an instant she was at the hedge that marked the mouth of the gravel turnaround. Here she stopped and kicked off her shoes. Gathering them in one hand, the skirt of her dress in the other, she started down a dirt path that ran left, back through a thicket of scrub pines toward the bluff. She had only gone a few yards when she was grabbed from behind. Fanny had her in so hard a vise she could barely breathe.

"Steady, girl!" Joan cried, laughing and squeezing her mother almost as hard. "You'll destroy my dress!"

"I can't believe how much you've changed!" Fanny said breathlessly, wiping her eyes, when the hysteria had passed. "Even after the pictures you sent, I didn't at first recognize you. You're so *thin.* And your *nose!* Has El seen you?"

"He stepped on my foot—six inches away from Hayden. I nearly had a stroke."

"Christ almighty, listen to the way you talk!"

"It happens, but I'm afraid I'm slipping back."

"Does he suspect?"

"Philip? I don't know." Joan glanced toward the house. "He suspects something but I don't know if it's that."

"You haven't talked to the old man yet."

"I haven't had the chance. I'm going to have to go back in and try again. I just can't wait any longer. I've told Philip I'm leaving tomorrow."

"*Why?*"

"Well, it's not working out quite like we planned—the whole idea is pretty ridiculous when you come right down to it. I mean, who's to say he'd even listen? And even if he did, what I have to tell him he must know or suspect already. Certainly that Harry Gilbert's dead. Either way, I just can't go on with it any longer. If I hadn't come all this way I probably wouldn't go on with it at all, but I'm here so if I haven't been able to talk to him alone by the end of the day, I'm just going to blurt the whole thing out and leave it at that. It doesn't matter who knows about me anymore, not after I've told Chick what I have to say. The damage—if one of them *is* a murderer—will have been done."

"What about Philip?"

"That he knows? That won't matter either. In fact, thanks to you, I really have no choice but to come clean."

"Me? What did I do?"

"Well, Jesus, Mum, there was no reason to have them thinking I was *dead*."

"I never actually said you were dead. I just said I hadn't heard from you."

"For *ten months?*"

"Well, the bastard deserved it, though it probably is time. But wait, you're *not* going back to Africa!"

"We'll talk about that tomorrow. I'll call you first thing. I want you to meet Rocky."

"I have already. We stood in the buffet line together."

"I hope you were discreet."

"Me?" Fanny gave her daughter a surprised look, but it was replaced almost immediately by a maternal glare. "Speaking of which, you never said anything to me about this Cleese fellow. When am I going to meet *him?*"

"Tomorrow. But now I have to get back or I'll be missed. Give me ten minutes. We really can't be seen together."

"Wait, wait! I haven't had a chance to tell you who's staying with us."

"Sir George Rawlins."

"Who? No, Paul 'It Was All My Fault' Dorman. The herb doctor emigrated to Israel and he wants to reconcile."

"Tell him I'm dead!"

"There you are, Juanita," Rocky called, "we were just talking about Paris. Come join us. It's a city you *must* see."

Rocky was sitting on the terrace with Hayden and Chick watching a spectacular mass of white clouds muscle up on the horizon. The wind it pushed ahead of it carried an ocean chill.

"I've always wanted to go to Paris," Joan said agreeably.

"Oh, dear, you should," said Hayden without a shred of feeling.

"Say, why not visit us in the fall? We've a house there, too, you know. Daddy, wasn't that Caroline's voice? Is she here?"

Hayden got up to find out, leaving Rocky and Joan alone with Chick—if they didn't count the dozen other people on the porch. The two women exchanged glances. Joan's heart felt as if it was in her mouth.

"Mr. Dumas, would dance with me?"

"You're sweet," he said, patting her hand, "and you're a great dancer—I watched you with Philip. But I'd rather sit."

"Not even one?" she said, preparing her next approach, which would be more direct: Chick, I *must* talk to you privately, it's a matter of life and death!

"No, but this dashing young cad will stand in for me, won't you, Walter? Juanita is trying to get me to dance. Would you mind taking her off my hands?"

"If you put it like that—"

"Forget it!"

"He's teasing—"

"I'm teasing."

"And the truth is this is the reason I came over. *Please*," he begged shamelessly, "dance with me."

"So, Juanita," he said, pulling her close and planting his cheek against the side of her head, "how do you find our little island?"

"Little."

He laughed. "I don't wonder. What I do wonder—what everyone is wondering—is what in the world you're doing here? I, for one, didn't get the impression you were all that keen on us."

"Keen may not be the right word." She leaned back to look at him. "Tell me, what does 'everyone' think?"

"Didi thinks you're after Philip. Hayden thinks you're after me. Charlotte, no doubt, thinks you're after her husband. And, well, Philip never says."

"And what do you think, Walter?"

"I think you're after buried treasure."

"Yes, well, in fact, I've come to ask Chick to give up his share of the long-lost Croesian Hoard."

"That's what I thought." He laughed and squeezed her harder.

Joan did not return with Walter to where Rocky, Chick, Hayden and now Diana and Philip were chatting on the terrace. Rather, under the weight of a growing depression, she sat down at a deserted table near the bar. The party swirled by her—a green-tinted blur of nostalgic music, party laughter, tan faces and the latest in fashion. She tried not to think of the last time she was here. But it was hopeless: Memories worked on her like cactus spines. Everything was so familiar, like the voices she was overhearing now.

"Hello there, Anika, what a pretty dress you're wearing."

"Thank you, Eldon."

"This is a lovely party!"

"Thank you."

"Have you been out sailing yet this year?"

"No. Tony's decided he doesn't like the water anymore."

"Oh, no? Doesn't he still use that blue kayak we used to see him out in?"

"Not really. It's been in storage for a number of summers now."

"Does anyone use it?"

"No."

"Where is it, down at the boat house?"

"No. It's over in Chick's Hat Box."

"I wonder, do you think he'd want to sell it? I've been dying to . . ."

Joan missed the rest. After what seemed like hours, she at last spotted Fanny standing in a small group at the edge of the lawn gazing out over Menemsha Pond. With as much discretion as she still had patience for she strolled over to her, squeezed her fleshy arm and excused them.

"What's the 'hat box'?" she asked as soon as they were out of earshot.

"Joannie! I thought we weren't supposed to—What are you talking about?"

"A *hat box!* The *Dumases'* 'hat box'! Anika was just saying something to Uncle Eldon about it! You've got to go ask him what it is! Something to do with a kayak! Quickly, *go!*"

"Will you let go of me. I don't have to. I know what it is. It's the Dumases' old boat house, out on Wasque. Well, it's not a boat house actually, it's a shack—you've seen it—it's oval-shaped, which is why they called it that. They own land out there and were going to build—"

But Joan was already running back up the lawn. In answer to Rocky's look, the younger woman mouthed the words *I've found it* and disappeared into the house.

— 36

A strapless silk dress by Chanel was not the best outfit for the job—in Walter's words, a treasure hunt—but there was too great a risk in going back to the Dumas house to change. It was enough of a miracle that she had been able to leave the party—or so she hoped—unnoticed. She glanced in the rearview mirror. Through the cloud of rust-colored dust churned up from the Sloan's long dirt driveway there were no signs of pursuit. In a moment she was turning Rocky's rental car—which was a discreet electric red—onto the pavement and stepping on the gas. The thing shuddered once as if with excitement and was off like a bullet.

For about twenty seconds. The rest of the way, which she had imagined driving at a thrilling, felonious speed, she traveled at between fifteen and twenty miles per hour, or the excruciating pace of the vacation traffic. She lost most of the cars at the turn for the Dyke Bridge but picked up a horse van following a hay wagon a minute later. The only thing speeding for the rest of the way out to the end of Wasque Road was Joan's heart.

Even if she had not remembered seeing the Hat Box before, she would have known roughly where it was. Almost exactly a year ago, in the rain, she had seen Philip heading toward it across the moor-like slope. What he was doing, she had never stopped to wonder. Coming over the rise she could just see it now—oval as Fanny had said— nestled in a clump of scrub pines. Fortunately it was set off from the other houses and shacks clustered on the slope. After several false tries, she found the right dirt track and in a moment was pulling the car alongside. Something touched her cheek. It had begun to rain.

It had not occurred to Joan that the place might be locked, which, of course, it was. Tossing her shoes into the car, she circled the building, which was more a small cottage than a shack. Peering through a filmy windowpane, she could see that it was one large room with a sleeping loft. It was obvious that the Hat Box had once been lived in—a wood-burning stove stood in the middle of the room and kitchen appliances still lined the back wall—but not, it seemed, for many years. The cabin had instead been relegated to storage space. The floor was hidden under Tony Sloan's blue kayak, a Sailfish, several masts, a half dozen oars, sundry fishing gear, a storm-tossed lobster pot, sun-bleached picnic table and chairs, a rusted barbecue, the tangle of a rope hammock.

Joan tried the window. It did not give. Nor did any of the others. She rattled the porch door. She rattled the back door, then ran around to the ocean side of the cottage, climbed back onto the porch and stood under the narrow lip of the roof, which only barely protected her from the rain. It hardly mattered. She was soaked and, she sud- denly noticed, shaking. Too violently for the warmth of the after- noon. What am I doing here? she asked herself. I must be out of my mind. And with that she picked up the conch shell that lay at her feet, sent it through the pane of glass nearest the latch, reached through and let herself in.

Now that she had gained illegal access to the haystack, the needle could only be a minor miracle away. For starters, she had no idea what she was looking for. It was reasonable to assume that whatever it was would be sealed against the corroding forces of the ocean air, which had left the stain of mold on every surface. She lifted the lid of a trunk with her dirty foot. It was empty. So, not surprisingly, were all the cabinets, closets and drawers in sight, the refrigerator, the oven, the potbelly of the wood stove. At least she needn't worry about hidden spaces under the eaves or behind a false wall. The Hat Box was a thin-skinned structure, completely unpaneled, through which the wind freely moved. It was a marvel it didn't leak. The problem was, this left fewer places to look. As it was, there were no couches or chairs with upholstery to slice open, no desks to rifle: Every object in the room was either transparent or solid. If the oars or masts were hollowed out, they were too convincingly resealed. If the stovepipe held the secret, it would continue to do so, as devising a way to get into it was beyond her. But it had to be there.

Or did it? After retracing her steps back and forth across the room, she finally dropped down onto one of the dust-layered picnic chairs (her dress was already streaked with perspiration, mud, soot, rain) and rested her chin in her hands. The most obvious question was not where it was but why in the world, if no one else in the family had managed to find it after all this time, she thought she could. Dejectedly she stared down at her feet. A few inches away a spider was making its way across the strip of badly worn Persian carpet that covered part of the floor. She watched it labor over the matted gray-green fibers, just a speck of no more consequence than a camel in the desert, she thought. Or Chick walking at sunset outside Uśák, over Werner's "deserted Central Anatolian plain."

In the next instant Joan was on her hands and knees, reaching around and under the objects that cluttered the room, her fingers running over the brittle fibers like a blind person searching for something dropped. Shoving the chairs aside she pushed her chin against the rug and scanned the floor. A weak light was coming from the windows, but the clouds were still thin enough in the far western sky and the panes were just low enough. In a moment she saw what she was looking for.

Sliding the kayak, then the Sailfish board and masts to the side of the room and throwing any smaller objects after them, she grabbed the edge of the rug and peeled it back until it uncovered the trapdoor whose slight bulge the slanting sun had revealed. With a heave, she dragged it open and peered into absolutely nothing.

For all that, it led nowhere more promising than the underside of the shack. Light filtered in from the latticed siding that enclosed the dank and empty space. Poking her head through, she saw some electrical wires, copper pipes, and a sloping clay floor. No treasure chest, no wooden crate, no footlocker, no trunk, not so much as a sagging cardboard box. However, given the choices, it was still where she would have hidden something. With this in mind—the alternative was to admit to the lunacy of almost a week's worth of behavior—she climbed down for a last-stand look around.

Climbing down meant lowering herself only four feet or so onto the clammy soil. Standing upright she could rest her arms comfortably on the dirty floorboards. Only by crouching could she inspect their undersides, which she could see bore no packages, parcels or containers of any kind wedged between the beams. The ground slanted in the direction of the sea and at the southernmost wall, under the small deck, she could just stand fully erect. It was here that she stood, a muddy bedraggled mess, looking miserably out through the tiny rectangular openings in the siding, hearing only the wind whine through the bayberry bushes that surrounded the house, and found the chest, directly under her feet.

It was almost too easy. She had not at this point even been trying. The ball of her bare foot had touched something solid in the soil and in a few minutes her fingers had dug around its edges to make out its shape. It had probably been buried at a greater depth originally, but runoff had washed enough soil away to leave it all but exposed.

The dampness had also packed the clay, however, and unearthing it would be impossible without a shovel. This she scrambled back to get. Popping her head through the trap, she placed her hands on the lip and, with a little hop, landed her smudged silk seat on the floor. It was from this sitting position that she looked up to see Charlotte standing five feet away.

If it had been anyone else, she might have had some explaining to do, but its being Charlotte, and Charlotte's having a gun pointed at her heart, there was not much to say. Charlotte was not very talkative herself.

"You've found it," she said in her sweet, childlike voice.

Joan nodded.

"I was afraid you might."

"Charlotte—"

"Of course, on the one hand I'm glad you did. We've been looking for it for an awfully long time."

"Charlotte—"

"But I also wish you hadn't. The trouble is, there's only one thing I can do with you now."

Charlotte raised the revolver slightly, pointed at Joan's head, steadied it with her other hand and squeezed the trigger. There was a shattering explosion and Joan Cook landed in a cold, motionless heap on the orange earth.

"Who wants tea with their denouement?" Rocky asked.

No one said anything. Everyone was already drinking something harder.

"Well, bring us a pot and some cups anyway, will you please," Rocky said to the Dumases' maid. "Now, where were we?"

"Well, *I* didn't know Juanita was Joan," Diana said.

"I didn't know Juanita was Joan," Hayden said, "but I knew Charlotte was after the Hoard."

"I knew Juanita was Joan, and I knew Charlotte was after the Hoard," Walter said, "but I sure didn't think she was capable of murder."

"If you all don't *mind*," said the little man standing at the center of the room, "you'll get your turn, but for now—*please*—one at a time. Mr. Dumas, I don't believe you've answered the question. Did you know that Juanita Castlerosse was really Joan Cook?"

They—Hayden, Philip, Diana, Walter and Rocky—had taken seats in the Dumases' living room in a semicircle around the diminutive figure of one semiretired Detective Sergeant Curtis Walsh, of the Edgartown Police Department. If the man had not had a case like this since he left the Philadelphia force twenty years ago, he did not seem thrilled to have another one dropped at his door. If there had still been enough daylight, he would rather have been fishing; as there was not, he would rather have been at home watching TV. This, and his overall distrust of the kind of people assembled before him, his tone, which varied between weary and sarcastic, made amply clear. However vigilant he had been in his youth, the man was now just doing his job.

But then it was late, and everyone was tired. Philip certainly looked it.

"Yes," he answered, "I did."

"But you said nothing to her."

"I didn't see any point."

"Even when she arrived here?"

"No."

He gave Philip a doubtful look, but didn't ask the obvious question that hung in the air. "All right, now," he said with a sigh, "will you please go on with the story. You went down to Zambezi with your stepmother, sister and Mrs. Devilliers. . . ."

"Zambia, yes. I had found out that she, Joan, was there—"

"How?"

"Is it important?"

"Probably not."

"—and planned to make the trip to try and see her. I used a visit to an archeological project outside Livingstone as an excuse. This backfired somewhat when my father and stepmother announced they wanted to come with me. My sister, who has told you she suspected Charlotte, decided to come as well and the next thing I knew"—he shot Hayden a glance—"made a party of it, inviting Mrs. Devilliers and Mr. Hudson."

"And did you have any reason to suspect your stepmother of planning to cause harm to your father or to anyone else?"

"Not really. But my sister, as she has said, was convinced—enough to move back into the house with our father—that Charlotte did not have my father's best interests at heart, and spoke of it enough to me to make me begin to wonder."

"Enough to take the precautionary measure of moving in with them yourself, too."

"Yes."

"Though you never informed your—Ms. Cook."

"No."

"But she—your stepmother—as far as you knew took no action against your father."

"She tried to poison him," Hayden said.

Detective Walsh glanced at Hayden and then back to Philip.

"None that we could prove," Philip said.

"But you now believe she may have had some hand in the demise of this man in Africa."

"Harry Gilbert, yes," Hayden said.

"If this was true, it was purely coincidental that you would plan a trip to Africa—almost a year after Ms. Cook left you—that would also suit your stepmother's purposes so well?"

"Perhaps it just gave rise to opportunity."

"Why did you chose this particular time to seek out your estranged girlfriend?"

"I had only just found out where she was."

"Did anyone else know the purpose of your visit?"

"No."

"Why didn't your father travel with his wife?"

"He became ill a few nights before."

"Ill."

"Drugged," Hayden said.

"Mrs. Channing, please," Walsh said.

"Intestinal," Philip said. "You'll have to ask him."

"Was your stepmother away from you at any time during the trip?"

"No."

"Yes," Hayden said firmly. "When we were at Chobe and Philip was still up at Njoko, with Juanita—Joan. Charlotte was alone at the hotel, except when she was with Sidney. She told me he took her for a drive to a lake or something."

Detective Sergeant Walsh looked down and began flipping slowly through the pages of a spiral notebook. "According to Mr. Cleese's statement, he was with other guests and saw her only briefly, that he found her . . . 'limping along the driveway at about 5 P.M., chastised her, drove her to look at falls and then back to hotel,' which he estimates took less than an hour."

Hayden shrugged. "She said she spent the day with him."

"He says she didn't. As far as he can tell, she spent it in her room. He understood that the chambermaid had been asked not to disturb her."

"Which would have given her enough time to fly to Harare and back," Hayden said with some satisfaction.

"Unnoticed?" Diana said. "Hardly."

"Well, it's not impossible," Rocky said. "The hotel has been packed. People fly back and forth between Livingstone and Harare all the time."

"How outstanding would it have been for someone to catch a cab to the airport, fly over and back?" Hayden asked.

"Not very."

"So the twisted ankle was faked?" Walter asked.

"Why not?" Hayden said.

"But how could she know Philip would stay in Njoko or we would go to Chobe?" Walter asked. "And if Sidney hadn't come back when he did we all would have ended up back at the hotel together. That's leaving an awful lot to chance."

"But not really," Rocky said. "It was still likely that you would have done something to fill at least part of the three days left over. A day trip was almost inevitable."

"Besides," Hayden said, "if she didn't get the chance then, she would know she had another one the day we all left. Sidney flew us up to Lusaka and we all flew out together to Paris, *except* for Charlotte, who was going to make a stop in Athens. Her flight had two stopovers, in Nairobi and Cairo. If she flew down to Harare, caught the Air Zimbabwe Harare-to-Athens direct, which left four and a half hours later than the Zambia Airways flight, she still would have been in Athens less than an hour behind schedule."

Philip looked impressed. "You checked?"

Hayden nodded. "Which would have given her plenty of time for a trip to Mafeking Towers and back."

"With the added convenience of darkness," Rocky said.

"Exactly."

"I still find it difficult to picture Charlotte smashing Harry's head against a hearth," Walter said.

"Harder than her shooting Joan?" Hayden asked. "She's not—"

"If you all don't *mind*," Walsh said in a loud voice. "May *I* ask the questions?" His tone, like the look he cast at each in turn, was that of an exasperated parent at a roomful of hyperactive children. Quiet returned. "Thank you," he said. "Now . . . you say there was another murder?"

"No, that was a coronary," Rocky said.

"It had to have been coincidental," Hayden said. "No one went near Cecil, according to Phyllis—his wife. Some student or scholar was there, but it was someone she knew, a friend of theirs—certainly not Charlotte. And he was the one who called the police."

"So it was only the death of this man in Africa which led Joan Cook, who had been in hiding for nine months, to come back—posing as Juanita Castlerosse—to save her former lover's father by digging up his millions of dollars worth of treasure . . . which turned out to be five thousand dollars worth of old wine."

"Yes," Rocky said firmly.

For a long moment nobody said anything. Detective Sergeant Walsh finally broke the silence.

"I must tell you frankly I think this is about as unbelievable a story as I've ever heard. In fact, it sounds like a soap opera to me." With a show of weariness, he got to his feet. "But I don't think there will be any criminal charges, unless Mr. Cleese didn't have a permit for that gun."

"I showed it to the inspector at the station just now," Sidney said from the door. Everyone's head turned. He looked damp and exhausted. But not nearly so damp and exhausted—and filthy—as the blanket-clad figure who followed him in.

Rocky bounded to her feet. "How *are* you, sweetheart?"

"I'm fine," Joan said weakly, "thanks to Sidney."

"Let me see your head. You really popped yourself didn't you."

"It's just a bump."

"My poor darling," then, looking down at what was left of Joan's dress, "My *God* what a mess!"

"How's Chick taking it?"

"Not too well. He's in bed. But he wants to see you."

"Not tonight. He knows Sidney wasn't trying to kill her?"

Rocky looked at Sidney with maternal concern. "I think he knows. . . . How are *you*, dear?"

"I'd appreciate your all staying around for a few days as I'm sure there'll be more questions," Walsh said from the door and disappeared.

No one else moved. Hayden looked at Diana. Diana looked at Philip. Philip, arms on the armrests as if he were about to spring from the chair, was staring at Joan, who was huddled under Sidney's arm and staring blankly off into space.

Sidney looked at Rocky. "Let's go, shall we?"

"You go. I think I'll stay here tonight."

"All right, then. See you tomorrow, I suppose. Joan, darling, shall we—"

"Joan," Philip said quietly, "I want to talk to you."

"Later," Sidney said.

"Joan," Philip said in a louder voice, "can I talk to you?"

"Dumas—"

Philip was on his feet.

"Phil—" Hayden said.

"*Hayden*—" Walter said.

"Joan," Philip said, angrily this time.

Joan took a deep breath. "Not tonight," she said, and turned to go.

"*Yes* tonight."

"Dumas."

"Heh, *Cleese!*" Walter said.

"Stop it, everybody!" Rocky barked. "Hayden, go see your father! Walter, go make Diana a drink! Sidney, wait in the car! Joan, *talk to Philip.*"

Philip lead Joan to the couch.

"Sit."

"I'll ruin it."

"Sit. Are you cold?"

"No."

"Drink this."

"You know how many glasses of 'this' I've had?"

"Does your head hurt?"

"Yes, as a matter of fact."

"It was just the edge of the trapdoor?"

"I assure you Charlotte missed me by a mile. Sidney's bullet hit her first."

"But you were knocked unconscious."

"No. I fainted."

"What was he doing there?"

"Sidney? He followed Charlotte."

"He had to kill her?"

"He didn't mean to. It happened too fast. He looked in the window, saw Charlotte taking aim and fired at her arm. He's never been much of a shot."

"Sweetheart . . . why didn't you tell anybody?"

She pulled the blanket more tightly around her. "I can't go through this now, Philip. The recriminations, the excuses, the Why didn't you just do this, Why didn't you just say that. I'm sorry for *my* deception, and that you might even have grieved for me. It was a dirty trick and selfish on my part, and stupid, and I regret it now. But I—"

"I mean why didn't you tell someone that you were going to the Hat Box?"

"Oh . . . well, who for instance? Hayden? Walter? *Didi?*"

"What about me?"

"I couldn't."

"Why not?"

When she didn't answer, he said, "I have things to be sorry for, too. I made a mistake—"

But Joan was getting up. "You're forgiven. You're forgiven and it's over. It's behind us. We can forget it. And leave it at that."

Philip gave her a puzzled look. "If you want," he said softly. "Maybe later. . . . Where are you going?"

"Back to Edgartown."

"Don't be silly, you're staying here."

"No, I'm not. Didn't you hear me? I said it's over."

"I thought you meant . . ." Then, as he grasped her meaning, he was on his feet, too. "No, Joannie, it's not *over*. It's never *been* over. Not for me. And not for you, either."

"I have a new life—"

"And you framed the whole damn thing around *me!* Even if only the *avoidance* of me! *Juanita Castlerosse?* Jesus Christ, you built a goddamn monument! Though how you ever came up with that name. . . ."

Joan turned once again toward the door.

"What are you going to do now?" Philip said angrily. "Run away again? Pretend you're somebody else? How will you die this time?"

"I'm not running away from you, Philip!" Joan snapped back. "There was never any *you* to run away from! Not for nine months! Not for the three months before that! You made your choice between Diana and me, now *live* with it!"

"Diana! What's she got to do with—"

"Goddamn you!" Joan shouted. By now, the whole house was hearing this. "I *did* damn near die for you! Over and over! Every time I thought of your *lies*—"

"Well, I'll admit I should have told you, but, come on, it really wasn't that big a lie—"

His smile inflamed her. *"Not that big a lie?"*

"Can you look at me and tell me you've stopped loving me?"

She looked right at him, shouted, *"I've—stopped—loving—me* . . . I mean *you!"* and stormed out the door.

— 38 —

Joan slept until almost noon the next day. She woke up to full sun, a sore head and an empty room. The note in her hand said *Coffee waiting on the porch, S.* She dug a T-shirt and running shorts out of Sidney's suitcase and went stiffly down to join him. Rocky was already there.

Joan smiled weakly. "It didn't turn out exactly as we thought, but, we did it."

"Well, we did *something*," Rocky said.

"Enough to write about."

"What? Oh. That. Yes. It should keep me busy. Though I think I'm going to go back to a curse."

"Of what?" Sidney asked. "Romanèe-Conti La Tâche '21? Speaking of which, you don't think they'd sell us a bottle, do you, Juanita—I mean Joan."

"I'm sorry about all that, Sidney," she said sheepishly, "but there *was* a reason. Or at least I thought there was. Now I feel embarrassed about the whole thing."

"Don't think about it anymore," he said, brushed her arm gently with the back of his hand, then went on in a brighter voice, "What's on the agenda for the Super Sleuths?"

"Well, they've asked me to stay a few more days and I think I will. How about you, Joan?"

"I'd like to see poor Chick. And I suppose I should speak to Philip—civilly—but I thought I'd give it a day. Fanny's on her way over. She's dying for the chance to really talk with you. No doubt she wants a full report."

"That'll be fun, but fear not, your secrets are safe with me."

"What's left of them."

"After that, Hayden wants to show me around."

"You're kidding."

"You know she's really not as bad as you thought."

"That's not saying much."

"You realize, it was Charlotte, of course, who wanted you out of the house. According to Didi, who got drunk with me and had a few ugly confessions of her own to make last night, it was Charlotte's idea to plant a story in the newspaper about Didi's having an affair with Philip. She knew you could be counted on to overreact, but just to be sure of something big, Charlotte arranged for you to find the article when Didi could be certain to be alone in Philip's room at the Ambassador Hotel—to answer the phone when you called. Didi's a determined woman. She evidently bribed the desk clerk to cover her tracks."

"The whole thing seems to me a bit risky," Sidney said. "I mean, what if Joan *had* confronted Philip? And he in turn had confronted Didi? Surely it would have gotten back to Charlotte."

"Not as long as Didi was in a position to deny it, which she was. It was hardly in her interest to own up to such a scheme. Her contacts at the newspaper weren't about to tattle on her, and no one at the hotel would jeopardize their jobs. . . . You see, Joan could simply have been wrong about the voice."

"How did they know she'd up and bolt?" Sidney asked.

"Of course they couldn't for sure, but even if she didn't, they knew she was going to be upset enough by the article that she would probably pressure Philip to move out, which was Charlotte's objective, if not precipitate a breakup—which was Didi's."

"Why would Charlotte want them out?"

"Elbow space. She could hardly turn around without running into someone in that house. Though, I agree there was a small risk of it backfiring. So why take it—and at that particular point—no one seems to know."

"She had to do something," Joan said. "I suppose I should be thankful she didn't try to shoot me ten months ago."

"But why did she have to do anything?" Sidney said.

Joan looked at Rocky. "You were asking me if I might have stumbled onto something without knowing it? Well, thinking it was Hayden, I'd been looking in the wrong place."

"You remembered something."

"A coin, with what looked at the time like a man's face on it, but that I now realize was a woman's. She had to have taken it from Cecil Barnard's things when she went to see Phyllis after his death and thought it was part of the treasure. I saw it in her jewelry bag just about two weeks before the newspaper story appeared. I asked her about it. Well, not it specifically—them: There were several. She seemed very eager to show them to me—tried to give me one, in fact—which threw me off. I never thought of it again."

Rocky's eyes brightened with recognition. "Chick said something about that this morning! Apparently Phyllis noticed it was gone because after Cecil died she'd been planning on giving it to Chick. He said each of the three men had one. But, my dear, it *wasn't* the face of Mynnia! You were right the first time in thinking it was a man—some overweight Roman emperor. The thing was worth practically nothing. They bought them in a tourist shop in the Istanbul Covered Bazaar on a drunk one night, incorporated them into an ad hoc blood-brother oathing ceremony—men and their mystic bonds!—and each kept them in a little case as a monument to . . . whatever."

"Like the wine they buried."

"Like the wine."

"So Gilbert's story to his housekeeper was—"

"The harmless fib of an old and lonely—and quite possibly stoned—man."

"And wishful thinking, no doubt."

"Did Chick think Charlotte had taken it?" Sidney asked.

"He won't say, but Hayden thinks he did. I tend to think so, too.

I was there when the police came in and gave him the news and he seemed a lot of things but not enormously surprised."

"Anyway," Joan said, "she couldn't risk my mentioning the coin to Philip or Chick, or maybe somehow piecing things together on my own, I don't know. . . . But it worked."

A waiter came up and asked if they had had enough.

"Quite," they all said at once, but no one laughed.

Sidney turned to Rocky. "Will you stay for a swim?"

"Surely." She put a soft stubby hand on Sidney's. "And as for you, how are you managing? I mean after all that."

"I would have to do it again, wouldn't I?"

"That doesn't answer my question."

"Then, yes, *I'm fine*, little mother."

"Does this mean, having saved my life once, you have to go on saving it ad infinitum?" Joan asked.

"Only until I can get you to save mine back, which effectively lets me off the hook. But there's no rush." He grinned at her. "I rather like being your hero for a bit."

Joan sat down on the edge of her bed. She could see through the windows that an evening calm had settled over the harbor. She wished a calm would settle over her. So much had happened, most of it utterly bizarre. Against ridiculous odds they'd arrived here on a Friday evening and by Sunday afternoon had uncovered a murderer and possibly saved a life. What more could she have hoped for? A simple sense of accomplishment, some satisfaction maybe. Why wouldn't it come?

She got to her feet. Sidney would be meeting her in an hour to take her out to dinner. Fanny would be joining them. That was something to look forward to. (With Paul Dorman making a nuisance of himself at the Cooks' house, she had decided not to move out of the inn.) She slipped out of her T-shirt and Sidney's shorts—which she'd worn to the beach—and took a shower. She felt a measure improved when fifty minutes later she was standing in a cool sleeveless shift and sandals on the porch with half of a strong drink left in her hand and a soft southwest wind blowing gently in her face. It had dried her hair, cooled her skin and given her the first inkling of ease she'd had in what seemed like weeks. She sighed. Whatever still needed to be said to Philip she simply would say. Then she'd get on a plane, fly back across the ocean and resume her ordered life in the small simple world of Livingstone, Zambia.

"What are you looking so unhappy about?" Sidney said, coming up behind her.

"Not unhappy," she said quickly. "Just a little awed."

"Well, it suits you. You're unspeakably enticing tonight."

"Thank you. I'm still trying to believe it's all over."

"Is it?"

"Unless there really is a curse," she said, purposely missing his meaning. "It's going to make one hell of a book."

"You don't suppose that's why she wants to stay on."

"Of course. Mary Lord is famous for exhaustive research. She's probably counting Hayden's facial hairs as we speak. Can I order you a drink?"

"Love one. When are we meeting the Queen Mum?"

"Not for an hour. Oh, which reminds me, I still have the earrings she wanted me to hold for her at the beach. They're in my—your shorts upstairs. Get me another one, too. I'll be right down."

Joan went upstairs feeling more optimistic still. Seeing Chick tomorrow would be an enormous relief, she thought as she found Sidney's shorts where she'd left them in his suitcase and fished out an earring: a gaudy little enameled disc—Fanny had no taste. He would no doubt take her hand in one of his and, as he asked her about herself and looked carefully into her eyes, would begin absently to pat the back of it with his other. She was sure she could make him understand, she told herself as her fingers found the mate and she straightened to gaze through the window across the channel at Chappaquiddick: The setting sun had muted its colors and softened its shapes. He wouldn't blame her, Joan knew and smiled inwardly, and glanced down at the shiny objects in her hand.

The next sequence of thoughts that moved—at first only clumsily—through her brain was not quite so serene. It started with the mundane: This was not the other earring. Groping under the clothes along the bottom of the suitcase, her fingers hit on several other possibilities before recognition had even begun to glimmer. Her hand came out folded over a quarter, a nickel, the ugly enamel disc that was Fanny's other earring and a little gold coin that matched the one in her other hand.

The earrings, quarter and nickel clattered noisily to the bare floor. Joan stared at what remained in her palm. The size of dimes, they were smooth, not perfectly round, and blank. She knew already what she would see before she flipped them over, but the familiar sight of the fleshy, androgynous profile still came with a breathtaking jolt. It came with something else, too. Something amorphous, like a cool draft that raised hairs on the back of her neck. In fact, exactly like a cool draft that actually did raise the hairs on the back of her neck. It had been drawn into the room when Sidney cracked the door open behind her.

He did not come all the way in, but stood with his hand on the knob, shaking his head slightly as if he were surveying the damage of some disaster. Not until Joan finally turned to see him did he move or speak, and that was only to close the door behind him and ask, "Didn't your mother ever tell you that it was impolite to snoop?"

39

Joan's mouth dropped open a little as she stared. She had the ridiculous urge to use the phrase "Say it ain't so," but this didn't last. The vague sensation that something was not right was already being rudely overrun by the first flush of fear. What she said instead, in a harmlessly conversational voice not quite her own, was:

"Gee, where did you get these?"

Sidney didn't answer.

"They're very old, aren't they?"

"Hmm." He was still gazing motionlessly at her but his mind seemed to have gone on to other things.

"Are they Greek?"

"Quiet for a minute, Joan."

"They look Greek. I saw some like this in a shop once."

"Shhhh."

"Let's see—where'd I drop those earrings?"

"Pick up the phone."

"Why?"

"Darling," he was looking at his watch, "do as I say."

"Who am I calling?"

"Your mother." He was still looking at his watch as if blocking out time. "Tell her you're tired, not feeling up to it, whatever—you can't make dinner. Don't tell her anything else, Joan. Just that."

"Sidney—"

"Joan." He spoke quietly, pleasantly even, but there was as much of a threat in his tone as there would have been had he pulled out a gun. Which, when Joan had the phone to her ear, he finally did.

"They're Cecil's and Harry's aren't they?" she asked from the chair he'd motioned her to after she'd finished with Fanny.

He said nothing as he methodically collected his things from around the room.

"How did you get them from Charlotte?"

"She gave them to me," he said without turning around.

"When?"

"Before she died." He was inspecting the small leather pouch from which the two gold coins had slipped. "Funny, but I knew I should have had this fixed."

She was looking at the back of his head, the powerful neck, the elegant set of his broad shoulders. In that linen jacket, from behind, she thought inconsequentially, he could almost pass for Walter. In fact, from across a room, or a square . . . Joan's mouth dropped open. "The Buci market!" she cried.

"Keep your voice down!"

"It was *you*. I *saw* you, in Paris, meeting Charlotte down the street from the Buci market! I thought it was *Walter!* That *he* was her lover! But, Sidney, it was . . . *you?*" Her hand went to her head as if it could somehow help her brain assimilate this extraordinary new fact. But hardly had she processed this one when another burst thunderously out of the fog.

"It was around the time Cecil died. *That's* how she got the coin! The one I found mixed in with her jewels! *Charlotte* didn't take it after he died—*you* did . . . when you killed him!"

Sidney glanced around. "I didn't kill him. Now, Juanita, please, pack your things."

"Why? Where are we going?"

"Vineyard Haven. We're taking the eight-thirty ferry to Woods

Hole. If we're lucky we can make it to Logan in time to catch the one o'clock to Switzerland tonight."

"But why do you have to take me?"

"You have to ask? But don't worry, darling, if you behave nothing will happen to you. As soon as we touch down on foreign soil you'll be free to turn right around, fly right back and reconcile with your estranged boyfriend. So you see, there's no need to panic."

Joan's heart was thudding but she was a long way from panic. Even if the tone of his voice had not been reassuring, she knew that Sidney Cleese, whatever else he had done, would never dream of hurting her. She quietly gathered up her things.

When she was done she sat back down. Sidney was lying on the bed with his gun on his chest and hands behind his head. They stared at each other from across the room.

"I didn't kill Cecil."

"He just happened to keel over dead while you were there?"

He shrugged, almost apologetically. "Yes, as a matter of fact."

"How convenient for you."

"Not really. It was too soon. He showed me this—" Sidney held up one of the two gold coins he'd taken from Joan's hand "—which, you're wrong, I took almost *two weeks* before he died—but he hadn't told me yet where the rest of it was. I'm convinced he would have, though. The man was *aching* to talk about it. Let me tell you something, besides being competitive and petty, archeologists are incredibly vain people. If you appeal to that inflated sense of their importance—it must come from chasing the ghosts of Agamemnon and Ulysses—they can't keep a secret to save their lives."

"Evidently not."

"I tell you, what I gave him might have made him a little more expansive than usual but it didn't kill him. Something else did. Captivity, maybe. The poor bastard had a king's fortune in his backyard all these years and couldn't do anything with it. *There's* a subject for a novel. He was kept by his prize. He couldn't sell it for fear of getting caught and wouldn't anyway because then, without his great secret, this ultimate *possession*, what would he have left? He never even told Phyllis. He and Gilbert had some weird pact not to tell their wives.

I mean if they couldn't trust Chick—and they were big male-bonders—who could they trust? The fool couldn't even look at it. He could only imagine it, which he could have done just as well if he'd never dug the bloody thing up. To take it from him would have been to liberate him, if he'd only lived to experience it."

"And Harry Gilbert tripped and fell."

"Yes and no. But that little cocksucker had it coming. I knew he'd do something and sure enough the old pothead went off on me. It was as if he'd figured it out—*after* he'd showed me this." Sidney held up the other coin. "He realized he'd said too much, he'd already started to hint about the Bosphorus, and suddenly went crazy—grabbed the thing back. If he hadn't been drunk as well as high as an airplane he wouldn't have shown me anything, but he probably would've had the good sense to tell me what I wanted to know and not tried to defend it with what was left of his pitiful burnt-out life. The maniac had a gun, you know."

"So which was it with Charlotte? An accident, too? Surely not self-defense."

"Listen, dearest, she was the one who brought me into this in the first place. She always suspected that the three of them had taken the Hoard and assumed over time that Chick would privately admit to it."

"Is that why she married him?"

"Partly. She was rather singularly directed when it came to money. It was the reason I never married her myself. I could never be sure she wouldn't poison my tea for the insurance one day."

"But you *were* lovers. Since when?"

"I met her in Ankara on her first dig with Chick." There was a momentary silence, then he went on. "The problem was he stuck with his story and she was beginning to lose patience. She tried drugging him—"

"Drugging him!"

"Well, a *mild* toxic—something I gave her to make him think he was on the way out, bad indigestion, harmless really—but there were no deathbed confessions of anything but gratitude, love and so on. She'd never said precisely what she wanted my herbal 'cure' for, though I suspected. Anyway, when it didn't work she grew a bit itchy and having had no luck on her own—in fact, Hayden was beginning to make rather a nuisance of herself—approached me with the proposition. She just wanted confirmation that the Croesian Hoard *existed* and I was to go to work on Cecil. This ended up taking only a matter of a few months—"

"You were the flattering student they were so keen on?"

"During which time, to Charlotte's annoyance, you and Philip showed up. I think she was ready to call it quits on the whole lot of you, but then suddenly," he rattled the coins in his hand, "we had the proof. After that, we figured it was just a matter of finding it. Of course, we had to get you out of the picture first."

"Because I saw the coin. How lucky for you that Philip cooperated by having his little affair," she said bitterly.

"Lucky?" He chuckled. "Darling, you underestimate our Charlotte. You and Rocky both. Of course, she had Didi's help—"

"And Philip's."

"Actually, in fairness to the poor bastard, without much help from him at all. You see, the triumph of her scheme was not the carefully timed revelation of an affair, but the convincing revelation of an affair," he smiled, "that never really was."

"What do you mean?"

"You work it out."

"But the picture—of Philip and Diana in Italy—"

"A child could have cut and pasted that one together. Now that arresting one of you at the pool *was* a piece of art. *Incredibly* convincing, I thought. How they—"

"Then why did he lie about his apartment being occupied?"

"Did he? I've no idea, you'll have to ask him, though my guess is he didn't want to have to explain to you why he had you both still living at Rue St. Dominique. Can you imagine him saying, Welcome darling but we're really only here to keep an eye on my dastardly stepmother, who's really only here to rob my father of his hidden treasure? You might have found it a little awkward, but who knows."

Joan looked away.

"Anyway, after you cut out—and with a flare, I must say . . . (The fact that you ended up in my hotel, purely by chance, really gives one pause, doesn't it?) . . . Charlotte thought she'd ease off for a time.

Hayden was like a bloodhound after Cecil's death and Hudson was starting to get into the act—he'd actually started tailing the poor woman. We were even afraid they might track *me* down. And then, just when the heat had finally died down, Philip comes up with the idea of going to *Zambia*, of all bloody places. I don't know who told him you were there, but at the time it was news to both of *us*. Nevertheless, Charlotte figured she could kill two birds with one stone. Spend some time with me and pay a visit to poor old Harry."

"So she arranged Chick's intestinal attack."

"She knew he'd insist she go anyway."

"And her little accident at Njoko?"

"I have to take my hat off to her for that one, too."

"As was your coincidental return to camp."

"Yes, but we did not imagine everybody and their uncle would be returning with us."

"But then of course they all went to Chobe, which gave you a chance to take a sidetrip to Harare."

"No, no. Charlotte never went with me to Harare. We spent a few memorable hours together at a lodge on Lake Kariba but I flew down myself the night everybody left."

"I suppose you went straight to her tent after mine?"

"Look who's calling the kettle black. . . ." He looked at his watch as he said this. "It's time to go."

In the hour that had passed the light had gradually faded and Sidney's face, like the details of the room, had grown less and less distinct until the whole thing seemed like a dream. His rising to his feet, the feel of his hand on her arm, the sound of their heels on the bare floor, did little to dispel it. Even when he opened the door and the hall light flooded in, making them squint, any sense of reality was smothered under the impossibility of what seemed to be happening to her. Joan walked down the stairs in almost a trance, stood by him demurely as he checked himself out (he did, after all, have a gun) and stepped onto the porch without so much as a meaningful glance back.

Here he leaned over to her and said calmly in her ear: "If you've ever loved him, or your life, make him go away."

She followed his gaze to where Philip was waiting for them on the bottom step.

— 40

After what she'd said to him already, she knew it wouldn't be too hard.

"Where are you going, Joan?" He was looking at Sidney.

"We're leaving."

"Without saying good-bye?"

"I said good-bye."

"What about Chick?"

"I just talked to him on the phone."

"It must have been a concise conversation."

"That's none of your business, Philip," she said slowly, unkindly. "I've said everything I have to say to your family. I've said everything I have to say to you. Let it go."

"Is it because of him? Has he told you to say this?"

Joan felt the gun nudge her ribs. She shouted, "No, it's not! It's you! Can't you get it through your head that I never want to see you again!"

"I don't believe—"

"Can't you see the trouble I went through to make it so that I'd never have to see you again? I've had ten months to think about it! The only reason I came back was for your father."

"You're lying."

"Accept it, Philip."

"Accept what? That—"

"That I've had all I wanted of you!" She dug deep for the look she gave him and the tone with which she said, "You've heard the Japanese expression 'I'd fuck you—once'?"

This did the trick.

Joan had stopped crying by the time they reached Vineyard Haven. The dam burst, besides finally exhuming her long-denied feelings for Philip, also had the effect of draining her of the spirit that had made her courteous abduction by Sidney in a perverse way something of an adventure. She felt tired and angry.

She could tell from his grip as he led her across the gangplank into the *Islander*'s noisy floodlit bay that he was tense himself. He held her close to him as they lingered to watch the rest of the passengers board. He'd made sure they were among the first on and so could be certain there were no familiar faces in the crowd. Not until the ferry's roaring engines were ground into gear did he finally take his eyes off the dock and turn to lead her up the metal stairs to the upper decks.

He bought them both a cup of coffee and carried them to practically the same booth she and Philip had collapsed gaily into at the end of last August. Through the porthole the outline of the island was black against the rosy western sky. It was dotted with homey clusters of electric lights.

Sidney sat down across from her. "Cream and sugar, right?"

"Did you mean to kill Charlotte?"

Sidney emptied a container of cream into both coffees and stirred them slowly. He had smiled slightly at her tone but answered politely, and informatively.

"The problem, for Charlotte, was that news of Gilbert's death, which arrived about a week ago, was like petrol on Hayden's fire and she began to imagine her baying hound of a stepdaughter was closing in. There was of course nothing that could possibly link Charlotte to him, but she was growing paranoid. She even accused me of planning to sell her out, which is the principal reason I decided to come over here in person. Blackmailing me was the next logical—or illogical—step. Whether I could have reasoned with her or not, we'll never know because you found the trunk. The problem for you at that moment of discovery was that Charlotte by then imagined she had everything riding on it. It wasn't just the quest for the Holy Grail anymore. It—or what she was convinced was *in* it—was her salvation, her means of getting out of Hayden's reach, out of Walter's, Chick's, out of mine. It was, as they say on your TV, 'her ticket out of town.' You could have been Mahatma Gandhi sitting on that thing and she still would have pulled the trigger."

"But you came along to save me. Or was it just the perfect opportunity to dissolve a partnership that had soured?"

"Don't be ungrateful. I could have let her kill you first." Sidney was smiling more broadly now. She could tell that he had begun to relax, as if the farther away from the island they got the more at ease he became. Come to think of it, and for no good reason, so had she. In fact, it was almost as if they were back sitting on the graceful porch of the Vic Grand, the Falls rumbling in the background, gossiping about one of the guests.

"Thanks," she said. "And you could've hit my mother a lot harder at Rue St. Dominique."

"I'm glad I didn't. You might have ditched then and there, never met Rocky and we wouldn't have had Zambia."

"What were you doing there, anyway?"

"Running a hotel. I thought you knew."

"No, on the third floor at Rue St. Dominique."

"A wild goose chase as it turned out. Charlotte got the idea in her head, from something in a letter Cecil wrote to Chick, that there was a hat box, *literally* a hat box, or something like it, hidden somewhere in Chick's house and of course that the coins were in that. I thought it odd that she hadn't known about the boat house, until I realized of course she would've searched it a dozen times by then—which is why she thought they were speaking in code. Anyway, she wanted me to come and have a look—I happened to be in Paris at the time—because Hayden and Walter were watching her so closely. If I was caught, which you'll remember I was, I could always get rough and flee as a burglar. Seen or not, it wouldn't matter. I knew by then that Chick didn't have the Hoard but thought it best to play along." He pulled a familiar piece of airmail stationery from his bag. "But here's how she could have been confused. . . . Cecil writes: *'. . . HARRY WANTS HIS SHARE NOW, AND I'M AFRAID I MUST AGREE. FEAR OF MORTALITY AT LAST POKING THROUGH? POSSIBLY. THE THOUGHT OF IT, THE ANTICIPATION, HAS BEEN FUN BUT I THINK, WHILE WE STILL CAN, WE SHOULD TAKE OUR PRIZE OUT OF THE HAT BOX AND CELEBRATE ITS OPENING. IT'S TIME YOU AND HARRY. . . .'*

"He was talking about the wine, of course. *I* knew about it because Cecil had told me. Twenty-five or so years ago they ceremoniously buried it—Rocky was right, these old boys were very big on symbols, oaths, secret handshakes and so on. Philip and Hayden should've known about it, but all this was before Charlotte's time and she evidently did not. It seemed all to fit, of course, when she saw you run off, followed, and found you poking around the Hat Box. Poor dear . . . but the *best* part of it"—Sidney's eyes widened a little with excitement—"was that Cecil *did* actually allude to the treasure, the real treasure, Croesus's treasure, farther down. Charlotte missed it entirely. . . . listen: *'. . . AS FOR THE REST, IT'S AS MUCH YOURS AS OURS AND I WANT YOU TWO TO HAVE IT NOW. I'M TIRED AND I THINK DYING, CHICK, AND THIS WAY YOU'LL KEEP THE FLAME ALIVE, BY GOD. IT'S BEEN MY LIFE. OUR LIFE TOGETHER. DON'T BE AN OLD FOOL. GO TO HARRY. PATCH IT UP WITH HIM AND GO BACK FOR IT . . .'*"

Sidney looked up and grinned.

"I don't understand," Joan said.

"I don't wonder, talk about tortured prose. The man was obviously drunk, and no doubt ambivalent. But what he was trying to tell Chick after all these years was that they *had* the stuff. He wanted him to go to Gilbert—whom he was working on to agree to let Chick in on their secret—and then for the two of them to go dig the stuff up. The damn thing's still in Turkey!"

"What damn thing?"

"Juanita! *Joan!* The Croesian Hoard, of course! Harry as good as told me. I didn't know myself *where* in Turkey until Charlotte let me look at this"—he shook the thin sheet—"for myself a few nights ago: *'THE PLACE IS EMPTY, UNUSED, JUST AS WE LEFT IT. SEE IF THE ROSES ARE STILL IN BLOOM. BRING ME BACK ONE IF THEY ARE, AND I'M STILL HERE. SENTIMENTAL IDIOT THAT I AM. . . . IF NOT, THEY'RE ALL YOURS. . . .'"*

Sidney looked at her with a self-satisfied smile. She struggled to understand. "But there *is* no treasure, Sidney."

"Not here, not under Chick's boathouse. It's in the Bosphorus."

"What are you *talking* about?"

"The roses," he said, reaching into his pocket. "The trove." He put the little gold coins on the table between them. Joan looked down at the two strange faces. She could not seem to tear her eyes away. "Except for these, they reburied the whole lot at Barnard's summer place on the Bosphorus. I don't know why I didn't think of it! In the garden! *Under his roses!*"

Joan looked up at Sidney. His face seemed to be leaning toward hers. His smile seemed all at once so broad as to be grotesque. Something was happening.

"But there *is* no treasure," she repeated, pressing a palm against her forehead and trying to concentrate. "This"—she took the coins in her other hand—"isn't Mynnia. It's not even a woman. It's a Roman—"

"Emperor?" He laughed. "Not even close."

"Sidney. . . ." She stared at the coins. They were staring back, making it hard to think. "You . . . killed Harry Gilbert . . . and Charlotte . . . over a pair of cheap Roman coins."

"No, darling," he leaned close again and murmured campily, "over *millions.*"

"You're *mad*," she said, alarmed. "Listen to yourself. There *is* no—"

But he was laughing and in the next second came the late and staggering realization that she wasn't going to get as far as Switzerland. Not by a long shot. He wasn't fleeing the law, he was going to Turkey to dig for treasure and he'd never take her that far. What had she been thinking about? This man had killed two, possibly three, people already. Why stop there? Given what he'd just told her, he *couldn't* stop there. He'd just turned her into his greatest liability:

Worse than his confession to murder, he'd told her what he was going to do next and where he was going to do it. Having done so he had no choice now but to get rid of her. Probably on the highway to Boston—leave her where her body wouldn't be found for weeks. Why spend the money for baggage you don't need? Even if you think you're coming into a fortune.

"You don't look well, Joan, perhaps you'd like some air."

"I don't feel very well," she murmured, dropping her head on her arms. It felt as if it weighed twenty pounds. She closed her eyes and the room began to spin. Sidney was going to try to throw her out of the car, she knew it, and she had to think of a way to get free before then. She had to think.

"Joan, darling. . . ."

Maybe just run for it, here, now, with all these people around. She should've done it before. He wasn't about to shoot her . . . well, he wasn't about to shoot up the whole boat.

"Up you go," he said, pulling her to her feet. "I think a little fresh air is just what you need."

It was simple. She would just make a break for it . . . if only she weren't so tired. She reached for her coffee cup and knocked it across the table.

"No," Sidney laughed, "you've definitely had enough of *that*." He had his arm around her and was leading her toward the door. "Atta girl," he said cheerfully. "Ooops! Hold on."

"Lemme rest a minute," she said thickly, eyes looping crazily in their sockets. "I'm so . . ."

"That's okay, darling, we'll just walk it off."

Joan was barely aware of a strange voice in her ear. "Is she all right?" it asked. "Oh, yes," Sidney answered with a little laugh. "I'm afraid my wife has a bit of a drinking problem."

"No, no, no, I'm not his wife, I'm not drunk, he's going to try and kill me!" Joan shouted at the stranger. But her mouth seemed to be full of cotton and all she or anyone else heard was a string of muffled syllables.

"So I see," the stranger snorted, and the next thing Joan knew they were stepping out into the roaring night air. For a split second the chilly wind made her lucid but almost immediately she was falling back against Sidney, trying to keep her eyes open, trying to keep her balance, vaguely aware that something was about to happen to her and that she was powerless to stop it. She could not even stop herself. She tried to pull her arms free, to stop her feet, but they kept walking down the side of the cabin, passed the lifeboats, passed a couple huddled in deck chairs, passed the rumbling smoke stack, toward the stern of the ship.

"Here we are, darling," he said leading her to the rail. "Breathe deeply, you'll feel much better."

"Sidney," she whispered.

"You oughtn't to drink so much, dear, you promised me you wouldn't."

Why was he talking this way?

"We're going to see a doctor when we get home. No more excuses, understand?"

Joan tried to turn her head but he held her tightly against the rail. Out of the corner of her eye she could see a man and a woman strolling by. Arm in arm they looked like it was Sunday afternoon and they were in a park. She tried to call to them but it came out like a groan and Sidney's hand was coming over her mouth.

"Do as I say, now, darling. Breathe deeply."

The couple was almost out of sight.

"That's my girl. One. Two."

Letting her go with one hand, he groped in his jacket pockets. He was going for his gun, Christ, he was going to shoot her! But then something else happened that she didn't at first understand. He nudged the top of her thigh and she felt something heavy slide into her pocket. The other thigh, the other pocket. They felt as heavy as bricks. But smooth. Like rocks. They *were* rocks! Rocks? Where'd he get rocks? They weighed a ton. She could barely stand, but he held her up. Holding her under the arms until it hurt. Then he was lifting her over the rail.

She tried to fight him but the uncoordinated flailing of her free arm had little effect. Already he had her straddling the rail. She could see the water below, it was black. Hissing white phosphorescent foam pushed out from the *Islander*'s wall-like metal sides in lovely curling waves. She wondered if it was going to be cold.

Sidney gave one last push and the rest of Joan's body toppled over the edge. Whimpering nonsensically she stuck there for a moment, like a doll, hooked awkwardly on her upper arms, struggling desperately to gain footing on the ledge. Then his hands were on her elbows and she knew it was over. A child could have pried her free and with barely a shove sent her tumbling backwards into the night air. She closed her eyes and waited. Mercifully she felt nothing as she fell through the blackness toward the water. She listened for the splash.

Oddly, it didn't come. What she heard instead was a strange animal grunt in her ear. Like a warthog, she thought, and opened her eyes in time to see Sidney's head crashing forward, making a loud *crack* against the rail. Then, suddenly, he dropped in a heap.

There was commotion all around. Shouts. Someone's running feet echoed on the metal deck. Dimly lit faces swarmed around hers. Hands were grabbing her arms. Evidently, she instructed herself, you are being saved. Either that or you are dead and this is the greeting team from the Afterlife. "We have you," one said. "Give me a hand," another said. "Here we are, just lay her down." Yes, you really must be dead, she told herself, because now her life was passing before her eyes. Rocky's face swam toward her out of the dark. "The poor girl's got rocks in her pockets," she said. "Sidney was always one for detail." Then Fanny's. "We should throw the bastard to the sharks!" she was saying. And finally Philip's. He was lifting her shivering body into his arms. "No point," he said, pressing his warm face against hers. "They'd just throw him back."

41

"So, what are we supposed to call you now?" Chick asked Joan.

Curled into a ball and nestled into a warm, comfortable spot under Philip's arm, she grinned sheepishly at him. "Whatever you think fits."

They were sitting out on the terrace under a black sky bright with stars. In another few hours the eastern horizon would begin to lighten, but nobody seemed in the mood for sleep. Joan was savoring the return of lucidity since Sidney's drug had worn off; Philip was savoring the return of Joan; Hayden, her victory over Charlotte; Walter, the symmetry of the moment. Rocky and Fanny were talking philosophically about men. Chick had a curiously expectant air.

"Why, by the way, did you wait so long to rush in and save me?" Joan asked Philip.

"Sitting where you were, we couldn't get near you without Cleese seeing us a mile away, which would have given him plenty of time to pull his gun on you."

"Or you."

"No, in that case I think he would have known that his best advantage would be to use you as a hostage. But we really didn't think he'd try anything before the ferry landed."

"Most of the time you were drinking your spiked coffee we were on the bridge with the captain, trying to convince the idiot to help us set a trap in Woods Hole," Fanny said. "You might have thought we were trying to steal his boat. Of course, when Philip went back to check on you, you were gone. It took some time to figure out where the bastard had taken you. The last thing any of us expected was for him to try to toss you over the side. But he must have been planning it all along. I mean he had to have gotten those stones while you were still on the island."

"It's hard enough to believe he would kill anybody, let alone *you*," Rocky said. "But that he of all people would convince himself there was a *treasure*. Charlotte I never knew, but Sidney—it's so unlike him. I always thought the corrupting potential of gold was overrated. It appears I was wrong . . . but then, considering everything that's happened, I don't suppose I knew him very well at all."

"He not only thought the trove existed," Joan said, emerging from Philip's hold to take a cup of coffee from Hayden, "but he was convinced it had corrupted Cecil and Harry. He thought the only reason both of them in turn showed them their coins was because he'd managed to flatter their egos. He was quite contemptuous of them." She lowered her voice slightly. "He drugged them, you know. At least he gave something to Cecil, to try to get him to talk. It may have. . . ."

"So we've begun to suspect," Philip said. "Poor Phyllis. After this I'm afraid they're going to want to re-examine his body."

Walter broke the short silence. "Well, who knows what Cleese appealed to, but it only got him a look at a couple of so-so late Roman pieces."

"Knowing Cecil," Hayden said, "he must have thought he had a live one on. I'd be surprised if it didn't occur to him to try to sell it to him."

Chick chuckled. "I'm sure it did."

"And there was also the matter of Cecil's letter," Joan said. "It seems he wrote rather tantalizingly about 'riches'. . . ."

"I remember," Chick said. "He was referring, as he has many times before, to *memories*. He was a terrible sentimentalist. He was right, however, about making amends with Harry. I should've done it a long time ago."

"Maybe Harry . . ." Philip did not finish his sentence.

"Maybe not," Chick said.

"Tell me, Philip," Fanny asked, "how did you know Joannie was in Africa?"

"Margot von Jhering told me."

"Margot?" Hayden said. "How did she know that?"

Joan swung around on Rocky. "You rat!"

"Well, I thought it was time he knew," she said unapologetically, with a wink at Philip. "You couldn't hide forever."

"You should talk," Chick said. Rocky looked over at him but said nothing. He gave her a little smile. "What are *you* doing holed up in Africa?"

"I'm writing a history of Shona civilization," she said, smiling, "although I may have to move somewhere else now. Sidney was giving me a break on the rates, local tourist attraction that I was. But no doubt the Vic Grand will be changing hands."

"Where will you go?"

"I thought of buying a small castle somewhere, digging a moat and filling it with ducks."

"Like Chantilly," Joan said, tilting her head to smile at Philip.

"That's Chan-tee-EE," Rocky corrected her.

"Someone's idea of a castle," Hayden said.

"I wouldn't know," Rocky said looking at Chick. "All *I* ever saw was the barn."

"You'll have to come back and see the whole thing some time, Vera."

"Vera?" Joan said.

Rocky blushed suddenly like a twelve-year-old girl. "I didn't think you'd remembered."

"You don't think I could ever forget?"

"Who's Vera?" Fanny said.

"I haven't been to Paris in years," Rocky said.

"*Vera?*" Joan said again. "Now wait just a minute—"

"It's changed," Chick said. "But some things are still the same."

"What's going on here?" Joan demanded.

"*You* haven't changed," Chick said.

"Daddy?" Hayden said.

"Yes, I have," Rocky said. "And so have you. We're *old*."

"Then we can't afford to waste any more time."

"What are you suggesting?"

"Well, I have a big house in Paris with a lot of empty rooms. I'd give you a deal on the rent."

"Daddy!" Hayden said.

"Rocky!" Joan cried. "You and Chick? You're the girl—You *lied* to me!"

"I think I'm going to cry," Fanny said.

"All right, old man," Rocky said, "let's discuss your terms."

There was a glow of dawn by the time they finally got up and were moving back through the house.

"*Vera*," Joan murmured.

"Short for Veronica," Rocky said. "Sort of."

"So you were never writing a novel at all, were you?"

"No, child, that was your idea. Which I must say came in very handy."

"You set this whole thing up!"

"Not the whole thing."

"Which also explains the sudden stage fright. Why didn't you tell me?"

"But I did finally, didn't I? Let's save it for the morning, shall we? Good night, all."

"Wait, what should I do with these?" Joan asked, holding out the coins she'd somehow managed to hang on to during her struggle with Sidney.

"Is that them there?" Chick said. "Let me see for a minute."

"Had I been of sounder mind, I'm sure I would have dropped them."

"Had Cleese been in less of a rush to kill you, I'm sure he would have asked for them back," Philip said. "What's wrong, Dad?"

Chick had started to chuckle. "Those sons of bitches," he murmured.

"What is it?"

"Those sons of bitches!" he said again, handed the coins to Philip, and started to laugh. Philip held one up to the light and in a moment was laughing himself.

"What *is* it?" Fanny asked.

"It's her," Philip said.

"Who's her?"

"Mynnia!"

"What do you mean?" Hayden said.

"Let me see," Walter said, taking the coin from him. "Bloody hell! So it is!"

"You mean—" Joan said.

"You mean there *is*—" Hayden said.

"Yes, there is," Chick said, his laughter dying down.

"In the *Bosphorus!*" Hayden said.

"Under Cecil's roses!" Joan said.

"So Sidney was right," Rocky said.

"And so was Charlotte," Walter said.

"They took it without telling me," Chick said, shaking his head. "Those sons of bitches."

Nobody said anything for several moments. Everybody was looking at Chick. Hayden broke the silence.

"We probably should leave it where it is," she said.

"Yes," Philip said, "look at the trouble it's caused."

"It does in its own way seem to be cursed," Rocky said.

"Yes, what would be the point?" Walter said.

Chick stopped halfway up the stairs and looked back at the rest of them. "You're all quite right," he said soberly.

They all gazed wordlessly at each other for several seconds, then Chick turned and continued up the stairs. Nobody else moved. They listened to the tromp of his feet as he climbed wearily to the top, the sound of his heavy tread as he made his way slowly down the hall, then, out of the silence, the gathering rumble of a thunderous laugh.